CORNELL WOOLRICH

PHANTOM LADY

CORNELL WOOLRICH was born in 1903. He began writing fiction while at Columbia University in the 1920s, and went on in the '30s and '40s to become, along with Raymond Chandler and James M. Cain, one of the creators of the *noir* genre, producing such classics as *Rear Window* (the basis for the 1954 Alfred Hitchcock film starring James Stewart and Grace Kelly), *The Bride Wore Black*, *I Married a Dead Man*, and the so-called "Black Series" of suspense novels. Under the pseudonyms William Irish and George Hopley, Woolrich made the elements of tension, tragedy, and terror the trademarks of his timeless thrillers. More of his work has been adapted to film, TV, and radio than any mystery author since Edgar Allan Poe; among these adaptations are *The Night Has a Thousand Eyes*, *Obsession*, *Deadline at Dawn*, *The Leopard Man*, *Nightmare*, and *The Black Angel*. Woolrich died an alcoholic recluse in 1968.

"No one has ever surpassed Cornell Woolrich for sheer suspense, or equaled him for exciting entertainment."

—Robert Bloch

"Woolrich can distill more terror, more excitement, more downright nail-biting suspense out of even the most commonplace happenings than nearly all his competitors."

—Ellery Queen

AVAILABLE NOW

ALFRED HITCHCOCK MYSTERIES
The Vertigo Murders by J. Madison Davis

ALO NUDGER MYSTERIES
by John Lutz
Nightlines • *The Right to Sing the Blues*
Ride the Lightning

AMOS WALKER MYSTERIES
by Loren D. Estleman
Motor City Blue • *Angel Eyes*
The Midnight Man • *The Glass Highway*
Sugartown • *Every Brilliant Eye*

CHARLOTTE MacLEOD CLASSIC MYSTERIES
The Resurrection Man

CORNELL WOOLRICH CLASSIC MYSTERIES
The Bride Wore Black

MASAO MASUTO MYSTERIES
by Howard Fast
Masuto Investigates
Masuto: The Hollywood Murders

MOSES WINE MYSTERIES
by Roger L. Simon
The Big Fix • *Wild Turkey*
Peking Duck • *California Roll*
The Straight Man • *The Lost Coast*

OTTO PENZLER HOLLYWOOD MYSTERIES
Laura by Vera Caspary
The Lady Vanishes by Ethel Lina White

PHILIP MARLOWE MYSTERIES
Raymond Chandler's Philip Marlowe
Anthology; Byron Preiss, Editor

SHERLOCK HOLMES MYSTERIES
Revenge of the Hound
by Michael Hardwick

Sherlock Holmes vs. Dracula
by Loren D. Estleman

TOBY PETERS MYSTERIES
by Stuart M. Kaminsky
Murder on the Yellow Brick Road
He Done Her Wrong • *Never Cross a Vampire*
The Devil Met a Lady

PHANTOM LADY

CORNELL WOOLRICH

ibooks
new york
www.ibooksinc.com

DISTRIBUTED BY SIMON & SCHUSTER, INC

An Original Publication of ibooks, inc.

Copyright © 2001 Sheldon Abend D/B/A The American Play Company
and American Publishing Company

Originally written under the pseudonym "William Irish"
Copyright © 1942 by William Irish

An ibooks, inc. Book

Distributed by Simon & Schuster, Inc.
1230 Avenue of the Americas, New York, NY 10020

ibooks, inc.
24 West 25th Street
New York, NY 10010

The ibooks World Wide Web Site Address is:
http://www.ibooksinc.com

ISBN 0-7434-2373-9
First ibooks, inc. printing August 2001
10 9 8 7 6 5 4 3 2 1

Cover illustration and design by Steranko

Printed in the U.S.A.

To Apartment 605, Hotel M—
in unmitigated thankfulness
(at not being in it any more)

Share your thoughts about Cornell Woolrich's
Phantom Lady
and other ibooks titles at *www.ibooksinc.com*

PHANTOM
LADY

I answer not and I return no more.

—John Ingall

1: The Hundred and Fiftieth Day
Before the Execution

THE night was young, and so was he. But the night was sweet, and he was sour. You could see it coming from yards away, that sullen look on his face. It was one of those sustained angers, pent-up but smoldering, that last for hours sometimes. It was a shame, too, because it was all out of tune with everything around him. It was the one jarring note in the whole scene.

It was an evening in May, at the get-together hour. The hour when half the town, under thirty, has slicked back its hair and given its billfold a refill and sauntered jauntily forth to keep *that date*. And the other half of the town, still under thirty, has powdered its nose and put on something special and tripped blithely forth to keep that *same date*. Everywhere you looked, the two halves of the town were getting together. On every corner, in every restaurant and bar, outside drugstores and inside hotel-lobbies and under jewelry-store clocks, and darned near every place there was that somebody else hadn't beat them to first. And the same old stuff went around and around, old as the hills but always new. "Here I am. Been waiting long?" "You look swell. Where'll we go?"

9

That was the kind of an evening it was. The sky was rouge-red in the west, as though it was all dolled-up for a date itself, and it was using a couple of stars for diamond clips to hold up its evening-gown. Neons were beginning to wink out along the street-vistas, flirting with the passersby like everyone else was tonight, and taxi-horns were chirping, and everyone was going someplace, all at one time. The air wasn't just air, it was aërated champagne, with a whiff of Coty for good measure, and if you didn't watch out it went to your head. Or maybe your heart.

And there he went, pushing that sore face in front of him, spoiling the whole scene. People glancing at him as he strode by wondered what he had to be that ill-tempered about. It wasn't his health. Anyone that could swing along at the gait he was, must be in the pink of condition. It wasn't his circumstances. His clothes had that carelessly expensive hang that can't be faked. It wasn't his age. If he had thirty beat at all, it was by months, not years. He wouldn't have been half bad-looking if he'd given his features a chance to unpucker. You could tell that around the edges where the scowl was thin.

He went striding along with that chip-on-the-shoulder look, his mouth a downturned ellipse, a horseshoe stuck under his nose. The topcoat slung across the crook of his arm bobbed up and down with the momentum of his pace. His hat was too far back on his head and it had a dent in the wrong place, as though he'd punched it on without adjusting it afterwards. Probably the only reason his shoes didn't strike sparks from the pavement was because they were rubber-heeled.

He hadn't intended going in where he finally did. You could tell that by the abrupt way he braked as he came opposite to it. There was no other word for the way he halted; it was as though a brace down his leg had locked, jamming him still. He probably wouldn't have even noticed the place if the intermittent neon over it hadn't glowed on just then, as he was passing. It said "Anselmo's" in geranium-red, and it dyed the whole sidewalk under it as though somebody had spilled a bottle of ketchup.

He swerved aside, on what was obviously an impulse, and went barging in. He found himself in a long, low-ceilinged room, three or four steps below street-level. It wasn't a large place nor, at the moment, a crowded one. It was restful on the eyes; the lighting was subdued, amber-colored, and directed upwards. There was a line of little bracketed nooks with tables set in them running down both walls. He ignored them and went straight back to the bar, which was semicircular, facing toward the entrance from the rear wall. He didn't look to see who was at it, or whether anyone was at it at all. He just dumped his topcoat on top of one of the tall chairs, dropped his hat on top of it, and then sat down on the next one over. His attitude plainly implied he was there for the night.

A blurred white jacket approached just above the line of his downcast vision and a voice said, "Good evening, sir."

"Scotch," he said, "and a little water. I don't give a damn how little."

The water stayed on untouched, after its companion-glass was empty.

He must have, subconsciously at the moment of sitting down, glimpsed a bowl of pretzels or some sort of accessory like that over to his right. He reached out that way without looking. His hand came down, not on a twisted baked shape but on a straight smooth one that moved slightly.

He swung his head around, took his hand off the other one that had just preceded his into the bowl. "Sorry," he grunted. "After you."

He swung his head around to his own business once more. Then he turned again, gave her a second look. He kept on looking from then on, didn't quit after that. Still in a gloomy, calculating way, though.

The unusual thing about her was the hat. It resembled a pumpkin, not only in shape and size but in color. It was a flaming orange, so vivid it almost hurt the eyes. It seemed to light up the whole bar, like a low-hanging garden-party lantern. Stemming from the exact center of it was a long thin cockerel feather, sticking straight up like the antenna of an insect. Not one woman in a thousand would have braved that color. She not only did, she got away with it. She looked startling, but good, not funny. The rest of her was toned-down, reticent in black, almost invisible against that beacon of a hat. Perhaps the thing was a symbol of some sort of liberation, to her. Perhaps the mood that went with it was, "When I have this on, watch out for me! The sky's the limit!"

Meanwhile, she was nibbling a pretzel and trying to seem unaware of his steady scrutiny. When she broke off nibbling, that was the only sign she gave of being aware that he had quitted his own chair, come over, and was standing beside her.

She inclined her head very slightly, in a listening attitude, as if to say: "I'm not going to stop you, if you try to speak. Whether I do after that or not, depends on what you have to say."

What he had to say, with terse directness, was: "Are you doing anything?"

"I am, and I'm not." Her answer was well-mannered, but

not encouraging. She didn't smile nor commit herself to receptiveness in any way. She carried herself well; whatever else she was, she wasn't cheap.

There was no trace of the masher in his own manner, either. He went on, briskly impersonal, "If you've got an engagement, just say so. I'm not trying to annoy you."

"You're not annoying me—so far." She got her meaning across perfectly: my decision is still held in the balance.

His eyes went to the clock up over the bar, facing both of them. "Look, it's ten after six, right now."

Her own eyes sought it in turn. "So it is," she agreed neutrally.

He had taken out a wallet, meanwhile, extracted a small oblong envelope from one of the compartments. This he opened in turn, and prodded forward two salmon-colored pasteboard strips, forking them apart as he did so. "I have two perfectly good tickets here for the show at the Casino. Row Double-A, aisle-seats. Care to take it in with me?"

"You're abrupt about it." Her eyes went from the tickets to his face.

"I have to be abrupt about it." He was scowling as deeply as ever. He wasn't even looking at her at all, he was looking at the tickets, with an air of resentment. "If you have a previous engagement say so, and I'll try to find somebody else to share them with me."

A flicker of interest showed in her eyes. "These tickets must be used up at all costs?"

"It's a matter of principle," he said sullenly.

"This could be mistaken for a very crude attempt at, shall we say, striking up an acquaintanceship," she let him know. "The reason I don't think it is, is it's so blunt, so unvarnished, it couldn't be anything but just what you say it is."

"It isn't." His face was still set in flinty lines.

She had veered slightly toward him on her chair by now. Her way of accepting was to remark, "I've always wanted to do something of this sort. I'd better do it now. The chance mayn't recur—at least not in a genuine form —for a long time."

He armed her down. "Shall we make an agreement before we start? It may make it simpler afterward, when the show is over."

"That depends on what it is."

"We're just companions for an evening. Two people having dinner together, seeing a show together. No names, no addresses, no irrelevant personal references and details. Just—"

She supplied: "Two people seeing a show together, companions for an evening. I think that's a very sensible, in fact necessary, understanding, so let's abide by it. It does away with a great deal of self-consciousness, and perhaps even an occasional lie." She offered him her hand, and they shook briefly on it. She smiled for the first time. She had a rather likeable smile; reserved, not too sugary.

He motioned the barman over, tried to pay for both drinks.

"I'd already paid for mine before you came in," she told him. "I was just coasting along on it."

The barman took a small tablet out of the pocket of his jacket, pencilled "1 Scotch—60" on the top leaf, tore it off and presented it to him.

They were numbered, he noticed, and he saw that he'd drawn a large, beetling, black "13" in the upper corner. He gave a wry grin, handed it back with the requisite amount, turned and went after her.

She had preceded him toward the entrance. A girl ensconced with a companion in one of the wall-booths leaned slightly outward to stare after the glowing hat as it went by. He, coming up in the rear, was just in time to catch that.

Outside she turned to him, questioningly. "I'm in your hands."

He forefingered a taxi waiting a few car-lengths away. One cruising past at the moment, for whom the signal had not been intended, tried to chisel in on the hail. The first one frustrated it by rolling up into position ahead of it, but not without a slight scraping of fenders and snatches of belligerent repartee. By the time the competition had sidled off again and the first driver had cooled sufficiently to turn his attention to his fares-to-be, she was already ensconced inside.

Her host had waited a moment by the driver's seat to give him the destination. "Maison Blanche," he said, and then followed her in.

The light was on, and they let it stay that way. Perhaps because to have turned it out would have been a suggestion of intimacy, neither one felt a dim-out was appropriate to the occasion.

Presently he heard her give a little gratified chuckle, and following the direction of her eyes, grinned sparingly in accompaniment. Cabmen's license-photos are seldom examples of great portrait-beauty, but this one was a caricature, with its pitcher-ears, receding chin, and pop-eyes. The name identifying it was memorably curt and alliterative: "Al Alp."

His mind took note of it, then let it go again.

The Maison Blanche was an intimate-type dining-room, renowned for the excellence of its food. It was one of those places over which a hush of appreciation seems to hang, even at their busiest hours. No music nor distraction of any other sort was allowed to interfere with its devotees' singleness of purpose.

In the foyer she separated from him. "Will you excuse me a moment while I go in and repair the ravages of Time? Go in and sit down awhile, don't wait, I'll find you."

As the powder-room door opened to admit her, he saw her hands start upward toward her hat, as if she intended to remove it. The door closed after her before she completed the gesture. It occurred to him that a temporary lapse of courage was probably the real reason behind this whole maneuver; that she had separated from him and was about to remove the hat in order to be able to enter the dining-room singly after he did, and thereby attract a degree less attention.

A headwaiter greeted him at the dining-room entrance. "One, sir?"

"No, I have a reservation for two." And then he gave the name. "Scott Henderson."

He found it on his list. "Ah, yes." He glanced over the guest's shoulder. "Are you alone, Mr. Henderson?"

"No," Henderson answered noncommittally.

It was the only vacant table in sight. It was in a secluded position, set back into an indentation in the wall, so that its occupants could only be seen frontally, were screened from the rest of the diners on three sides.

When she appeared at the dining-room entrance presently, she was hatless, and he was surprised at how much the hat had been able to do for her. There was something flat about her. The light had gone out; the impact of her personality was soggy, limp. She was just some woman in black, with dark-brown hair; something that blocked the background, that was all. Not homely, not pretty, not tall, not small, not chic, not dowdy; not anything at all, just plain, just colorless, just a common denominator of all feminine figures everywhere. A cipher. A composite. A Gallup poll.

Not a head that turned remained turned a second longer than necessary, or carried back any continuing memory of what it had seen.

The headwaiter, momentarily engaged in tossing a salad, was not on hand to guide her. Henderson stood up to show her where he was, and she did not strike directly through the room, he noticed, but made her way unobtrusively around two sides of it, which was the longer but the far less conspicuous way.

The hat, which she had been carrying at arm's length beside her, she placed on the third chair of their table, and partly covered it with the edge of the cloth, possibly to protect it from stains.

"Do you come here often?" she asked.

He pointedly failed to hear her.

"Sorry," she relented, "that comes under the heading of personal background."

Their table-waiter had a mole on his chin. He couldn't help noticing that.

He ordered for them without consulting her. She listened attentively, gave him an appreciative glance when he had finished.

It was uphill work getting started. There were heavy restrictions on her choice of topics, and she had his leaden mood to combat as well. Man-like, he left most of the effort to her, made very little attempt to keep his own end up. Though he gave a sketchy appearance of listening, his thoughts were obviously elsewhere most of the time. He would bring them back again each time, and with an effort that was almost a physical wrench, only when his abstraction had become so noticeable it threatened to be flagrantly discourteous.

"Don't you want to take your gloves off?" he said at one point. They were black, like everything else about her but the hat. They hadn't appeared awkward with the cocktail or purée, but with the sole came a slice of lemon that she was trying to mash with her fork.

She stripped the right one off immediately. She took a little longer with the left, seemed about to leave it on after all. Then finally, with a touch of defiance, she followed suit with that.

He carefully refrained from seeing the wedding-band, looked out and across at something else. But he could tell she knew that he had.

She was a good conversationalist, without being spectacular about it. She was dexterous, too, managed to eschew the obvious, the banal, the dry; the weather, the newspaper-headlines, the food they were engaged with.

"This crazy South American, this Mendoza, in the show we're seeing tonight: when I first saw her a year or so ago, she had hardly any accent at all. Now, with every engagement she has up here, she seems to unlearn more English, acquire a heavier one than the time before. One more season and she'll be back in pure Spanish."

He gave one-third of a smile. She was cultured, he could tell that about her. Only someone cultured could have gotten away with what she was doing tonight and not made a ghastly mess of it, either in one direction or the other. She had balance, to take the place of either propriety or recklessness. And there again, if she had leaned a little more one way or the other, she would have been more memorable, more positive. If she had been a little less well-bred, she would have had the piquancy, the raffishness, of the parvenu. If she had been a little more, she would have been brilliant—and therefore memorable in that respect. As it was, polarized between the two, she was little better than two-dimensional.

Toward the end, he caught her studying his necktie. He looked down at it questioningly. "Wrong color?" he suggested. It was a solid, without any pattern.

"No, quite good, in itself," she hastened to assure him. "Only, it doesn't match—it's the one thing that doesn't go with everything else you— Sorry, I didn't mean to criticize," she concluded.

He glanced down at it a second time, with a sort of detached curiosity, as though he hadn't known until now, himself, just which one it was he had put on. Almost as though he were surprised to find it on him. He destroyed a little of the tonal clash she had indicated by thrusting the edge of his dress-handkerchief down out of sight into his pocket.

He lit their cigarettes, they stayed with their cognacs awhile, and then they left.

It was only in the foyer—at a full-length glass out in the foyer—that she finally put her hat on again. And at once she came alive, she was something, somebody, again. It was wonderful, he reflected, what that hat could do to her. It was like turning on the current in a glass chandelier.

A gigantic theatre-doorman, fully six-four, opened the cab-door for them when it had driven up, and his eyes boggled comically as the hat swept past, almost directly under them. He had white walrus-tusk mustaches, almost looked like a line-drawing of a theatre-doorman in the *New Yorker.* His bulging eyes followed it from right to left as its wearer stepped down and brushed past him.

Henderson noted this comic bit of optic by-play, to forget it again a moment later. If anything is ever really forgotten.

The completely deserted theatre-lobby was the best possible criterion of how late they actually were. Even the ticket-taker at the door had deserted his post by now. An anonymous silhouette against the stage-glow, presumably an usher, accosted them just inside the door, sighted their tickets by flashlight, then led them down the aisle, trailing an oval of light backhand along the floor to guide their advancing feet.

Their seats were in the first row. Almost too close. The stage was an orange blur for a moment or two, until their eyes had grown used to the foreshortened perspective.

They sat patiently watching the montage of the revue, scene blending into scene with the superimposed effect of motion-picture dissolves. She would beam occasionally, even laugh outright now and then. The most he would do was give a strained smile, as though under obligation to do it. The noise, color, and brilliance of lighting reached a crescendo, and then the curtains rippled together, ending the first half.

The house-lights came on, and there was a stir all around them as people got up and went outside.

"Care for a smoke?" he asked her.

"Let's stay where we are. We haven't been sitting as long as the rest of them." She drew the collar of her coat closer around the back of her neck. The theatre was stifling already, so the purpose of it, he conjectured, was to screen her profile from observation as far as possible.

"Come across some name you've recognized?" she murmured presently, with a smile.

He looked down and found his fingers had been busily turning down the upper right-hand corner of each leaf of his program, one by one, from front to back. They were all blunted now, with neat little turned-back triangles superimposed one on the other. "I always do that, fidgety habit I've had for years. A variation of doodling, I guess you'd call it. I never know I'm doing it, either."

The trap under the stage opened and the orchestra started to file back into the pit, for the second half. The trap-drummer was nearest to them, just across the partition-rail. He was a rodent-like individual, who looked as though he hadn't been out in the open air for ten years past. Skin stretched tight over his cheekbones, hair so flattened and glistening it almost looked like a wet bathing-cap with a white seam bisecting it. He had a little twig of a mustache, that almost seemed like smudge from his nose.

He didn't look outward into the audience at first; busied himself adjusting his chair and tightening something or other on his instrument. Then, set, he turned idly, and almost at once became aware of her and of the hat.

It seemed to do something to him. His vapid, unintelligent face froze into an almost hypnotic fascination. His mouth even opened slightly, like a fish's, stayed that way. He would try to stop staring at her every once in a while, but she was on his mind, he couldn't keep his eyes away very long, they would stray back to her each time.

Henderson took it in for a while, with a sort of detached, humorous curiosity. Then finally, seeing that it was beginning to make her acutely uncomfortable, he put a stop to it in short order, by sending such a sizzling glare at him that he turned back to his music rack forthwith and for good. You could tell, though, even with his head turned the other way, that he was still thinking about her, by the rather conscious, stiff way he held his neck.

"I seem to have made an impression," she chuckled under her breath.

"Perfectly good trap-drummer ruined for the evening," he assented.

The gaps behind them had filled up again now. The house-lights dimmed, the foots welled up, and the overture to the second act began. He went ahead moodily pleating the upper corners of his dog-eared program.

Midway through the second half there was a crescendo build-up, then the American house-orchestra laid down its instruments. An exotic thumping of tom-toms and rattling of gourds onstage took its place, and the main attraction of the show, Estela Mendoza, the South American sensation, appeared.

A sharp nudge from his seat-mate reached him even before he had had time to make the discovery for himself. He looked at her without understanding, then back to the stage again.

The two women had already become mutually aware of the fatal fact that was still eluding his slower masculine perceptions. A cryptic whisper reached him: "Just look at her face. I'm glad there are footlights between us. She could kill me."

There was a distinct glitter of animosity visible in the expressive black eyes of the figure onstage, over and above her toothsome smile, as they rested on the identical replica of her own headgear, flaunted by his companion there in the very first row, where it couldn't be missed.

"Now I understand where they got the inspiration for this particular creation," she murmured ruefully.

"But why get sore about it? I should think she'd be flattered."

"It's no use expecting a man to understand. Steal my jewelry, steal the gold-fillings from my teeth, but don't steal my hat. And over and above that, in this particular case it's a distinctive part of her act, part of her trademark. It's probably been pirated, I doubt that she'd give permission to—"

"I suppose it is a form of plagiarism." He watched with slightly heightened interest, if not yet complete self-forgetfulness.

Her art was a simple thing. As real art always is. And as getting away with something at times is too. She sang in Spanish, but even in that language there was very little intellect to the lyric. Something like this:

"Chica chica boom boom
Chica chica boom boom"

Over and over. Meanwhile she kept rolling her eyes from side to side, throwing one hip out of joint at every step she took, and throwing little nosegays out to the women-members of the audience from a flat basket she carried slung at her side.

By the time she had run through two choruses of the thing, every woman in the first two or three rows was in possession of one of her floral tokens. With the notable exception of Henderson's companion. "She purposely held out on me, to get even for the hat," she whispered knowingly. And as a matter of fact, every time the hitching, heel-stamping figure on the stage had slowly worked her way past their particular vantage-point, there had been an ominous flash, an almost electrical crackling, visible in her fuse-like eyes as they glided over that particular location.

"Watch me call her on it," she remarked under her

breath for his benefit. She clasped her hands together, just below her face, in vise-formation.

The hint was patently ignored.

She extended them out before her, at half arm's length, held them that way in solicitation.

The eyes on the stage slitted for a minute, then resumed their natural contour, strayed elsewhere.

Suddenly there was a distinct snap of the fingers from Henderson's companion. A crackling snap, sharp enough to top the music. The eyes rolled back again, glowered maniacally at the offender. Another flower came out and winged over, but still not to her.

"I never know when I'm beaten," he heard her mutter doggedly. Before he knew what she meant, she had risen to her feet, stood there in her seat, smiling beatifically, passively claiming her due.

For a moment there was a deadlock between the two. But the odds were too unequal. The performer, after all was said and done, was at the mercy of this individualistic spectator, for she had an illusion of sweetness and charm to maintain at all costs in the sight of the rest of the audience.

The alteration in the stature of Henderson's seat-mate also had an unforeseen result in another respect. As the hiphiker slowly made the return trip, the spotlight, obediently following her and slanted low, cut across the head and shoulders of this lone vertical impediment, standing up on the orchestra floor. The result was that the similarity of the two hats was brought explosively to everyone's attention. A centripetal ripple of comment began to spread outward, as when a stone is dropped into heretofore still waters.

The performer capitulated and capitulated fast, to put

an end to this odious comparison. Up came a blackmail-extorted flower, out it went over the footlights in a graceful little curve. She covered up the omission by making a rueful little moue, as if to say "Did I overlook you? Forgive me, I didn't meant to." Behind it, however, could be detected the subcutaneous pallor of a lethal tropical rage.

Henderson's companion had deftly caught the token and subsided into her seat again with a gracious lip-movement. Only he detected the wordage that actually emerged: "Thank you—you Latin louse!" He choked on something in his throat.

The worsted performer slowly worked her way off into the wings with little spasmodic hitches, while the music died down like the clatter of train-wheels receding into the distance.

In the wings they glimpsed a momentary but highly revealing vignette, while the house was still rocking with applause. A pair of shirt-sleeved masculine arms, most likely the stage-manager's, were bodily restraining the performer from rushing back onstage again. Obviously for some purpose over and above merely taking bows. Her hands, held down at her sides by his bear-hug embrace, were visibly clenched into fists and twitching with punitive intent. Then the stage blacked out and another number came on.

At the final curtain, as they rose to go, he tossed his program into the discard, onto the seat he had just quitted.

To his surprise she reached down for it, added it to her own, which she was retaining. "Just as a memento," she remarked.

"I didn't think you were sentimental," he said, moving slowly up the choked aisle at her heels.

"Not sentimental, strictly speaking. It's just that—I like

to gloat over my own impulsiveness at times, and these things will help."

Impulsiveness? Because she had joined forces with him for the evening, without ever having seen him before, he supposed. He shrugged—inwardly, if not visibly.

As they were fighting their way toward a taxi, in the mêlée outside the entrance, an odd little mischance occurred. They had already claimed their cab, but before they could get into it, a blind beggar approached, hovered beside her in mute appeal, alms-cup all but nudging her. The lighted cigarette she was holding was jarred from her fingers in some way, either by the beggar himself or someone nearby, and fell into the cup. Henderson saw it happen, she didn't. Before he could interfere the trustful unfortunate had thrust probing fingers in after it, and then snatched them back again in pain.

Henderson quickly dug the ember out for him himself, and put a dollar bill in his hand to make amends. "Sorry, old timer, that wasn't intentional," he murmured. Then noting that the sufferer was still blowing ruefully on his smarting finger, he added a second bill to the first, simply because the incident could have been so easily misconstrued as the height of calloused mockery, and he could tell by looking at her it hadn't been intended as such.

He followed her into the cab and they drove off. "Wasn't that pathetic?" was all she said.

He had given the driver no direction as yet.

"What time is it?" she asked presently.

"Going on quarter of twelve."

"Suppose we go back to Anselmo's, where we first met. We'll have a night-cap and then we'll part there. You go your way and I'll go mine. I like completed circles."

They're usually empty in the middle, it occurred to him,

but it seemed ungallant to mention this, so he didn't.

The bar was considerably more crowded now, when they got there, than it had been at six. However, he managed to secure a stool for her all the way around at the very end of the bar, up against the wall, and posted himself at her shoulder.

"Well," she said, holding her glass just an inch above bar-level and eyeing it speculatively, "hail and farewell. Nice having met you."

"Nice of you to say so."

They drank; he to completion, she only partially. "I'll remain here for a short while," she said by way of dismissal. She offered him her hand. "Good night—and good luck." They shook briefly, as acquaintances of an evening should. Then just as he was about to turn away, she crinkled her eyes at him in remonstrative afterthought. "Now that you've got it out of your system, why don't you go back and make up with her?"

He gave her a slightly surprised look.

"I've understood all evening," she said quietly.

On that note they parted. He moved toward the door, she turned back to her drink. The episode was over.

He glanced back, when he had reached the street-entrance, and he could still see her sitting there, all the way over against the wall, at the end of the curved bar, looking down pensively, probably fiddling idly with the stem of her glass. The bright orange of the hat showed through a V-shaped opening left between two pairs of shoulders around the turn of the bar from her.

That was the last thing of all, the bright orange of her hat peering blurredly through the cigarette-haze and shadows, all the way back there behind him, as in a dream, as in a scene that wasn't real and never had been.

2: The Hundred and Fiftieth Day
Before the Execution

MIDNIGHT

TEN minutes later and only eight blocks away in a straight line—two straight lines: seven blocks up one way and then one over to the left—he got out of the cab in front of an apartment-house on the corner.

He put the change left over from the fare into his pocket, opened the vestibule-door with his own key, and went inside.

There was a man hanging around in the lobby waiting for somebody. He was on his feet, drifting aimlessly around, from here to there, from there to the next place, the way a man waiting in a lobby does. He didn't live in the building; Henderson had never seen him before. He wasn't waiting for the car to take him up, because the indicator was unlighted; it was motionless somewhere up above.

Henderson passed him without a second glance, and pushed the button for himself, to bring it down.

The other had found a picture on the wall now, and was staring at it far beyond its merits. He stood with his back to Henderson. In fact he made it a point to seem unaware there was anyone else in the lobby with him at all, which was overdoing it a little.

He must have a guilty conscience, Henderson decided. That picture wasn't worth all that close attention. He must be waiting for someone to join him down here, someone whom he had no right to escort out.

Henderson thought: what the hell did he care, what was it to him anyway?

The car arrived and he stepped in. The heavy bronze door swung closed by itself after him. He thumbed the six-button, the top of the rack. The lobby started to drop from sight, seen through the little diamond-shaped glass insert let into the shaft-door. Just before it did so he saw the picture-gazer, evidently impatient at being kept waiting this long by his prospective date, finally detach himself and take a preliminary step over toward the switchboard. Just a vignette, that was no possible concern of his.

He got out on the sixth floor and fumbled for his latchkey. The hall was quiet; there wasn't a sound around him but the slight tinkle of the loose change in his own pocket as he sought for the key.

He fitted it into his own door, the one to the right as you came off the car, and opened it. The lights were out, it was pitch-dark on the other side of it. At this, for some reason or other, he gave a sound of scornful disbelief, deep in his throat.

He snapped a light-switch, and a small neat foyer came into existence. But the light only took care of just this one cubicle. Beyond the arched opening facing him across it, it was still as dark, as impenetrable, as ever.

He closed the door behind him, flung down his hat and coat on a chair out there. The silence, the continuing darkness, seemed to irritate him. The sullenness was starting to come back into his face again, the sullenness that had been so conspicuously there at six, out on the street.

He called out a name, called it through into the darkness lying beyond the inscrutable arched opening. "Marcella!" He called it imperatively, and not particularly friendlily.

The darkness didn't answer.

He strode into it, speaking in that same harsh, demanding tone as he went. "Come on, cut it out! You're awake, who do you think you're kidding? I saw the light in your bedroom-window, from the street just now. Grow up, this isn't going to get us anywhere!"

The silence didn't answer.

He cut diagonally through the dark, toward some particular point on the wall, known to him by heart. He was grumbling in a less strident voice now. "Until I come back, you're wide awake! The minute you hear me, you're sound asleep! That's just dodging the issue!"

His arm was reaching out before him. The click came before it had touched anything. The sudden bath of light made him jump slightly; it had come too soon, before he was expecting it.

He looked along his own arm, and the switch was still inches out past it; they hadn't come together yet. There was a hand just leaving it, sidling away from it along the wall. His eyes raced up the sleeve the hand protruded from and found a man's face.

He gave a startled half-turn, and there was another one looking at him from that direction. He gave an additional turn, still further rearward, having nearly reversed himself now, and there was a third, directly behind him. The three stood impassive, motionless as statues, in a half-circle around him.

He was so stunned for a minute by the triple, deathly-silent apparition that he stared questioningly around the room in search of recognition, of orientation, to see if he was in the right place at all, if it was his own apartment he'd entered.

His eyes came to rest on a cobalt-blue lamp-base on a table over by the wall. That was his. On a low-slung chair cocked out from a corner. That was his. On a photograph-folder standing on a cabinet. One panel held the face of a beautiful, pouting, doe-eyed girl with masses of curly hair. The other held his own face.

The two faces were looking in opposite directions, aloofly, away from one another.

So it was his own home he'd come back to.

He was the first one to speak. It seemed as if they were never going to. It seemed as if they were going to stand staring at him all night. "What're you men doing in my apartment?" he rapped out.

They didn't answer.

"Who are you?"

They didn't answer.

"What do you want here? How'd you get in?" He called her name again. This time parenthetically, as though demanding of her an explanation of their presence here. The door toward which he'd turned his head as he did so, the only other door that broke the walls besides the arched opening through which he'd just come, remained obliviously closed. Secretively, inscrutably closed.

They'd spoken. His head snapped back to them. "Are you Scott Henderson?" They had narrowed the semicircle about him a little now.

"Yes, that's my name." He kept looking around toward that door that didn't open. "What is it? What's up?"

They continued, with maddening deliberation, to ask their own questions instead of answering his. "And you live here, is that right?"

"Certainly I live here!"

"And you're the husband of Marcella Henderson, is that right?"

"Yes! Now listen, I want to know what this is about."

One of them did something with his palm, made some sort of a gesture with it that he failed to get in time. It only struck him after it was already over.

He tried to get over to that door and found that one of them, somehow, was in his way. "Where is she? Is she out?"

"She's not out, Mr. Henderson," one of them said quietly.

"Well if she's in there, why doesn't she come out?" His voice rose exasperatedly. "*Talk,* will you? Say something!"

"She can't come out, Mr. Henderson."

"Wait a minute, what was that you showed me just now, a police badge?"

"Now, take it easy, Mr. Henderson." They were executing a clumsy sort of a group dance, the four of them. He'd shift a little one way, and they'd shift with him. Then he'd shift back again the other way, and again they'd shift with him.

"Take it easy? But I want to know what's happened! Have we been robbed? Has there been an accident? Was she run over? Take your hands off me. Let me go in there, will you?"

But they had three pairs of hands to his one. Each time he'd get rid of one pair, two more would hold him back somewhere else. He was rapidly working himself up into a state of unmanageable excitement. The next step would have been blows. The rapid breathing of the four of them filled the quiet room.

"I live here, this is my home! You can't do this to me! What right've you got to keep me out of my wife's bedroom—"

Suddenly they'd quit. The one in the middle made a little sign to the one nearest the door, said with a sort of reluctant indulgence: "All right, let him go in, Joe."

The obstructive arm he had been pressing against dropped so suddenly, he opened the door and went through almost off-balance, careening the first step or two of the way.

Into a pretty place, a fragile place, a place of love. All blue and silver, and with a sachet clinging to the air that he knew well. A doll with wide-spread blue satin panniers, sitting plumped on a vanity table, seemed to look over at him with helpless wide-eyed horror. One of the two crystal sticks supporting blue silken shades had fallen athwart her lap. On the two beds, blue satin coverlets. One flat and smooth as ice, the other rounded over someone's hidden form. Someone sleeping, or someone ill. Covered up completely from head to foot, with just a stray wisp or two of curly hair escaping up at the top, like bronze foam.

He'd stopped short. A look of white consternation crossed his face. "She's—she's done something to herself! Oh, the little fool—!" He glanced fearfully at the nightstand between the two beds, but there was nothing on it, no drinking-glass or small bottle or prescription-box.

He took sagging steps over to the bedside. He leaned down, touched her through the coverlet, found her rounded shoulder, shook it questioningly. "Marcella, are you all right—?"

They'd come in past the doorway after him. Vaguely he had an impression everything he did was being watched, being studied. But he had no time for anyone, anything but her.

Three pairs of eyes in a doorway, watching. Watching him fumble with a blue satin coverlet. His hand whipped down a narrow triangular corner of it.

There was a hideous, unbelievable moment, enough to scar his heart for life, while she grinned up at him. Grinned with a cadaverous humor that had become static. Her hair was rippling about her on the pillows in the shape of an open fan.

Hands interfered. He went backwards, draggingly, a step at a time. A flicker of blue satin and she was gone again. For good, forever.

"I didn't want *this* to happen," he said brokenly. "*This* wasn't what I was looking for—"

Three pairs of eyes exchanged glances, jotted that down in the notebooks of their minds.

They took him out into the other room and led him over to a sofa. He sat down on it. Then one of them went back and closed the door.

He sat there quietly, shading his eyes with one hand as though the light in the room was too strong. They didn't seem to be watching him. One stood at the window, staring out at nothing. The other was standing beside a small table, leafing through a magazine. The third one was sitting down across the room from him, but not looking at him. He was prodding at one of his fingernails with something, to clean it. The way he pored over it, it seemed the most important thing in the world to him at the moment.

Henderson took his shielding hand away presently. He found himself looking at her wing of the photograph-portfolio. It slanted his way. He reached over and closed it.

Three pairs of eyes completed a circuit of telepathic communication.

The ceiling of leaden silence began to come down closer, to weigh oppressively. Finally the one sitting across from him said, "We're going to have to talk to you."

"Will you give me just a minute more, please?" he said wanly. "I'm sort of shaken up—"

The one in the chair nodded with considerate understanding. The one by the window kept looking out. The one by the table kept turning the pages of a woman's magazine.

Finally Henderson pinched the corners of his eyes together as if to clear them. He said, quite simply: "It's all right now. You can begin."

It began so conversationally, so off-handedly, it was hard to tell it had even begun at all. Or that it was anything but just a tactful chat, to help them fill in a few general facts. "Your age, Mr. Henderson?"

"Thirty-two."

"Her age?"

"Twenty-nine."

"How long were you married?"

"Five years."

"Your occupation?"

"I'm in the brokerage business."

"About what time did you leave here tonight, Mr. Henderson?"

"Between five-thirty and six."

"Can you come a little closer than that?"

"I can narrow it for you, yes. I can't give you the exact minute the door closed after me. Say, somewhere between quarter of and five of six. I remember I heard six o'clock striking, when I'd gotten down as far as the corner; from the little chapel over in the next block."

"I see. You'd already had your dinner?"

"No." A split second went by. "No—I hadn't."

"You had your dinner out, in that case."

"I had my dinner out."

"Did you have your dinner alone?"

"I had my dinner out, without my wife."

The one by the table had come to the end of the magazine. The one by the window had come to the end of the interest the view held for him. The one in the chair said with tactful over-emphasis, as if afraid of giving offense: "Well, er, it wasn't your usual custom, though, to dine out without your wife, was it?"

"No, it wasn't."

"Well, as long as you say that, how is it you did tonight?" The detective didn't look at him, looked at the cone of ash he was knocking off his cigarette into a receptacle beside him.

"We'd arranged to take dinner out together tonight. Then at the last minute she complained of not feeling well, of having a headache, and—I went alone."

"Have words, anything like that?" This time the question was inaudible, it was so minor-keyed.

Henderson said, in an equally minor key, "We had a word or two, yes. You know how it is."

"Sure." The detective seemed to understand perfectly how little domestic misunderstandings like that went. "But nothing serious, that right?"

"Nothing that would make her do anything like this, if that's what you're driving at." He stopped, asked a question in turn, with a momentary stepping-up of alertness. "What was it, anyway? You men haven't even told me yet. What caused—?"

The outside door had opened and he broke off short. He watched with a sort of hypnotic fascination, until the bedroom door had closed. Then he made a half-start to his feet. "What do *they* want? Who are they? What are they going to do in there?"

The one in the chair had come over and put his hand to his shoulder so that he sat down again; without, however, any undue pressure being exerted. It was more like a gesture of condolence.

The one who had been by the window, looked over, mentioned: "A little nervous, aren't you, Mr. Henderson?"

A sort of instinctive, natural dignity, to be found in all human beings, came to Henderson's aid. "How should I be—at ease, self-possessed?" he answered with rebuking bitterness. "I've just come home and found my wife dead in the house."

He'd made that point. The interlocutor by the window noticeably had nothing further to say on that score.

The bedroom door had opened again. There was awkward, commingled motion in it. Henderson's eyes dilated, they slowly coursed the short distance from door to arched opening, leading out into the foyer. This time he gained his feet fully, in a spasmodic jolt. "No, not like *that!* Look what they're doing! Like a sack of potatoes— And all her lovely hair along the floor—she was so careful of it—!"

Hands riveted to him, holding him there. The outer door closed muffledly. A little sachet came drifting out of the empty bedroom, seeming to whisper: "Remember? Remember when I was your love? Remember?"

This time he sank down suddenly, buried his face within his two gouging, kneading hands. You could hear his breath. The tempo was all shot to pieces. He said to them in helpless surprise, after his hands had dropped again, "I thought guys didn't cry—and now I just have."

The one who had been in the chair before passed him
a cigarette, and even lit it for him. His eyes looked bright,
Henderson's, in the shine of the match.

Whether it was that that had interrupted it, or it had
died out of its own accord for lack of anything further to
feed on, the questioning didn't resume. When they resumed talking again, it was pointless, inane, almost as
though they were talking just to kill time, for the sake
of having something to say.

"You're a very neat dresser, Mr. Henderson," the one
in the chair observed at random.

Henderson gave him a half-disgusted look, didn't answer.

"It's great the way everything you've got on goes together."

"That's an art in itself," the former magazine-reader
chimed in.

"Socks, and shirt, and pocket-handkerchief—"

"All but the tie," the one by the window objected.

"Why do you have to discuss anything like that at a
time like this?" Henderson protested wearily.

"It should be blue, shouldn't it? Everything else is blue.
It knocks your whole get-up silly. I'm not a fashion-plate,
but y'know just looking at it does something to me—"
And then he went on innocently, "How'd you happen to
slip up on an item as important as the tie, when you went
to all the trouble of matching everything else up? Haven't
you got a blue tie?"

Henderson protested almost pleadingly, "What're you
trying to do me? Can't you see I can't talk about trifles
like—"

He'd asked the question again, as tonelessly as before.
"Haven't you got a blue tie, Mr. Henderson?"

Henderson ran his hand up through his hair. "Are you
trying to drive me out of my mind?" He said it very
quietly, as though this small-talk was almost unendurable.
"Yes, I have a blue tie. Inside, on my tie-rack, I think."

"Then how'd you come to skip it when you were putting on an outfit like this? It cries out for it." The detective gestured disarmingly. "Unless, of course, you did
have it on to begin with, changed your mind at the last
minute, whipped it off and put on the one you're wearing
instead."

Henderson said, "What's the difference? Why do you
keep this up?" His voice went up a note. "My wife is dead.
I'm all cracked-up inside. What's the difference what color
tie I did or didn't put on?"

It went on, as relentlessly as drops of water falling one
by one upon the head. "Are you sure you didn't have it on
originally, then change your mind—?"

His voice was smothered. "Yes, I'm sure. It's hanging
from my tie-rack in there."

The detective said guilelessly, "No, it isn't hanging
from your tie-rack. That's why I'm asking. You know
those little vertical notches running down your tie-rack,
like a fish's backbone? We found the one it belongs on, the
one you usually kept it strung through, because that was
the only vacant one on the whole gadget. And that was
the lowest one of all, in other words all the ties on the
upper ones overlapped it as they hung down straight. So
you see, it was removed from *under* all the other ties,
which means you must have gone there and selected it
originally, not just pulled it off at random from the top.
Now what bothers me is why, if you went to all the
trouble of lifting up all your other ties and selecting that
one from underneath, and withdrawing it from the rack,

you then changed your mind and went back to the one you'd already been wearing all day at business, and which didn't go with your after-dark outfit."

Henderson hit himself smartly at the ridge of the forehead with the heel of one hand. He sprang up. "I can't stand this!" he muttered. "I can't stand any more of it, I tell you! Come out with what you're doing it for, or else stop it! If it's not on the tie-rack, then where is it? I haven't got it on! Where is it? You tell me, if you know! What's the difference where it is, anyway?"

"A great deal of difference, Mr. Henderson."

There was a long wait after that; so long that he started to get pale even before it had come to an end.

"It was knotted tight around your wife's neck. So tight it killed her. So tight it will have to be cut loose with a knife to get it off."

3: The Hundred and Forty-ninth Day
Before the Execution

DAYBREAK

A THOUSAND questions later, the early light of day peering in the windows made the room look different, somehow, although everything in it was the same, including the people. It looked like a room in which an all-night party has taken place. Cigarette-ends spilling-over in every possible container, and many that weren't intended as such. The cobalt-blue lamp was still there, looking strange in the dawn with its halo of faded electric light. The photographs were still there; hers a lie now, a picture of someone that no longer existed.

They all looked and acted like men suffering from a hangover. They had their coats and vests off, and their shirt-collars open. One of them was in the bathroom, freshening up at the cold-water tap. You could hear him snorting through the open door. The other two kept smoking and moving restlessly around. Only Henderson was sitting quiet. He was still sitting on the same sofa he'd been on all night. He felt as though he'd spent all his life on it, had never known what it was to be anywhere but in this one room.

The one in the bathroom, his name was Burgess, came to the door. He was pressing drops of excess water out of his hair, as though he'd ducked his whole head in the wash-basin. "Where're all your towels?" he asked Henderson, with odd-sounding commonplaceness.

"I was never able to find one on the rack myself," the latter admitted ruefully. "She— I'd always be given one when I asked for it, but I don't know to this day just where they're kept."

The detective looked around helplessly, dripping all over the doorsill. "D'you mind if I use the edge of the shower-curtain?" he asked.

"I don't mind," Henderson said with a sort of touching wistfulness.

It began again. It always began again just when it seemed to have finally stopped for good.

"It wasn't just about two theatre-tickets. Why do you keep trying to make us believe it was that?"

He looked up at the wrong one first. He was still used to the parliamentary system of being looked at when spoken to. It had come from the one who wasn't looking at him.

"Because it was that. What should I say it was about, if that's all it was about? Didn't you ever hear of two people having words about a pair of theatre-tickets? It can happen, you know."

The other one said, "Come on, Henderson, quit stalling. Who is she?"

"Who is who?"

"Oh, don't start that again," his questioner said disgustedly. "That takes us back an hour and a half or two hours, to where we were about four this morning. Who is she?"

Henderson dug wearied fingers through his hair, let his head droop over in futility.

Burgess came out of the bathroom, tucking his shirt in. He took his wristwatch out of his pocket, strapped it on. He scanned it idly, then he drifted aimlessly out into the foyer. He must have picked up the house-phone. His voice came back. "All right now, Tierney." Nobody paid any attention, least of all Henderson. He was half-asleep there with his eyes open, staring down at the carpet.

Burgess sauntered in again, moved around after that as if he didn't know what to do with himself. Finally he ended up at the window. He adjusted the shade a little, to get more light in. There was a bird on the sill outside. It quirked its head at him knowingly. He said, "C'mere a minute, Henderson. What kind of a bird is this, anyway?" And then when Henderson didn't move the first time, "C'mere. Hurry up, before he goes away." As though that were the most important thing in the world.

Henderson got up, and went over and stood beside him, and thus his back was to the room. "Sparrow," he said briefly. He gave him a look as if to say: That wasn't what you wanted to know.

"That's what I figured it was," Burgess said. And then, to keep him looking forward, "Pretty decent view you got from here."

"You can have it, bird and all," Henderson said bitterly. There was a noticeable lull. All questioning had stopped.

Henderson turned away, then stopped where he was. There was a girl sitting there on the sofa, in the exact place where he'd just been himself until now. There hadn't been a sound to mark her arrival. Not the creak of a door-hinge, not the rustle of a garment.

The way the eyes of the three men dug into his face, all the skin should have peeled off it. He got a grip on it from the inside, held it steady. It felt a little stiff, like cardboard, but he saw to it that it didn't move.

She looked at him, and he at her. She was pretty. She was the Anglo-Saxon type, more so even than the Anglo-Saxons themselves are any more. Blue-eyed, and with her taffy-colored hair uncurled and brushed straight across her forehead in a clean-looking sweep. The part was as distinct as a man's. She had a tan camel-hair coat drawn over her shoulders, with the sleeves left empty. She was hatless, but was clutching a handbag. She was young, at that stage when they still believe in love and men. Or maybe she always would, was of an idealistic temperament. You could read it in the way she looked at him. There was practically incense burning in her eyes.

He moistened his lips slightly, nodded barely percepti-bly, as to a distant acquaintance, whose name he could not recall, nor where they had met, but whom he didn't want to slight.

He seemed to have no further interest in her after that.

Burgess must have made some esoteric sign in the back-ground. All of a sudden they were alone together, there was no one else in the room with them any more.

He tried to motion with his hand, but it was too late. The camel-hair coat was already propped up empty in the corner of the sofa, without her inside it. Then it slowly wavered and collapsed into a huddle. She had flung herself against him like some sort of a projectile.

He tried to get out of the way, side-step. "Don't. Be careful. That's just what they want. They're probably listening to every word—"

"I have nothing to be afraid of." She took him by the arms and shook him slightly. "Have you? Have you? You've got to answer me!"

"For six hours I've been fencing to keep your name out of it. How did they come to drag you into it? How did they hear of you?" He smacked himself heavily on the shoulder. "Damn it, I would have given my right arm up to here to keep you out!"

"But I want to be in things like this with you, when you're in them. You don't know very much about me, do you?"

The kiss kept him from answering. Then he said, "You've kissed me before you even know whether or not—"

"No I haven't," she insisted, breathing close to his face. "Oh, I couldn't be *that* wrong. Nobody could be. If I could be that wrong, then my heart ought to be put in an institution for mental defectives. And I've got a smart heart."

"Well, tell your heart for me it's okay," he said sadly. "I didn't hate Marcella. I just didn't love her enough to go on with her, that's all. But I couldn't have killed her. I don't think I could kill anyone, not even a man—"

She buried her forehead against his chest, in a sort of

ineffable gratitude. "Do you have to tell me that? Haven't I seen your face when a stray dog came up to the two of us on the street? When a dray-horse standing at the curb— Oh, this is no time to tell you, but why do you suppose I love you? You don't think it's because you're so handsome, do you? Or so brilliant? Or so dashing?" He smiled and kept stroking her hair. And he'd interrupt the strokes, softly, with his lips. "It's all inside you, what I love, where no one but me can see it. There's so much goodness in you, you're such a swell fellow—but it's all inside, for me alone to know, to have to myself."

She raised her face at last, and her eyes were all wet.

"Don't do that," he said gently, "I'm not worth it."

"I'll set my own price-tags, don't try to jew me down," she rebuked him. She glanced over at the oblivious door, and the light on her face dimmed a little. "What about *them?* Do they think—?"

"I think it's about fifty-fifty, so far. They wouldn't have kept at me this long— How did they come to drag you into it?"

"Your message was there from six o'clock, when I got in last night. I hated to go to sleep without knowing one way or the other, so finally I called you back here, around eleven. They were already here in the place, and they sent someone right over to talk to me. I've had someone with me ever since."

"That's great, keeping you up all night long!" he said resentfully.

"I wouldn't have wanted to be asleep, knowing you were in trouble." Her fingers swept the curve of his face. "There's only one thing that matters. Everything else is beside the point. It'll be straightened out, it's got to be. They must have ways of finding out who actually did it—

How much have you told them?"

"About us, you mean? Nothing. I was trying to keep you out of it."

"Well maybe that's what the hitch has been. They could sense you were leaving out something. I'm in it now, so don't you think it's better to tell them everything there is to know about us? We have nothing to be ashamed or afraid of. The quicker you do, the quicker it'll be over with. And they've probably already guessed, from my own attitude, we're pretty off-base about each—"

She stopped short. Burgess was back in the room. He had the pleased look of a man who has gained his point. When the other two followed him in, Henderson even saw him give one of them the wink.

"There's a car downstairs that'll take you back to your own address, Miss Richman."

Henderson stepped over to him. "Look, will you keep Miss Richman out of this? It's unfair, she really has nothing—"

"That depends entirely on yourself," Burgess told him. "We only brought her over here in the first place because you made it necessary for us to remind you—"

"Anything I know, anything I can tell you, is yours," Henderson assured him earnestly, "if you see that she's not annoyed by newspapermen, that they don't get hold of her name and make a big thing of it."

"Always providing it's the truth," Burgess qualified.

"It will be." He turned to her, said in a softer voice than the one he'd been using, "You go now, Carol. Get some sleep, and don't worry, everything'll be all right in a little while."

She kissed him in front of all of them, as though proud to show the way she felt toward him. "Will you let me hear from you? Will you let me hear from you as soon as you can—sometime right today if you can?"

Burgess went to the door with her, said to the cop posted outside it: "Tell Tierney nobody is to come near this young lady. No name, no questions answered, no information of any kind."

"Thanks," Henderson said fervently when he'd come back, "you're a regular guy."

The detective eyed him without acknowledgement. He sat down, took out a notebook, ran a wavy cancellation-line down two or three closely-scribbled pages, turned over to a fresh one. "Shall we start in?" he said.

"Let's start," Henderson acquiesced.

"You said you had words. Does that stand?"

"That stands."

"About two theatre-tickets? Does that stand?"

"About two theatre-tickets and a divorce. That stands."

"Now that comes in it. Then there was bad feeling between you?"

"No feeling of any kind, good or bad. Call it a sort of numbness. I'd already asked her for a divorce some time ago. She knew about Miss Richman. I'd told her. I wasn't trying to hide anything. I was trying to do it the decent way. She refused the divorce. Walking out was no good. I didn't want that. I wanted Miss Richman for my wife. We stayed away from each other all we could, but it was hell, I couldn't stand it. Is all this necessary?"

"Very."

"I had a talk with Miss Richman night-before-last. She saw it was getting me. She said, 'Let me try, let me talk to her.' I said no. She said, 'Then you try again yourself. Try in a different way this time. Talk to her reasonably, try to win her over.' It went against the grain, but I gave it a spin. I telephoned from work and reserved a table for two at our old place. I bought two tickets to a show, first row on the aisle. At the last minute I even turned down an invitation from my best friend to go out on a farewell party with him. Jack Lombard, he's going to be in South America for the next few years; it was my last chance of seeing him before he sailed. But I stuck to my original intention; I was going to be nice to her if it killed me.

"Then when I got back here, nothing doing. She wasn't having any reconciliation. She liked things the way they were, and she was going to keep them that way. I got sore, I admit. I blew up. She waited until the last minute. Let me go ahead and shower and change clothes. Then she just sat there and laughed. 'Why don't you take *her* instead?' she kept needling me. 'Why waste the ten dollars?' So I phoned Miss Richman from here, right in front of her.

"I didn't even have that satisfaction. She wasn't in. Marcella laughed her head off. She made me know it.

"You know how it is when they laugh at you. You feel like a fool. I was so sore I couldn't see straight any more. I yelled: 'I'm going out on the street and invite the first girl I run into to come with me in your place! The first thing in curves and high heels that comes along, no matter who it is!' And I slammed on my hat and slammed out the door."

His voice ran down like a clock that needs winding. "And that's all. I can't do any better than that for you, even if I tried. Because that's the truth, and the truth can't be improved on."

"And after you left here, does that timetable of your movements you already gave us still go?" Burgess asked.

"That still goes. Except that I wasn't alone, I *was* with someone. I did what I'd told her I'd do: stepped up to someone and invited her along. She accepted, and I was

with her from then until just about ten minutes before I
came back here."

"What time did you meet her, about?"

"Only a few minutes after leaving here. I stopped in at
some bar or other, over on Fiftieth Street, and that was
where I met her—" He did something with his finger.
"Wait a minute, I just remembered. I can give you the
exact time I met her. We both looked at the clock together,
as I was showing her the theatre-tickets. It was ten after
six, to the dot."

Burgess ran his nail along underneath his lower lip.
"What bar was this?"

"I couldn't say, exactly. It had a red come-on over it,
that's all I can remember at the moment."

"Can you prove you were in there at ten after six?"

"I've just told you I was. Why? Why is that so important?"

Burgess drawled: "Well, I could string you along, but
I'm funny that way. I'll give it to you. Your wife died at
exactly *eight after six*. The small wristwatch she wore
shattered against the edge of the vanity-table as she fell to
her death. It stopped at exactly—" He read from something: "6–08–15." He put it away again. "Now nothing
with two legs, or even wings, could have been here at that
time, and over on Fiftieth Street one minute and forty-
five seconds later. You prove you were over there at ten-
past, and all this is over."

"But I've told you! I looked at the clock."

"That isn't proof, that's an unsupported statement."

"Then what would proof be?"

"Corroboration."

"But why does it have to be at that end? Why can't it
be at this?"

"Because there's nothing at this end to show that anyone

but you did it. Why do you suppose we've been sitting up with you all night?"

Henderson let his wrists dangle limp over his knees. "I see," he breathed at last. "I see." The silence coursed and swirled around the room after that, for awhile.

Burgess spoke again at last. "Can this woman you say you met in the bar corroborate you on what time it was?"

"Yes. She looked at the clock when I did. She must remember that. Yes, she can."

"All right, then that's all there is to it. Providing she satisfies us, her corroboration is given in good faith, and you didn't put her up to it. Where does she live?"

"I don't know. I left her where I first met her, back at the bar."

"Well, what was her name?"

"I don't now. I didn't ask, and she didn't give it to me."

"Not even a first name, not even a nickname? You were with her for six hours, what did you call her?"

" 'You,' " he answered glumly.

Burgess had got out his notebook again. "All right, describe her for us. We'll have to send out after her ourselves and have her brought in."

There was a long wait.

"Well?" he said finally.

Henderson's face was getting paler by the minute. He swallowed hard. "My God, I can't!" he blurted out finally. "I've lost her completely, she's rubbed out." He circled his hand helplessly in front of his own face. "I could have told you when I first came back here last night, maybe, but now I can't any more. Too much has happened since. The shock of Marcella— And then you guys pegging away at me all night. She's like a film that's been exposed to too much light, she's completely faded out. Even while I was with her I didn't notice her very closely, my mind was too full of my own affairs." He looked from one to the other of them, as if in search of help. "She's a complete blank!"

Burgess tried to help him out. "Take your time. Think hard. Now, here. Eyes?"

Henderson flexed his clenched hands open, in futility.

"No? All right, hair, then. What about hair? What color hair?"

He plastered hands to his eye-sockets. "That's gone too. Every time I start to say one color, it seems to me it was another; and then when I start to say the other, I think it was the first again. I don't know; it must have been sort of in-between. Not brown, not black. Most of the time she had it under a hat." He looked up half-hopefully. "I can remember the hat better than anything else. An orange hat, will that do any good? Yeah, orange, that's it."

"But suppose she's taken it off since last night, suppose she don't show up anywhere in it for the next six months? Then where are we? Can't you remember anything about *her* herself?"

Henderson kneaded his temples in brain-agony.

"Was she fat? Skinny? Tall? Short?" Burgess peppered at him.

Henderson writhed his waist, first to one side, then the other, as if to get away from the questions. "I can't, that's all, I can't!"

"I think you're taking us for a ride, aren't you?" one of the others suggested stonily. "It was only last night. Not last week or last year."

"I never did have a very good memory for faces, even when I'm—at peace, nothing to bother me. Oh, she had a face, I suppose—"

"No kidding?" the one who had assumed the role of end-man jeered.

He kept going from bad to worse, because he was making the mistake of thinking aloud, instead of rehearsing his words. "She was shaped like other women, that's about all I can tell you—"

That did it. Burgess' face had been slowly lengthening for some time, without his giving any other sign of truculence. He was evidently of a slow-moving temperament. Instead of reclipping his stymied pencil into his pocket, he flung it with a sort of angered deliberateness, almost as if taking aim, at the wall opposite him. Then he got up and went over and got it. His face had turned good and red. He shrugged into his long-discarded coat, pulled the knot of his tie around frontward.

"Come on, boys," he said surlily, "let's get out of here, it's getting late."

He stopped a moment at the arched opening leading out to the foyer, eyed Henderson flintily. "What do you take us for anyway?" he growled. "Easy-marks? You're out with a woman, for six solid hours, only last night, and yet you can't tell us what she looked like! You're sitting shoulder-to-shoulder with her at a bar, you're sitting across a table from her for a whole table d'hôte meal from celery to coffee, you're in the seat right next to her for three full hours at a show, you're in the same taxi with her coming and going—but her face is just a blank space under an orange hat! You expect us to swallow that? You try to hand us a myth, a phantom, without any name or form or height or width or eyes or hair or anything else, and we're supposed to take your word for it you were with *that* and not home here when your wife was getting killed! You're not even plausible about it. A ten-year-old kid could see through what you're trying to put over. It's one of two things. Either you weren't with any such person, and just made her up out of your own mind. Or more likely still,

you weren't with any such person but *did* see her in the
crowd around you sometime during the evening, and are
trying to foist her on us as having been with you, when
she wasn't at all. Which is why you're purposely making
her blurred, so we can't get a very good line on her and
find out the truth!"

"Come on, stir!" one of the others ordered Henderson,
in a voice like a buzz-saw going through a pine-knot.
"Burge don't burn very often," he added half-humorously,
"but when he does, he burns good and strong."

"Am I under arrest?" Scott Henderson asked Burgess
as he got up and moved toward the door in the grasp of
the other man.

Burgess didn't answer him directly. The answer was to
be found in the parting instruction he gave the third man,
over his shoulder.

"Turn out that lamp, Joe. There won't be anybody using it around here for a long time to come."

4: The Hundred and Forty-ninth Day
Before the Execution

SIX P. M.

THE car was standing waiting there by the corner when
the unseen belfry somewhere close at hand began tolling
the hour. "Here it comes," Burgess said. They'd been
waiting about ten minutes for this, motor running.

Henderson, neither free nor indicted yet, sat on the
rear seat between him and one of the other two headquarters men who had taken part in the questioning up at

his apartment the previous night and morning.

A third man whom they referred to as "Dutch" stood outside the car, on the sidewalk, in a sort of fatuous idleness. He had been kneeling crouched in mid-sidewalk tightening up his shoeslaces just before the first stroke sounded. He straightened now.

It was the same kind of a night like the one before. The get-together hour, the sky with its make-up on in the west, everyone going someplace all at one time. Henderson gave no sign, sitting there between two of his captors. It must have occurred to him, though, what a difference a few hours can make.

His own address was just a few doors behind them, at the next corner to the rear. Only he didn't live there any more; he lived in a detention-cell in the prison attached to police headquarters now.

He spoke dully. "No, a store-length further back," he said to Burgess. "I'd just come up to that lingerie-store window when the first stroke hit. I can remember that, now that I'm looking at it—and hearing the same sound—over again."

Burgess relayed it to the man on the sidewalk. "Back up one store-length and take it from there, Dutch. That's it. All right, start walking!" The second stroke of six had sounded. He did something to the stop-watch he was holding in his hand.

The tall, rangy, red-headed man on the sidewalk struck out. The car at the same time eased into gliding motion, keeping abreast of him out beyond the curb.

"Dutch" looked self-conscious for a moment or two, his legs worked a little stiffly; then it wore off gradually.

"How is he for pace?" Burgess asked presently.

"I think I was a little faster than that," Henderson said. "When I'm sore I walk fast, I notice, and I was going at a pretty good clip last night."

"Quicken it up a little, Dutch!" Burgess coached.

The rangy one accelerated slightly.

The fifth stroke sounded, then the last.

"How is it now?" Burgess asked.

"That's about me," Henderson concurred.

An intersection sidled past under them. A light held the car up. Not the walker. Henderson had disregarded them the night before. The car caught up with him midway down the next block.

They were on Fiftieth now. One block of it ticked off. Two.

"See it yet?"

"No. Or if I have, it doesn't click. It was awfully red, redder than that one. The whole sidewalk was like red paint."

The third block. The fourth.

"See it?"

"It doesn't click."

Burgess warned: "Watch what you're doing, now. If you string it out very much longer, even your theoretical alibi won't be any good. You should have been inside it already by now; it's eight-and-a-half past."

"If you don't believe me anyway," Henderson said drily, "what's the difference?"

"It don't hurt to figure out the exact walking-time between the two points," the man on the other side of him put in. "We might just happen to find out when you *actually* got there, and then all we do is subtract."

"Nine minutes past!" Burgess intoned.

Henderson was holding his head low, scanning the slowly-moving belt of sidewalk-fronts from under the car-ceiling.

A name drifted by, colorless glass tubes unlighted. He turned quickly after it. "That's it! I think that's it, but it's out. Anselmo's, it was something like that, I'm almost sure of it. Something foreign—"

"In, Dutch!" Burgess hollered. He drove the plunger down, killed his stop-watch. "Nine minutes, ten and a half seconds," he announced. "We'll give you the ten and a half seconds to allow for variations, such as the density of the crowd you had to buck and the cross-traffic at inter-sections, which is never the same twice. Nine minutes flat, walking-time, from the corner below your apartment to this bar. And we'll give you another minute from the apartment itself down to that first corner, where the first chime-stroke caught you. We've already tested that lap out. In other words—" He turned and looked at him, "you find some way of proving that you got into this bar as late as *six-seventeen*—but no later—and you'll still clear yourself automatically, even now."

Henderson said: "I can prove I got in here as early as six-ten, if I can only find that woman."

Burgess swung open the car-door. "Let's go inside," he said.

"Ever see this man before?" Burgess asked.

The barman held his chin in a vise. "Looks kind of fa-miliar," he admitted. "But then, my whole job is just faces, faces, faces."

They gave him a little more time. He took an angle-shot at Henderson. Then he went around the opposite side and took it from there. "I don't know," he still hesitated.

Burgess said, "Sometimes the frame counts as much as the picture. Let's try it differently. Go on back behind the bar, barman."

They all went over to it. "Which stool were you on, Henderson?"

"Somewhere along about here. The clock was straight over, and the pretzel-bowl was about two up from me."

"All right, get on it. Now try it, barman. Forget about us, take a good look at him."

Henderson inclined his head morosely, stared down at the surface of the bar, the way he had the other time.

It worked. The barman snapped his fingers. "That did it! Gloomy Gus. I remember him now. Only last night, wasn't it? Must have been just a one-drink customer, didn't stick around long enough to sink in."

"Now we want the time."

"Sometime during my first hour on duty. They hadn't thickened up yet around me. We had a late start last night; sometimes happens."

"What is your first hour on duty?"

"Six to seven."

"Yeah, but about how long after six, that's what we want to know."

He shook his head. "I'm sorry, gents. I only watch the clock toward the *end* of my shift, never around the beginning. It might have been six, it might have been six-thirty, it might have been six-forty-five. It just wouldn't be worth a damn for me to try to say."

Burgess looked at Henderson, raised his eyebrows slightly. Then he turned to the barman again. "Tell us about this woman that was in here at that time."

The barman said with catastrophic simplicity, "What woman?"

Henderson's complexion went slowly down the color-scale, from natural to pale to dead white.

A flick of Burgess' hand held him mute.

"You didn't see him get up and go over and speak to a woman?"

The barman said, "No sir, I didn't see him get up and go over and speak to anyone. I can't swear to it, but my impression was there was no one else at the bar at that time *for* him to speak to."

"Did you see a woman sitting here by herself, without seeing him get up and go over to her?"

Henderson pointed helplessly two bar-stools over. "An orange hat," he said, before Burgess could stop him.

"Don't do that," the detective warned him.

The barman was suddenly becoming irritable, for some reason or other. "Look," he said, "I've been in this business thirty-seven years. I'm sick of their damn faces, night after night, just opening and closing, opening and closing, throwing the booze in. Don't come in and ask me what color hats they had on, or if they picked each other up or not. To me they're just orders. To me they're just drinks, see, to me they're just drinks! Tell me what she had and I'll tell you if she was in here or not! We keep all the tabs. I'll get 'em from the boss' office."

They were all looking at Henderson now. He said, "I had Scotch and water. I always have that, never anything else. Give me just a minute now, to see if I can get hers. It was all the way down near the bottom—"

The barman came back with a large tin box.

Henderson said, rubbing his forehead, "There was a cherry left in the bottom of the glass and—"

"That could be any one of six drinks. I'll get it for you. Was the bottom stemmed or flat? And what color was the dregs? If it was a Manhattan the glass was stemmed and dregs, brown."

Henderson said, "It was a stem-glass, she was fiddling with it. But the dregs weren't brown, no, they were pink, like."

"Jack Rose," said the barman briskly. "I can get it for you easy, now." He started shuffling through the tabs. It took a few moments; he had to sift his way through them in reverse, the earlier ones were at the bottom. "See, they come off the pads in order, numbered at the top," he mentioned.

Henderson gave a start, leaned forward. "Wait a minute!" he said breathlessly. "That brought something back to me, just then. I can remember the number printed at the top of my particular pad. Thirteen. The jinx-number. I remember staring at it for a minute when he handed it to me, like you would with that number."

The barman put down two tabs in front of all of them. "Yeah, you're right," he said. "Here you are. But not both on the same tab. Thirteen—one Scotch and water. And here are the Jack Roses, three of them, on number seventy-four. That's one of Tommy's tabs, from the shift before, in the late afternoon; I know his writing. Not only that, but there was some other guy with her. Three Jack Roses and a rum, this one says, and no one in their right mind is going to mix those two drinks."

"So—?" Burgess suggested softly.

"So I still don't remember seeing any such woman, even if she stayed over into my shift, because she was Tommy's order, not mine. But if she *did* stay over, my thirty-seven years' experience tending bar tells me he didn't get up and go over and speak to her, because there was already a guy with her. And my thirty-seven years' experience also tells me he was with her to the end, because nobody buys three Jack Roses at eighty cents a throw and then walks out and leaves his investment behind for somebody else to cash in on." And he took a definitive swipe to the counter with his bar-rag.

Henderson's voice was shaking. "But you remembered *me* being here! If you can remember me, why can't you remember her? She was even better to look at."

The barman said with vicious logic: "Sure I remembered you. Because I'm seeing you now over again, right before my eyes. Bring her back in front of me the same way, and I'll probably remember her too. I can't without that."

He was hanging onto the rim of the bar with both hands, like a drunk with unmanageable legs. Burgess detached one of his arms, grunted, "Come on, Henderson."

He still clung to it with the other, straining toward the barman. "Don't do this to me!" he protested in a choked voice. "Don't you know what the charges are? Murder!"

Burgess quickly sealed a hand to his mouth. "Shut up, Henderson," he ordered curtly.

They led him out backward. He kept straining away from them toward that bar.

"You sure did draw the thirteen-tab," one of them grunted in a wry undertone, as they emerged to the street with him, pressed closely around him in a sort of perambulatory vise.

"Even if she shows up from now on, at any later point in the evening, it's already too late to do you any good," Burgess warned him as they sat waiting for the taxi-driver to be traced and brought in. "It had to be in that bar by six-seventeen. But I'm curious to see whether she will show up at some later point, and if so, just how long after. That's why we're going to retrace your movements, step by step, throughout the entire evening, from beginning to end."

"She will, she's got to!" Henderson insisted. "*Some-body*'ll remember her, in one of the other places we went that night. And then, once you get hold of her in that way, she herself will be able to tell you just where and at what time she first met me."

The man Burgess had sent out on the assignment came in, reported: "The Sunrise Company has two drivers on the line outside Anselmo's. I brought them both down. Their names are Budd Hickey and Al Alp."

"Alp," Henderson said. "That's the funny name I've been trying to think of. That's the name I told you we both laughed at."

"Send Alp in. Tell the other guy never mind."

He was as funny-looking in real life as on his license-picture; even funnier, for he was in full color in real life.

Burgess said, "Did you have a haul last night from your stand to the Maison Blanche Restaurant?"

"Mason Blantch, Mason Blantch—" He was going to be a little doubtful at first. "I pick 'em up and put 'em down so many times a night—" Then a memory-quickening method of his own seemed to come to his aid. "Mason Blantch; about sixty-five cents on a dry night," he mumbled. He went back into full-voice again. "Yeah, I did! I had a sixty-five cent haul last night, in between two thirty-cent pulls."

"Look around you. See anyone here you gave it to?"

His eyes slid past Henderson's face. Then they came back again. "It was him, wasn't it?"

"We're asking you, don't ask us."

He took the question-mark off. "It was him."

"Alone or with somebody else?"

He took a minute with that. Then he shook his head slowly. "I don't remember noticing nobody else with him. Alone, I guess."

Henderson gave a lurch forward, like somebody who suddenly turns an ankle. "You must have seen her! She got in ahead of me and she got out ahead of me, like a woman does—"

"Sh, quiet," Burgess tuned him out.

"Woman?" the driver said aggrievedly. "I remember you. I remember you perfect, because I got a dented fender picking you up—"

"Yes, yes," Henderson agreed eagerly, "and maybe that's why you didn't see her step in, because your head was turned the other way. But surely when we got there—"

"When we got there," the driver said sturdily, "my head *wasn't* turned the other way, no cabman's ever is when it comes time to collect a fare. *And I didn't see her get out either.* Now how about it?"

"We had the light on, all the way over," Henderson pleaded. "How could you help seeing her, sitting there in back of you? She must have shown in your rear-sight mirror or even against your windshield—"

"Now I *am* sure," the driver said. "Now I'm positive—even if I wasn't before. I been hacking eight years. If you had the top-light on, you were by yourself. I never knew a guy riding with a woman to leave the top-light on yet. Any time the top-light's on, you can bet the guy behind you is a single."

Henderson could hardly talk. He was feeling at his throat as though it bothered him. "How could you remember my face, and not remember hers?"

Burgess stepped all over that, before the man could even answer. "You didn't remember her face yourself. You were with her six solid hours—*you* say. He had his back to her for twenty minutes." He ended the interview. "All right, Alp. Then that's your statement."

"That's my statement. *There was nobody with this man when I had him in my cab last night.*"

They hit the Maison Blanche at the dismantlement stage. The cloths were off the tables, the last long-lingering gourmets had departed. The help was eating in the kitchen, judging by the unbridled sounds of crockery and silverware in work that emanated from there.

They sat down at one of the denuded tables, drawing up chairs like a peculiar ghost-party of diners about to fall to without any visible utensils or comestibles.

The headwaiter was so used to bowing to people that he bowed now as he came out to them, even though he was off-duty. The bow didn't look so good because he'd removed his collar and tie, and had a lump of food in one cheek.

Burgess said, "Have you seen this man before?"

His black-pitted eyes took in Henderson. The answer came like a finger-snap. "Yes, surely."

"When was the last time?"

"Last night."

"Where did he sit?"

He picked out the niche-table unerringly. "Over there."

"Well?" Burgess said. "Go on."

"Go on with what?"

"Who was with him?"

"Nobody was with him."

There was a line of little moist needle-pricks starting out

along Henderson's forehead. "You saw her come in a moment or two after me, and join me. You saw her sitting there during the whole meal. You must have. Once you even passed close by and bowed and said, 'Everything satisfactory, m'sieu?'"

"Yes. That is part of my duties. I do it to each table at least once. I distinctly recall doing it to you, because your face was, how shall I say, a little discontented. I also distinctly recall the two vacant chairs, one on each side of you. I believe I straightened one a little. You have quoted me yourself. And if I said 'monsieur,' as I did, that is the surest indication there was no one with you. The correct inquiry for a lady and gentleman together is 'm'sieu-et-dame.' It is never altered."

The black centers of his eyes were as steady as buckshot fired deep into his face and lodged there. He turned to Burgess. "Well, if there is any doubt, I can show you my reservation-list for last night. You can see for yourselves."

Burgess said with an exaggeratedly slow drawl that meant he liked the idea very much, "I don't think that would hurt."

The headwaiter went across the dining-room, opened a drawer in a buffet, brought back a ledger. He didn't go out of the room, he didn't go out of their sight. He handed it to them unopened, just as he had found it; let them open it for themselves. All he said was, "You can refer to the date at the top."

They all formed a cluster of heads over it but himself. He remained detached. It was kept in impromptu pencil, but it was sufficient for its purpose. The page was headed "5–20, Tues." Then there was a large corner-to-corner X drawn across the page, to show that it was over and done with. It cancelled without impairing legibility.

There was a list of some nine or ten names. They went like this, columnarly:

Table 18—Roger Ashley, for four. (Lined out)
Table 5—Mrs. Rayburn, for six. (Lined out)
Table 24—Scott Henderson, for two. (Not lined out)

Beside the third name was this parenthetic symbol: (1).

The headwaiter explained, "That tells its own story. When a line is drawn through, that means the reservation has been completed, filled up. When there is no line drawn through, that means they never showed up. When there is no line drawn through, and a number is added, that means only part of them showed up, the rest are still expected. Those things in the little brackets are for my own guidance, so I will know where they go when they do show up, where to put them, without having to ask a lot of questions. No matter if they come only at the dessert, so long as they come at all, the line goes through. What you see here means, therefore: m'sieu had a reservation for two, m'sieu showed up by himself, and the other half of his party never reached here."

Burgess traced hypersensitive finger-pads over that particular section of the page, feeling for erasures. "Texture unmarred," he said.

Henderson pronged his hand, elbow to tabletop; let it catch his head as it toppled forward.

The headwaiter shovelled with his hands. "My book is all I have to go by. My book says—to me—Mr. Henderson was alone in this dining-room last night."

"Then your book says that to us too. Take his name and address, usual stuff, case wanted further questioning. All right, next. Mitri Maloff, table-waiter."

A change of figures before Henderson's eyes, that was

all. The dream, the practical joke, the whatever it was, went on and on.

This was going to be comedy-stuff. To the rest of them, anyway, if not to him. He caught sight of one of them writing something down. He hooked his finger around to his thumb, like in that old hair-tonic ad. "No, no. Beg pardon, shentlemen. There is a D in it. It is silent, you don't speak it."

"Then what's the good of having it?" one of them wondered to the man next to him.

"I don't care what there is in it," Burgess said. "All I want to know is, do you have table twenty-four?"

"From ten, over there, all the way around to twenty-eight, that is me."

"You waited on this man at twenty-four last night?"

He was going to make a social introduction of it. "Ah, sure, certainly!" he lighted up. "Good evening! How are you? You coming back again soon, I hope!" He evidently didn't recognize them as detectives.

"No he isn't," said Burgess brutally. He flattened his hand, to kill the flow of amenities. "How many were there at the table when you waited on him?"

The waiter looked puzzled, like a man who is willing to do his best but can't get the hang of what is expected of him. "Him," he said. "No more. Shust him."

"No lady?"

"No, no lady. What lady?" And then he added, in perfect innocence, "Why? He lose one?"

It brought on a howl. Henderson parted his lips and took a deep breath, like when something hurts you unbearably.

"Yeah, he lost one all right," one of them clowned.

The waiter saw he had made a hit, batted his eyes at them coyly, but still, apparently, without any very clear idea of how he had chalked up his success.

Henderson spoke, in a desolate, beaten-down sort of voice. "You drew out her chair for her. You opened the menu-card, offered it to her." He tapped his own skull a couple of times. "I *saw* you do those things. But no, you didn't see her."

The waiter began to expostulate with Eastern European warmth and lavishness of gesture, but without any rancor: "I draw out a chair, yes, when there is a lady there for it. But when there is no lady there, how can I draw out a chair? For the air to sit down on it, you think I'm going to draw out a chair? When is no face there, you think I'm going to open bill-of-fare and push it in front of?"

Burgess said, "Talk to us, not him. He's in custody."

He did, as volubly as ever, simply switching the direction of his head. "He leave me tip for one-and-a-half. How could there be lady with him? You think I'm going to be nice to him today, if is two there last night and he leave me tip for only one-and-a-half?" His eyes lit with Slavonic fire. Even the supposition seemed to inflame him. "You think I forget it in a horry? I remember it for next two weeks! Hah! You think I ask him to come back like I do? Hah!" he snorted belligerently.

"What's a tip for one-and-a-half?" Burgess asked with jocular curiosity.

"For one is thirty cents. For two is sixty cents. He give me forty-five cents, is tip for one-and-a-half."

"Couldn't you get forty-five cents for a party of two?"

"Never!" he panted resentfully. "If I do, I do like this." He removed an imaginary salver from the table, fingers disdainfully lifted as if it were contaminated. He fixed a baleful eye on the imaginary customer, in this case Henderson. Sustained it long enough to shrivel him. His thick underlip curled in what was meant for a lopsided leer of derision. "I say, 'Thank you, sor. Thank you very motch, sor. Thank you *very very* motch, sor. You sure you able to do this?' And if is lady with him, he feel like two cents, he stick in some more."

"I kind of would myself," Burgess admitted. He turned his head. "How much do you say you left, Henderson?"

Henderson's answer was forlornly soft-spoken. "What he says I did; forty-five cents."

"One thing more," Burgess said, "just to round the whole thing out. I'd like to see the check for that particular dinner. You keep them, don't you?"

"Manager got them. You have to ask him." The waiter's face took on an expression of conscious virtue, as though now he felt sure his veracity would be sustained.

Henderson was suddenly leaning alertly forward, his licked listlessness was gone again.

The manager brought them out himself. They were kept in sheaves, in little oblong clasp-folders, one to a date, apparently to help him tally his accounts at the end of each month. They found it without difficulty. It said "Table 24. Waiter 3. 1 Table d'hote—2.25." It was stamped in faint purple, "Paid—May 20th" in a sort of oval formation.

There were only two other checks for Table Twenty-four in that day's batch. One was "1 tea—0.75," from late afternoon, just before the dinner hour. The other was dinner for four, a party that had evidently come in late, just before closing.

They had to help him get back into the car. He walked in a kind of stupor. His legs were balky. Again there was the dream-like glide of unreal buildings and unreal streets moving backward past them, like shadows on glass.

He broke out suddenly, "They're lying—they're killing me, all of them! What did I ever do to any of them—?"

"Y'know what it reminds me of?" one of them said in an
aside. "Them Topper pictures, where they fade off and on
the screen right in front of your eyes. Did y'ever see one
of them, Burge?"

Henderson shuddered involuntarily and let his head go
over.

There was a show going on outside, and the music, and
laughter, and sometimes handclapping, would trickle into
the small, cluttered office, diluted.

The manager was sitting waiting by the phone. Business
was good, and he tried to look pleasantly at all of them,
savoring his cigar and leaning far back in his swivel-chair.

"There can be no question that the two seats were paid
for," the manager said urbanely. "All I can tell you is that
nobody was seen going in with him—" He broke off
with sudden anxiety. "He's going to be ill. Please get him
out of here as quickly as you can, I don't want any com-
motion while there's a performance going on."

They opened the door and half-carried, half-walked
Henderson toward it, his back inclined far over toward the
floor. A gust of singing from out front surged in.

> "Chica chica boom boom
> Chica chica boom boom—"

"Ah, don't," he pleaded chokingly. "I can't stand any
more of it!" He toppled onto the back seat of the police
sedan, made a knot of his two hands, gnawed at them as if
seeking sustenance for his sanity.

"Why not break down and admit there *was* no dame

with you?" Burgess tried to reason with him. "Don't you see how much simpler it would be all around?"

Henderson tried to answer him in a rational, even voice, but he was a little shaky at it. "Do you know what the next step would be after that, if I did, if I *could*, make such an admission as you're asking me to? My sanity would start to leave me. I'd never be sure of anything again in my life. You can't take a fact that you know to be true, as true as—as that your name is Scott Henderson—" He clapped himself on the thigh; "—as true as that this is my own leg, and let yourself begin to doubt it, deny it, without your mental balance going overboard. She was beside me for six hours. I touched her arm. I felt it in the curve of my own." He reached out and briefly tweaked Burgess' muscular underarm. "The rustle of her dress. The words she spoke. The faint fragrance of her perfume. The clink of her spoon against her consommé-plate. The little stamp of her chair when she moved it back. The little quiver of the shaky taxi-chassis when she stepped down from it. Where did the liquor go to, that my eyes saw in her glass when she raised it? When it came down again, it was empty." He pounded his fist against his knee, three, four, five times. "She was, she was, she was!" He was almost crying; at least his face was wreathed in those lines. "Now they're trying to tell me she *wasn't!*"

The car glided on through the never-never land it had been traversing all evening.

He said a thing that few if any suspects have ever said before. Said it and meant it with his whole heart and soul. "I'm frightened; take me back to the detention-pen, will you? Please, fellows, take me back. I want walls around me, that you can feel with your hands. Thick, solid, that you can't budge!"

"He's shivering," one of them pointed out with a sort of detached curiosity.

"He needs a drink," Burgess said. "Stop here a minute, one of you go in and bring him out a couple fingers of rye I hate to see a guy suffer like that."

Henderson gulped it avidly, as though he couldn't get it down fast enough. Then he slopped back against the seat. "Let's go back, take me back," he pleaded.

"He's haunted," one of them chuckled.

"That's what you get when you raise a ghost."

Nothing further was said until they were out of the car again and filing up the steps at Headquarters in phalanx. Then Burgess steadied him with a hand to his arm, as he fumbled one of the steps. "You better get a good night's sleep, Henderson," he suggested. "And a good lawyer. You're going to need both."

5: The Ninety-first Day Before the Execution

". . . You have heard the defense try to claim that the accused met a certain woman, in a place called Anselmo's Bar, at ten minutes after six on the night the murder was committed. In other words, two minutes and forty-five seconds after the time established by police investigation as that of the death of the victim. Very clever. You can see at once, ladies and gentlemen of the jury, that *if* he was at Anselmo's Bar, Fiftieth Street, at ten past six, he could not have been at *his own* apartment two and three-quarter minutes before then. Nothing on two legs could have covered the distance from one to the other in that length of time. No, nor on four wheels, nor with wings and a propellor either, for that matter. Again I say, very clever. *But;* not clever enough.

"Convenient, wasn't it, that he should just happen to meet her on that one night, and not any other night during the year. Almost as though he had a premonition he was going to need her on that particular night. Strange things, premonitions, aren't they? You have heard the defendant admit, in answer to my questions, that he did *not* go out and accost unknown women other nights of the year. That he had never done such a thing before during the entire course of his married life. Not once, mind you. Those are the accused's own words, not mine. You heard them yourselves, ladies and gentlemen. Such a thought had never even entered his mind until then. It was not his habit to do that sort of thing. It was foreign to his nature. On this one night of all nights, however, they would have us believe that he did. Quite a handy coincidence, what? Only—"

Shrug, and a long pause.

"Where is the woman? We've all been waiting to see her. Why don't they show her to us? What's keeping them? Have they produced such a woman here in court?"

Singling out a juror at random with index-finger. "Have *you* seen her?" Another. "Or you?" A third, in the second tier. "Or you?" Gesture of empty-handed helplessness. "Has anyone of us seen her? Has she been up there on that witness-chair at any time from first to last? No, of course not, ladies and gentlemen. Because—"

Another long pause.

"Because there *is* no such woman. There never was. They can't produce a person who doesn't exist. They can't breathe life into a figment, a figure of speech, a nebula, a thing that *isn't*. Only the good Lord can create a full-grown woman in all her heighth and breadth and thickness. And even He needs eighteen years to do it, not two weeks."

Laughter, from all parts of the room. Brief smile of grateful appreciation on his part.

"This man is being tried for his life. If there was such a woman, do you think they would have neglected to bring her here? Wouldn't they have seen to it that she was on the job here, speaking her piece at the right time? You bet they would! *If—*"

Dramatic pause.

"—there was such a woman. Let's leave ourselves out of it. We're here in a courtroom, miles from the places that he insists he visited with her that night, and months have passed. Let's take the word of those who were right there, *at* those same places, *at* the same time, as he supposedly was with her. Surely they should have seen her, if anyone did. *Did* they? You heard for yourself. They saw him, yes. Every one of them can recall, no matter how vaguely, no matter how hazily, glimpsing him, Scott Henderson, that night. It seems to end there, as though they all had a blindness in one eye. Doesn't that strike you as a little odd, ladies and gentlemen? It does me. When people travel around in pairs, one of two things happens: either neither one of them is remembered afterward, or, if one is, then the other is also. How can the human eye see one person without seeing the other—if the other is right there alongside the first at the time? That violates the law of physics. I can't account for it. It baffles me."

Coy bunching of the shoulders.

"I'm open to suggestions. In fact I'll make a few myself.

Possibly her skin was of a peculiar transparency that let the light through, and so they looked right through her to the other side without—"

General laughter.

"Or possibly she just didn't happen to be there with him. Nothing more natural than that they should fail to see her if she didn't happen to be there at the time."

Change of manner and of voice. General tightening-up.

"Why go ahead? Let's keep this serious. A man's on trial here for his life. I'm not anxious to make a farce out of it. The defense is the one that seems to be. Let's leave hypotheses and theories, and go back to facts. Let's stop talking about phantoms and will o' the wisps and mirages; instead let's talk about a woman of whose existence there has never at any time been any doubt. Everybody saw Marcella Henderson in life, and everybody saw her just as plainly afterward in death. *She* was no phantom. She was murdered. The police have photographs showing that. That's the first fact. All of us see that man over there in the prisoner's dock, with his head bowed low through all of this— no, now he's raising it to stare defiantly over at me. He's on trial here for his life. That's the second fact."

In a confidential, theatrical aside: "I like facts much better than fancies, don't you, ladies and gentlemen? They're much easier to handle.

"And the third fact? Here's the third fact. He murdered her. Yes, that's as concrete, as undeniable, a fact as the first two. Every detail of it is a fact, already proven once here in this room. We're not asking you to believe in phantoms, in wraiths, in hallucinations, like the defense!" Raising his voice. "We have documents, affidavits, evidence, for every statement we make, every step of the way!" Bringing his fist crashing down on the rail before the jury-box.

Impressive pause. Then in a quieter voice. "You've already been made acquainted with the circumstances, the domestic background, immediately preceding the murder. The accused himself doesn't deny their accuracy. You've heard him confirm them; under pressure, unwillingly perhaps, but confirm them nevertheless. There hasn't been a false statement made about them; don't take my word for that, take his. I asked him that yesterday on the stand, and you all heard his answer. I'll run over them once more, briefly, for you.

"Scott Henderson fell in love outside of his own home. He's not up here for having done that. The girl he fell in love with is not on trial here. You've noticed that her name hasn't been mentioned in this courtroom, she hasn't been dragged forward, compelled to testify, involved in any way in this brutal, inexcusable murder. Why? Because she doesn't deserve to be. She had nothing to do with it. It's not our purpose to punish the innocent here in this courtroom, to subject her to the notoriety and humiliation that would follow. The crime was his—that man whom you see there—and his alone. Not hers. She's blameless. She's been investigated both by the police and by the prosecution, and absolved of any connection, or incitement, or even knowledge of what had happened, until it was all over. She's suffering enough right now through no fault of her own. We're in general agreement on that one point, all of us, defense as well as prosecution. Her name and identity is known to us, but we've called her 'The Girl' throughout, and we'll continue to do so.

"Very well. He was already dangerously in love with The Girl by the time he remembered to tell her he was married. Yes, I say dangerously—from his wife's viewpoint. The Girl wouldn't have him on those terms. She was, and is, a decent person, a fine human being; every one of us who has spoken to her feels that way strongly about her. I do myself, ladies and gentlemen; she's a lovely, unfortunate person who happened to meet the wrong man. So as I say, she wouldn't have him on those terms. She didn't want to hurt anyone else. He found he couldn't have his cake and eat it too.

"Very well, he went to his wife and he asked her to divorce him. Cold-bloodedly, just like that. She refused him a divorce. Why? Because, to her, marriage was a sacred institution. Not just a passing affair, to be broken off short at a whim. Strange wife, wasn't she?

"The Girl's suggestion, when he told her this, was that they forget all about one another. He couldn't see it that way. He found himself caught between the horns of a dilemma. His wife wouldn't give him up, and he wouldn't give The Girl up.

"He bided his time and then he tried once more. And if you'd speak of the first method as cold-blooded, what would you say of the way he went about it the second time? He put himself out to *entertain* her the way a customer's man entertains an out-of-town buyer with whom he is trying to transact a business-deal. That should give you a good insight into his character, ladies and gentlemen; that should tell you what calibre man he is. That was all a scrapped marriage, a broken home, a discarded wife, were worth to him. An evening's paltry entertainment.

"He bought two tickets for the theatre, he reserved a table at a restaurant. He came home and told her he was taking her out. She couldn't understand this sudden attentiveness. She mistakenly thought, for a moment, that perhaps there was a reconciliation in the air. She sat down at her mirror and she began to get ready.

"A few moments later he returned to the room and he found her still sitting there at her dressing-table, without going any further in her preparations. She understood a little better what his purpose was now.

"She told him that she wouldn't give him up. She told him, in effect, that she valued her home higher than two orchestra-seats and a course dinner. In other words, without giving him time to ask her, she had refused him a divorce a second time. That was one time too many.

"He was at the final stage of his own preparations. He had his necktie open in his hands, measured off, ready to insert it under his collar. Instead, in a blind ungovernable rage at being outguessed and out-generaled, he dropped it over her head as she sat there at her mirror. He tightened it around her neck, he twined the ends together with unimaginable cruelty and strength and will to kill. The police-officers have told you how it had to be cut off, practically *pared* off, it was so imbedded in her soft throat. Did you ever try to tear one of these seven-fold rep silk ties between your hands, ladies and gentlemen? It can't be done; the edges will slice your fingers like a knife, but you can't sever them.

"She died. She flung her arms out once or twice, just in the beginning, and then she died there, between her husband's hands. The man that had sworn to cherish and protect her. Don't forget that.

"He held her like that, upright at her own mirror, letting her look on at her own death-struggles, so to speak, for long minutes. Long, long minutes. So that she was dead long before he let her fall over from that upright position he'd held her in. Then when he was sure that she was dead, that she was good and dead, that she was dead beyond re-

call, that she was out of his way once and for all—what
did he do then?

"Did he try to bring her back, did he feel any remorse,
did he show any regret? No, I'll tell you what he did. *He
calmly went ahead and finished his own dressing*, right
there in the room with her. He picked up another necktie
and put that on, to take the place of the one he'd garrotted
her with. He put on his hat and his coat, and just before he
left he called The Girl up. Luckily for her, and it was the
luckiest thing that ever happened to her in her life, she
wasn't there at the time to get that call. She never knew
about it until hours afterward. And why did he call her
up, with his hands still moist and reeking from taking his
wife's life? Not in remorse, not to confess what he'd just
done and ask her to help him or advise him. No, no. To
use her for a catspaw. To make a living alibi out of her,
without her knowledge. To ask her to go out with him
instead, on those same tickets, on that same table reservation. He probably would have set his own watch back,
just before meeting her, and commented on it, so that she
would be sure to remember afterwards, and come forward
in good faith and shield him with her honestly-given testimony.

"Is that a murderer for you, ladies and gentlemen, or
isn't it?

"But that didn't work, he couldn't get her. So he did the
next best thing. He went out alone, cold-bloodedly went
through the whole routine he had prepared for himself
and his wife, without missing a single stop, from six to
midnight. At the time it didn't occur to him to do what he
now says he did: pick up some stray along the way and
use her for his alibi. He was too excited, too confused, just
then. Or perhaps it did enter his mind, but he lacked the

nerve; was afraid to trust a stranger, afraid his manner would betray him. Or then again maybe it was because he reasoned that it was already too late for that to do him any good; too much time had passed by now since he'd left his own house. His living alibi could have been made just as easily to count against him as for him, once the crime was more than just a few minutes old. A little adroit questioning would have been able to extract the exact time he had *really* met her, and not the time he wished it to be believed he had met her. He thought of all that.

"So what was better than that, even? Why, an imaginary companion, of course. A phantom at his side, purposely left vague, left blurred, so that she could never be retrieved later on to damn his story of when they had met. In other words, which was preferable for his purposes: an unsupported alibi or a refuted one? I leave that up to you yourselves, ladies and gentlemen. An unsupported one could never be completely confirmed, but it would always seem to leave a reasonable doubt open. A refuted one would be automatically cast back in his face and leave him no further defense. That was the best he could do, that was the best he could get, and he made his decision accordingly.

"In other words, he deliberately injected a myth into the proceedings, *knowing* she did not exist, *knowing* she could never be found, and perfectly content to have her *not* found, for only while she remains *not* found is his fractional alibi of any service to him.

"In conclusion, let me ask you ladies and gentlemen just one simple question. Is it natural, is it likely, when a man's very life depends on his ability to remember certain details in the appearance of another, for him to be unable to recall a single, solitary one of them? Not one, mind you!

He is unable to recall the color of her eyes, or the color of her hair, or the contour of her face, or her height, or her girth, or anything else about her. Put yourselves in his place. Would *you* be likely to forget so completely, so devastatingly, if your lives depended on it? Self-preservation can be a wonderful spur to the memory, you know. Is it at all plausible that he would forget her so totally, if he really wished her to be found? If she exists, or ever did, *to be* found? I leave you with that thought.

"I don't think there's much more I have to say to you, ladies and gentlemen of the jury. It's a simple case. The issue is clear, without anything to confuse it."

Pointing with dramatic prolongation. "The State accuses that man whom you see there, Scott Henderson, of murdering his wife.

"The State demands his life in return.

"The State rests its case."

6: *The Ninetieth Day Before the Execution*

"WILL the accused please rise and face the jury?

"Will the foreman of the jury please stand?

"Ladies and gentlemen of the jury, have you reached a verdict?"

"We have, your honor."

"Do you find this defendant guilt or not guilty of the charge made against him?"

"Guilty, your honor."

Strangled voice from the direction of the prisoner's dock: "Oh my God—no—!"

7: *The Eighty-seventh Day Before the Execution*

"PRISONER at the bar, have you anything to say before this court passes sentence upon you?"

"What is there to say, when they tell you you have committed a crime, and you and you alone know you haven't? Who is there to hear you, and who is there to believe you?

"You're about to tell me that I must die, and if you tell me I must, I must. I'm not more afraid of dying than any other man. But I'm just as afraid of dying as any other man. It isn't easy to die at all, but it's even harder to die for a mistake. I'm not dying for something I've done, but for a mistake. And that's the hardest way to die of all. When the time comes, I'll meet it the best I can; that's all I can do anyway.

"But I say to you now, all of you, who won't listen and don't believe: I didn't do that. I didn't do it. Not all the findings of all the juries, not all the trials in all the courts, not all the executions in all the electric chairs—in the whole world—can make what isn't so, so.

"I'm ready to hear it now, your honor. Quite ready."

Voice from the bench, in a sympathetic aside: "I'm sorry, Mr. Henderson. I don't think I've ever heard a more compelling, dignified, manly plea from anyone who has stood before me for sentence. But the verdict of the jury in this case gives me no alternative."

Same voice, slightly louder: "Scott Henderson, having

been tried and found guilty of murder in the first degree, I
hereby sentence you to die in the electric chair, in the
State Prison at ———, during the week beginning October
20th, said sentence to be carried out by the warden of the
prison, and may God have mercy on your soul."

8: The Twenty-first Day Before the Execution

Low voice, just outside the cell in the Death House corridor: "Here he is, in this one."

Louder, above a jangle of keys: "Somebody here to see
you, Henderson."

Henderson doesn't speak or move. Gate is opened, then
closed again. Long, awkward pause, while they look at
one another.

"Guess you don't remember me."

"You remember the people that kill you."

"I don't kill people, Henderson. I turn people who commit crimes over to those whose job it is to try them."

"Then you come around afterward to make sure they
haven't gotten away, to satisfy yourself they're still there
where you put them, getting it rubbed into them, day by
day and minute by minute. It must worry you. Well, take
a look. I'm here. I'm safe on ice. Now you can go away
happy."

"You're bitter, Henderson."

"It doesn't sweeten you any to die at thirty-two."

Burgess didn't answer that. No one could have, ade-
quately. He shuttered his eyes rapidly a couple of times to
show that it had hit. He went over to the skinny canal of
opening and looked out.

"Small, isn't it?" Henderson said, without turning his head to look.

Burgess promptly turned and came away from it, at that, as though it had closed up on him. He took something out of his pocket, stopped before the bunk the other was sitting crouched on. "Cigarette?"

Henderson looked up derisively. "What's the matter with them?"

"Ah, don't be like that," the detective protested throatily. He continued to hold them out.

Henderson took one grudgingly at last, more as if by doing so to get him to move away from him than because he really wanted one. His eyes were still bitter. He wiped the small cylinder insultingly on his sleeve before putting it to his mouth.

Burgess gave him a light for it. Henderson looked his scorn at him even for that, holding his eyes steady, above the small flame, on the other's face. "What's this, the day of the execution already?"

"I know how you feel—" Burgess began in mild remonstrance.

Henderson reared up suddenly on the slab. "*You* know how I feel!" he flared. He snapped ashes down toward the detective's feet, by way of indicating them. "They can go anywhere they feel like!" He jabbed his thumb toward his own. "But *they* can't!" His mouth looped downward at one corner. "Get out of here. Get out. Go back and kill somebody else. Get fresh material. I'm second-hand, I've been worked-over once already."

He lay back again, blew a tracer of smoke out along the wall. It mushroomed when it hit the top of the bunk, came down toward him again.

They had quit looking at one another. But Burgess was

standing still, hadn't gone. He said finally, "I understand your appeal's been turned down."

"Yes, my appeal's been turned down. Now there are no more hitches, no more impediments, nothing further to interfere with the ceremonial bonfire. Now I can skid straight down the chute without anything more to stop me. Now the cannibals won't have to go hungry. Now they can make a nice, swift, clean-cut job of it. Streamlined." He turned and looked at his listener. "What're *you* looking so mournful about? Sorry because the agony can't be prolonged? Sorry because I can't die twice over?"

Burgess made a wry face as though his cigarette tasted rotten. He stepped on it. "Don't hit below the belt, Henderson. My dukes aren't even up."

Henderson looked at him intently for awhile, as though noticing something in his manner for the first time through the red haze of anger that had hovered over his perceptions until now. "What's on your mind?" he asked. "What brings you around here like this, anyway, months afterward?"

Burgess felt the back of his neck. "I don't know how to put it myself. It's a funny thing for a dick to do," he admitted. "I know my job with you ended when you were indicted by the Grand Jury and bound over for trial— It's sort of hard to bring out," he ended lamely.

"Why? It shouldn't be. I'm just a condemned guy in a cell."

"That's just why it is. I came up to—well, what I'm here to say is—" He stopped a minute, then blurted out: "I believe you're innocent. Well, there it is, for what it's worth, and it's not worth anything—to you or me either. I don't think you did it, Henderson."

Long wait.

"Well, say something. Don't just sit there looking at me."

"I don't know what to say when a guy digs up the corpse he helped to bury and says, 'Sorry, old man, I guess I've made a mistake.' You better tell me what to say."

"I guess you're right. I guess there's nothing to say. But I still claim I did my part of the job right, on the evidence there was to go by. I'll go further than that. I'd do the same thing over again tomorrow, if it had to be done a second time. My personal feelings don't count; my job is to work with concrete things."

"And what brought on this profound change of conviction?" Henderson asked, with a dull sort of irony.

"That's as hard to explain, to make clear, as any of the rest of it. It's been a slow thing, it's taken weeks and months to soak through me. About as slow as water soaking through a stack of blotters. It started in at the trial, I guess. It worked by a sort of reverse process. All the things that they made to count against you so heavily, they seemed to point the other way around, to me, later on when I ran over them in my own mind.

"I don't know if you can quite get what I mean. Framed alibis are always so clever, so smooth, so chock-full of plausible details. Yours was so lame, so blank. You couldn't remember a single thing about this woman. A ten-year-old child would have been able to do a better job of description. As I sat in the back of the courtroom listening, it slowly damned on me: hey, that must be the truth he's telling! Any lie, any lie at all, would have more meat on its bones than that. Only a man who was *not* guilty could frustrate his own chances as thoroughly as you did. The guilty are smarter than that. Your life was at stake, and all you could muster to protect yourself was two nouns and an adjective. 'Woman,' 'hat,' and 'funny.' I thought to myself, 'How true to life that is.' A guy is all riled up inside from a row at home, he picks up someone he's not interested in in the first place. Then right on top of that comes the mental cloudburst of finding out there's been a murder in his house and hearing himself accused of it—"

He gestured expressively. "Which is more likely: that he'd remember such a stranger in exhaustive detail, or that what little impression remained of her in the first place would be completely washed away, leaving the slate blank?

"It's been on my mind a long time now. It's kept coming back to me with more and more pressure each time. Once before I already started to come up here, but then I turned around and backed out again. Then I talked to Miss Richman once or twice—"

Henderson elongated his neck. "I begin to see light."

The detective said, sharply and at once: "No you don't, at all! You probably think she came to see me and finally influenced me— It was the other way around. I first looked her up, and went to have a talk with her—to tell her pretty much what I've told you today. Since then, I admit, she's been to see me several times—not at Headquarters but at my own place—and we've had several more talks about it. But that's neither here nor there. Miss Richman nor nobody else can put anything in my mind if it wasn't in there already. If there's any changing with me, it's got to be done on the inside, and not from the outside in. If I'm up here to see you today, it's on my own hook. I'm not here at her suggestion. She didn't know I was coming up here. I didn't myself—until I did."

He started to walk back and forth. "Well, I've got it off my chest now. I still won't retract. I did my part of

the job the only way it could have been done, the way the
evidence called for it to be done. And you can't ask any
more of a man than that."

Henderson didn't answer. He sat staring moodily at the
floor. It was a sort of quiescent brooding. He seemed less
actively bitter than in the beginning. The shadow made
by Burgess' pacing kept passing and repassing him. He
didn't bother to look up at its source.

Then the shadow stood still, and he could hear the sound
of coins jangling thoughtfully inside a pocket-lining.

Burgess' voice said: "You've got to get hold of someone that can help you. That can work at it full-time for
you."

He jingled some more. "I can't, I've got work of my
own. Oh, I know in movies and such, there are these glori-
fied detectives that chuck everything just to go off on
some sideline of their own. I've got a wife and kids. I need
my job. And you and me are strangers, after all."

Henderson didn't move his head. "I didn't ask you to,"
he murmured quietly.

Burgess quit jingling finally, came part of the way back
to him. "Get someone that's close to you, that's all for
you—" He tightened his fist and hoisted it in promise,
"—and I'll back him up all I can."

Henderson looked up for the first time, then down again.
He said one word, dispiritedly. "Who?"

"It needs someone that'll put a passion into it, a belief,
a fervor. Someone who isn't doing it for money, nor for
his own advancement. Someone who's doing it for you,
because you're Scott Henderson, and no other reason.
Because he likes you, yes even loves you, because he'd
almost rather die himself than have you die. Someone that
won't be licked, even when he is. Someone that won't

know it's too late, even when it is. That's the kind of flame it needs, that's the kind of juice. That and only that'll swing it."

His hand had come to rest on Henderson's shoulder while he spoke, in an accolade of insistence.

"You've got a girl that feels that way about you, I know. But she's just a girl. She's got the flame, but not the experience. She's doing what she can, but it isn't enough."

For the first time Henderson's bleak expression softened a little. He shot a brief look of gratitude, meant for her, by proxy at the detective. "I might have known—" he murmured.

"It needs a man. Someone that knows his way around. And yet has that feeling for you she has. You must have someone like that. Everyone has someone like that in his life."

"Yes, when they first start out. I used to, I guess, like everyone else. They seem to drop off along the way, as you get older. Especially after you get married."

"They don't drop off, if they're what I'm talking about," Burgess insisted. "Whether you keep in touch with them or not has nothing to do with it. If it's once there, it's there."

"There was a guy once, he and I we were as close as brothers," Henderson admitted. "But that was in the past—"

"There's no time-limit on friendship."

"He isn't here right now, anyway. The last time I met him he told me he was leaving the next day for South America. He had a five-year contract with some oil company."

He quirked his head at the detective. "For a fellow in your line of work, you seem to have quite a few illusions left intact, haven't you? That would be asking something, wouldn't it? Expect someone to come back three thousand miles and can his whole immediate future, to go to bat for a friend at the drop of a hat. And not a current friend either, mind you. Remember, you get thicker-skinned as you get older. Some of the idealism peels off. The man of thirty-two isn't the same pal to you the lad of twenty-five was, and you're not to him."

Burgess cut across his objections. "Just answer one thing. Would he have once done it?"

"He would have once done it."

"Then if he would have once done it, he'll still do it. I tell you again there's no age-limit on that kind of loyalty. If he had it, then he has it. If he hasn't it, then that only proves he never did have it."

"But that's an unfair test, that's putting the hurdle too high."

"If he's the sort of a guy that would weigh a five-year-contract against your life," Burgess argued, "then he's no good to you anyway. If he isn't, then he's the guy you need. Why not give him a chance to come through first, before you start to talk as though he won't?"

He took a memorandum-book out of his pocket, tore off a blank leaf, poised his knee for a writing-rest, foot to the edge of the bunk.

NN29 22 CABLE VIA NBN =   ———, SEPT 20

NLT JOHN LOMBARD =
Compania Petrolera Sudamericana
Head Office, Caracas, Venezuela

Have been sentenced for Marcellas death since you left a certain key witness can clear me if found my lawyer here has reached the end of his resources this is to ask

you to come up and help me have no one else to turn
to and no other chance of pulling through sentence set
for third week October and appeal has been turned
down give me a hand will you

                        SCOTT HENDERSON

9: *The Eighteenth Day Before the Execution*

HE still had some of the tan on him from warmer latitudes.
He'd come up so quick he'd brought it with him, like
people do when they travel nowadays; a cold in the head
flies with them from the West Coast to the East; a three-
day boil on the neck lasts from Rio to La Guardia Field
before it pops.

He looked about the age Scott Henderson had once
been; the former Scott Henderson of five or six months
ago, not the pinched death-mask lingering on in a cell,
who counted years by hours.

He was still wearing the clothes he'd put on in South
America. A snowy panama that was out of season up here
right now, and a gray flannel suit that was too light, both
in shade and weight, for an American autumn. It needed
the blazing Venezuelan sunshine to make it seem less conspicuous.

He was moderately tall, and easy-moving with it; no
effort at all to get around. You could think of him as always chasing after a street-car, even when it was already
a block away, because it was so easy for him to catch up
with it. He was anything but a natty dresser, in spite of
his vernal clothes. His small mustache could have stood a

touch of the scissors, and his necktie needed steaming, it kept curling around on itself all the way down, like a spiral of spun-sugar candy. The impression he gave, in short, was that he'd be a lot better at bossing a crew of men or poring over a draughting-board than dancing on a ball-room-floor with the ladies. There was a certain gravity about him that indicated that, if outward indications are ever any good. What used to be called, in the days of simpler cataloguing, a man's man.

"How's he taking it?" he asked the guard in an under-tone as he followed him along the tier.

"Just about." Meaning, what can you expect?

"Just about, eh?" He shook his head, muttered under his breath: "Poor cuss."

The guard had reached it, was opening it up.

He held back a moment, swallowed hard as if to get his throat working smoothly, then turned the corner of the cell-grate into view. He went into the cell with a wry grin on his face and an outstretched hand leading the way. As though he was running into him in the lounge of the Savoy-Plaza.

"Well lookit old Hendy," he drawled. "What're you doing, trying to be funny?"

There was none of the bitterness present in Henderson's reaction there had been the day the detective had visited him. You could tell this man was an old friend. His drawn face lighted up. He answered him in kind. "I live here now. How d'ye like that?"

They pumped hands as if they'd never get through. They were still working away at it after the guard had locked up and gone off again.

That link of hands carried messages for them, unspoken

but plainly understood. Henderson's was a warmly grateful: "You came. You showed up. So that stuff about a real friend isn't the bunk."

And Lombard's was a fervent, encouraging: "I'm with you. I'm damned if they're going to do it."

After that, they steered clear of the subject the first few minutes. They said everything but what they really wanted to. A sort of skittishness, a diffidence, that a particular topic, when it is too vital, bleeding, and raw, will sometimes bring about.

Thus Lombard said: "Gee, that was a dusty ride on the train, getting up here."

And Henderson: "You look good, Jack. Must agree with you down there."

"Agree, hell! Don't talk about it, will you? Of all the lousy, godforsaken holes! And the food! *And* the mosquitoes! I was a sucker ever to sign up for five years like I did."

"But there was good money in it, I suppose, wasn't there?"

"Sure. But what am I going to do with it down there anyway? Nowhere to spend it. Even the beer has a kerosene flavor."

Henderson mumbled, "I feel low, spiking it for you, though."

"You did me a favor," Lombard protested gallantly. "The contract's still on, anyway. This is just time off I wangled."

He waited a moment or two more. Then finally he edged up to it; the *it* that was on both their minds. He quit looking at his friend, looked somewhere else instead. "What about this thing anyway, Hendy?"

Henderson tried to smile. "Well, there's a member of

the Class of '30 going to take part in an electrical experiment two and a half weeks from today. What was it they gave me in the year-book? 'Most likely to get his name in the papers.' Good prophecy. I'll probably make every edition that day."

Lombard's eyes turned to stare at him truculently. "No you won't. Let's quit horsing around. We've known each other half our lives; may as well kick off our shoes and drop the company-manners."

"Sure," Henderson agreed forlornly. "What the hell, life's so short." He belatedly realized the unintentional appropriateness of that, grinned sheepishly.

Lombard slung one hip across the rim of the washbowl in the corner and relieved the leg that supported it of floor-duty. He took it by the ankle with both hands and held it up. "I only met her once," he said thoughtfully.

"Twice," Henderson corrected. "There was that time we ran into you on the street, remember?"

"Yeah, I remember. She kept pulling you by the arm, from behind, to break it up."

"She was on her way to buy some clothes, and you know how they are when that's in the wind. Neither time nor tide—" Then he apologized still further, in behalf of someone who was dead and gone, apparently without realizing how perfectly unimportant it was now. "We were always going to have you up for dinner, but I dunno—somehow—you know how those things are."

"I know how it is," Lombard agreed with diplomatic understanding. "No wife ever yet liked her husband's pre-marriage friends." He took out the pow-wow cigarettes, threw them across the narrow cell. "Don't mind if they make your tongue swell up and your lips blister. They're from down there; part gunpowder and part insecticide.

I haven't had time to change back to ours yet."

He took a thoughtful drag. "Well, I guess you better give me the dope."

Henderson pulled up a sigh from way in. "Yeah, I guess I better. I've been over it so many times already, I think I could reel it off backwards, or in my sleep."

"To me it's like a blackboard without anything written on it yet. So don't skip anything if you can help it."

"That marriage of mine and Marcella's was just a prelim, not the main event it should have been at all. A guy don't usually go around admitting that, even to his friends, but this is the death house and it seems foolish to have reticences here. A little over a year ago, the main bout suddenly came up. And too late for me to take part in. You never met her, don't know her, so there's no reason for me to mention her name. They were decent enough to do that for me at the trial too. All through it they just called her The Girl. I'll do that here, I'll call her My Girl to you."

"Your Girl," Lombard assented. He had his arms folded, cigarette sticking out from behind his elbow, and was staring down himself broodingly at the floor, listening hard.

"My Girl, poor girl. It was It, the real thing, the McCoy. If you're not married, and It comes along—you're safe. Or if your marriage itself happens to be It, that's better still, you're on pure velvet. Or if you're married, and It never comes along—you're still safe, even if you're only half-alive and don't know it. It's when you're married, and It shows up only after it's too late—that you want to look out."

"That you want to look out," murmured Lombard with a sort of musing compassion.

"It was a clean little thing. I told My Girl about Marcella the second time I saw her. That was supposed to be the last time we saw each other. The twelfth time we saw each other we were still trying to make it the last time. We tried to steer clear of each other—like steel-filings try to steer clear of a magnet.

"Marcella knew about her within thirty days after it had started. I saw to it that she did, I went and told her. It wasn't a case of any sudden shock, get that. She just smiled about it a little, and she waited. Like someone watching two flies under a tumbler turned upside-down.

"I went to her and asked for a divorce. This was at about mid-point. That slow, thoughtful smile came out on her again. She hadn't seemed to set any particular store by me until then, that I could notice. Just that thing that dropped shoes in the next aisle over from her. She said she'd have to think it over. She thought it over. The weeks went by, the months. She took her time thinking it over, she kept me dangling like that. I'd get that slow, mocking smile every now and then. She was the only one of the three of us having a good time out of it.

"It was pulling me inside-out. I'm a grown man, and I wanted My Girl. I wasn't going to let myself be gypped, I didn't want any affair, I wanted my wife. And the woman in my house, she wasn't my wife."

The hands before his face that he stared down through, they shook a little even at this late day.

"My Girl said to me, 'There must be some way out. We're in her hands and she knows it. This sullen silence on your part, that's the wrong attitude. That brings out an equally sulky opposition on her part. Go to her as a man goes to a friend. Take her out some night, have a heart-to-heart talk with her. When two people once loved one another, as you and she did, there must be something left of it, if it's only a memory in common. There must be some vestige of good will, of kindly feeling for you, you can reach in her. Make her see it's the best thing for her own sake, as well as yours and mine.'

"So I bought tickets for a show, and I reserved a table for us at our old place, where we used to go in the days before our marriage. And I went home and said, 'Let's go out together again, shall we? Let's go out tonight like we used to.'

"Came that slow smile again, and she said 'Why not?' As I stepped into the shower, she was sitting there at the glass beginning to get ready. All the old ways I knew by heart, the first little touches here and there. I whistled in the shower. I liked her very much in the shower. I realized what the trouble was; I saw I'd always liked her, and I'd mistaken it for love."

He let the cigarette fall from his hand, flattened it. Then kept looking there. "Why didn't she refuse at once? Why did she let me whistle in the shower? Watch me in the glass take pains with the part in my hair? Get satisfaction out of the way my handkerchief looked in the breast-pocket of my coat? Be happy all over for the first time in six months? Why did she pretend she was going, when she knew from the first she didn't intend to? Because that was her way. That was her. Because she loved to keep me dangling in suspense. Even about that smaller matter, as well as the larger one.

"I caught on little by little. Her smile, reflected in the glass. The way she wasn't really getting anywhere with those little touches of hers. I was holding my necktie out in my hands, ready to sling it on. And finally even the little touches had quit, she was sitting there not moving

her hands any more, just sitting there doing nothing. Only
the smile stayed on, the smile at a man in love. A man in
love and at your mercy.

"There are two stories, theirs and mine. And both are
identical up to that point; not a hairsbreadth variation between the two. They didn't bring out a single detail that
wasn't true. Every slightest motion I made, up to there,
they had down pat. They did their research-work well,
perfect. And then, as I stood behind her looking into the
same glass with my necktie stretched out between my
hands, the two stories split as far apart as the hands of a
clock at six. Mine goes all the way over this way, theirs
goes all the way over that.

"I'm telling you mine now. I'm telling you the true one.

"She was just waiting for me to ask her. That's all she
was sitting there for like that. The smile, the still hands,
demurely folded on the table-edge. Finally I did, after I'd
watched her for a moment. I said, 'Aren't you going?'

"She laughed. Gee how she laughed. How hard, how
long and hearty. I'd never known until then what a terrible weapon laughter can be. I could see my face, over
there above hers in the glass, getting white.

"She said, 'But don't waste the tickets. Why throw out
good money? Take *her* instead. She can have the show.
She can have the dinner. She can have you altogether. *But
she can't have you in the only way she wants you.*'

"That was her answer. That was always going to be
her answer, from then on, I knew it then. Forever, for the
rest of our lives. And that's an awful long time.

"Then here's what happened next. I clenched my teeth
and drew my arm back, in a line with the side of her jaw.
I don't remember what happened to the necktie I'd been
holding. It must have dropped to the floor. I only know it

didn't go around her neck.

"I never let fly. I couldn't. I'm not that way. She even tried to get me to. I don't know why. Or maybe because she knew she was safe, I was incapable of doing it. She'd seen me in the glass, of course, she didn't have to turn her head. She jeered, 'Go ahead, hit me. Casey at the bat. That won't get it for you either. Nothing will get it for you; whether you're sweet or whether you're sour, whether you're gentle or whether you're rough.'

"Then we both said things we shouldn't have, like people do. But it was just mouth-fireworks, that was all. I never laid a hand on her. I said, 'You don't want me; then what the hell are you hanging onto me for?'

"She said, 'You might come in handy, in case of burglars.'

"I said, 'You bet that's all there'll be to it from now on!'

"She said, 'I wonder if I'll be able to tell the difference?'

"I said, 'That reminds me. You've got something coming to you,' I took two dollars out of my wallet and I threw them on the floor behind her. I said, 'That's for being married to you! And I'll pay the piano-player on my way downstairs.'

"Sure, it was low, it was rotten. I grabbed my hat and coat and I got out of there fast. She was still laughing there at the glass when I left. She was laughing, Jack. She wasn't dead. I didn't touch her. Her laughter followed me through the door, even after I'd closed it. It drove me down the stairs on foot, without waiting for the car to come up. It drove me nuts, I couldn't get away from it fast enough. It even followed me all the way down to the next landing, and then finally it faded away."

He stopped for a long time, while the scene he had re-kindled slowly cooled and died again, before he could go ahead. There were traces of sweat in the creases running across his contracted forehead.

"Then when I came back," he said quietly, "she was dead and they said I did it. They said it happened at eight minutes and fifteen seconds after six. Her watch told them. It must have happened within ten minutes after I'd slammed the door behind me. That part of it still gives me the creeps, even now, when I think of it. He must have been lurking right there inside the building already, whoever he was—"

"But you say you went down the stairs yourself?"

"He might have been hidden up on the last stretch, between our floor and the roof. I don't know. Maybe he heard the whole thing. Maybe he even watched me go. Maybe I slammed the door so hard it rebounded instead of catching on, and he got in that way. He must have been in on her before she knew it. Maybe the very sound of her own laughter helped to cover him up, kept her from hearing anything until it was late."

"That makes it sound like some sort of a prowler, doesn't it?"

"Yes, but what *for?* The cops were never able to figure out what for, that's why they wouldn't give it any serious consideration. It wasn't robbery; nothing was taken. There was sixty dollars in cash right in the drawer in front of her, not even covered over. It wasn't attack, either. She was killed right where she'd been sitting, and left right where she'd been killed."

Lombard said, "One or the other could have been intended, and he got frightened off before he carried out the object of the intrusion. Either by some outside sound or by the very act he had just committed itself. That's happened a thousand and one times."

"Even that won't do," Henderson said dully. "Her diamond solitaire was lying there *loose* on the dressing-table
the whole time. It wasn't even on her finger. All he had to
do was scoop it up as he ran out. Frightened or not, how
long would that take? It stayed behind." He shook his
head. "The necktie damned me. It came out from underneath all the others on the rack. And the rack was fairly
deep within the closet. And that particular tie went with
every stitch I had on. Sure, because I took it out myself.
But I didn't twist it around her. I lost track of it in the
heat of the quarrel. It must have fallen unnoticed to the
floor. Then I grabbed up the one I'd come home with,
and whipped that around my collar, and stormed out.
Then he came creeping in, and it caught his eye as he
advanced unsuspectedly on her, and he picked it up—
God knows who he was, and God only knows why he
did it!"

Lombard said, "It may have been some impulse without
rhyme or reason, just an urge to kill for the sake of killing,
unleashed in some stray mental case hanging around outside. It may have been whipped up by the very scene of
violence between you, especially after he had detected that
the door wasn't securely closed. He realized he could commit it almost with impunity, and you'd be blamed for it.
There have been things like that, you know."

"If it was anything along those lines, then they'll never
get him. Those kind of killers are the hardest to track
down. Only some freak or fluke will ever open it up. Some
day they may get him for something else entirely, and
then he'll confess this one along with it, and that's the
first inkling they'll have. Long after it'll do me any good."

"What about this key-witness you mentioned in your
message?"

"I'm coming to that now. It's the one slim ray of hope in the whole thing. Even if they never get on to who really did it, there's a way for me to be cleared of it. The two findings aren't necessarily one and the same, in this case; they can be separate and distinct, and yet equally valid each in its own right."

He began punching one hand into the flat of the other, over and over while he spoke. "There's a certain woman, somewhere or other, right at this moment, as we sit here in this cell talking it over, who can clear me—simply by telling them at what time I met her at a certain bar eight blocks from where I lived. That time was ten minutes after six. And she knows it just as I know it; wherever and whoever she is, she knows it. They proved, by reënacting it, that I couldn't have reached that bar at that time and still have committed the murder back at my house. Jack, if you hope to do anything for me, if you want to pull me through this, you've got to find that woman. She and she alone is the answer."

Lombard took a long time. Finally he said, "What's been done about finding her, so far?"

"Everything," was the devastating answer, "everything under the sun."

Lombard came over and slumped down limply on the edge of the bunk beside him. "Whew!" he said, blowing through his clasped hands. "And if the police failed, your lawyer failed, everyone and everything failed, right at the time it happened and with all the time they needed— what a chance I have, months after it's cold and with eighteen days to do it in!"

The guard had showed up. Lombard stood up, let his hand trail off Henderson's slumped shoulder as he turned away to be let out.

Henderson raised his head. "Don't you want to shake hands?" he said falteringly.

"What for? I'll be back again tomorrow."

"You mean you're going to take a fling at it anyway?"

Lombard turned and gave him a look that was almost scathing, as if irked by the obtuseness of such a question. "What the hell gave you the idea I wasn't?" he growled surlily.

10: *The Seventeenth, the Sixteenth Days Before the Execution*

LOMBARD shuffled around the cell, hands in pockets, looking down at his own feet as though he'd never noticed how they worked before. Finally he stopped and said, "Hendy, you've got to do better than that. I'm not a magician, I can't just pull her out of a hat from nothing."

"Listen," Henderson said weariedly, "I've gone over the thing in my own mind until I'm sick of it, until I dream about it at nights. I can't squeeze a drop more detail out of it."

"Didn't you look at her face *at all?*"

"It must have gotten in the way plenty of times, but it didn't take."

"Let's start in again at the beginning and run through it once more. Don't look at me like that, it's the only thing we *can* do. She was already sitting on a stool at the bar when you walked in. Suppose you give me your first impression of her if you can. Try to recapture it. Sometimes there's a clearer visualization to be gained from a fleeting first impression than from all the more deliberate studies you can make later on. Well then, your first impression?"

"A hand reaching for pretzels."

Lombard eyed him scathingly. "How can you leave your own barstool, walk over to another, and accost somebody, without seeing them? Show me that trick sometime. You knew it was a girl, didn't you? You didn't think it was a mirror you were addressing? Well *how* did you know it was a girl?"

"She had on a skirt, so she was a girl, and she wasn't using crutches, so she was able-bodied. Those were the only two things I cared about. I was looking through her, seeing My Girl in my mind's eye the whole time I was with her; what do you expect me to be able to tell you?" Henderson flared in turn.

Lombard took a minute off to let the two of them calm down. Then: "What was her voice like? Did that tell you anything? Where she came from? What her background was?"

"That she'd been to high-school. That she was city-bred. She talked like we all do here. Pure metropolitan. About as colorless as boiled water."

"Then this was her home-town, if you couldn't notice any variation in accent. Whatever good that does us. In the taxi, what?"

"Nothing; the wheels went around."

"In the restaurant, what?"

Henderson arched his neck rebelliously. "Nothing. It's no use, Jack. Nothing. It won't come. I can't. I can't. She ate and she talked, that was all."

"Yes, but about what?"

"I can't remember. I can't remember a word of it. It wasn't meant to be remembered. It was just meant to pass the time, keep silence at a distance. The fish was excellent.

Wasn't the war terrible? No, she didn't care for another cigarette, thank you."

"You're driving me crazy. You sure must have loved Your Girl."

"I did. I do. Shut up about it."

"In the theatre, what?"

"Only that she stood up in her seat; I've already told you that three times. And you said yourself, that doesn't tell you what she was like, that only tells you what she did at one point."

Lombard came in closer. "Yes, but *why* did she stand up? That keeps eluding you. The curtain was still up, you say. People don't stand like that for no reason."

"I don't know why she stood up. I wasn't inside her mind."

"You weren't even inside your own, from what I can gather. Never mind, we can come back to that later. Once you've got the effect, the cause is bound to follow eventually." He moiled around for awhile, letting a brief pause rest them up.

"When she stood up like that, you looked at her then at least?"

"Looking is a physical act, with the pupils of the eyes; seeing is a mental one, with the cells of the brain. I looked at her all night long; I didn't see her once."

"This is torture," Lombard grimaced, squeezing the bridge of his nose up close beneath the brows. "I can't seem to get it from you. There must be *some*body I can get it from, *some*body who saw you with her that night. Two people can't go around town for six hours together without *some*body at least seeing them."

Henderson smiled wryly. "That's what I thought too. I found out I was wrong. There must have been a case of mass-astigmatism all over town that night. Sometimes they've got me wondering myself if there really was such a person, or if she wasn't just a hallucination on my part, a vagary of my own feverish imagination."

"You can cut that out right now," Lombard ordered curtly.

"Time's up," a voice said from outside.

Henderson got up, picked up a charred match-stick from the floor, and carried it over to the wall, where there were rows of little charred dabs, in parallel rows. The top lines had all been intercrossed into x's; the last few on the end were still single downward strokes. He added a cross-line to one, and made that into an x.

"And cut that out too!" Lombard added. He spit forcefully into his own hand, took a quick step over, gave the wall a violent sweep, and the whole bunch of them, crossed and uncrossed, were gone at once.

"All right, move over," he said, taking out pencil and paper.

"I'll stand for a change," Henderson said. "There's only room for one on the edge of that thing."

"Now you know what I want, don't you? Raw material, that hasn't already been worked-over. Second-string witnesses, people who weren't subpoenaed to appear at the trial, people who were overlooked both by the cops and Gregory, your lawyer."

"You don't want much. Ghosts, once-removed. Second-degree ghosts to help us get a line on a first-degree ghost. We better get a medium in on this with us."

"I don't care if they only brushed elbows with you, walked past on one side of the street while you two walked past on the other. The point is, I want to be the first to

get to them, if possible. I don't want anyone else's left-
overs. There must be some place we can drive a wedge in,
split this thing open. I don't care how diaphanous it is, I
want to rig up some kind of a list between us. All right,
here we go again. The bar."

"The inevitable bar," Henderson sighed.

"The barman's been used up already. Anyone else at it
but the two of you?"

"No."

"Take your time. Don't try to force it. It won't come
that way, when you try to force it. It drives it back."

(Four or five minutes.)

"Wait. A girl in a booth turned her head to look around
after her. I noticed that as we were leaving. Want that?"

Lombard's pencil moved. "Give me that sort of thing.
That's exactly the sort of thing I want. Can you tell me
anything else about this girl?"

"No. Even less than the woman I was with. Just the turn
of a head."

"Come on, now."

"The taxi. That's been used up. He was the big comic
relief at the trial."

"The restaurant comes next. Was there a hat-check girl
at this Maison Blanche?"

"She's one of the few with a legitimate excuse for not
remembering her. I *was* alone when I went up to her alcove; the phantom had separated from me to go into the
powder-room."

Lombard's pencil moved again. "There may have been
an attendant in there. Still, if she wasn't noticed with you,
there's even less chance she was noticed without you. Now
how about the restaurant, any heads turn there?"

"She joined me separately."

"That brings us to the theatre."

"There was a doorman with funny fish-hook mustaches, I remember that much. He did a double take-em on her hat."

"Good. He's in."

He jotted something. "How about the usher?"

"We got there late. Just a pocket-light in the dark."

"No good. How about the stage itself?"

"You mean the performers? I'm afraid the show ran off too fast."

"When she stood up like that it might have been seen. Were any of them questioned by the police?"

"No."

"It won't hurt for me to check. We're not passing up anything in this, understand, anything? If a *blind man* was anywhere near you that night, I'd want— What's matter?"

"Hey," Henderson had said sharply.

"What is it?"

"You just brought something back to me then. One was. A blind pan-handler tagged us as we were leaving—" Then as he saw Lombard's pencil briefly scrawl something, "You're kidding," he protested incredulously.

"Think so?" Lombard said levelly. "Wait and see." He cocked his pencil once more.

"That's all there is, there isn't any more."

Lombard put the list away in his pocket, stood up. "I'll make a dent in that somewhere along the line!" he promised grimly. He went over and whacked at the grate, to be let out. "And keep your eyes off that wall!" he added, catching the direction of Henderson's inadvertent glance, over to where the erased box-score had once been kept. "They're not going to get you in there." He thumbed the opposite direction along the corridor from the one he was about to take.

"They say they are," was Henderson's ironically-murmured answer.

Personal Columns, all newspapers:

"Will the young lady who was seated in a wall-booth at Anselmo's Bar with a companion, at or around 6.15 in the evening, May 20th last, and who may recall an orange hat that caused her to turn her head as its wearer was leaving, kindly get in touch with me. She was facing toward the back. If she remembers this it is vital that I hear from her without delay. A person's happiness is involved. All replies held in strictest confidence. Communicate J. L., Box 654, care of this newspaper."

No replies.

11: The Fifteenth Day Before the Execution

LOMBARD

A BLOWSY woman, with her graying hair in her eyes and an aura of cabbage around her, opened the door.

"O'Bannon? Michael O'Bannon?"

That was as far as he got. "Now listen, I've already been over to your office once today, and the man there said he'd give us until Wednesday. We're not trying to gyp the poor penniless company that needs the money so bad. Sure it must be down to its last fifty thousand bucks it must!"

"Madam, I'm not a collector. I simply wish to speak to the Michael O'Bannon who worked as doorman at the Casino last Spring."

"Yes, I can remember when he had that job," she agreed caustically. She turned her head slightly aside, raised her voice a little, as if she wished someone other than Lombard to overhear her. "They lose one job, and then they never move the seat of their pants off the chair from that day on to try and get another. They sit and wait for it to come to them!"

What sounded like the hoarse grunt of a trained seal came from somewhere in the interior.

"Someone to see you, Mike!" she bellowed. And then to Lombard, "You better go in to him yourself, he's got his shoes off."

Lombard advanced down a "railroad" hall that threatened to go on indefinitely, but didn't. It ended finally in a room whose center was occupied by an oilcloth-covered table.

Sidewise to this lolled the object of his visit, stretched across two straight-backed wooden chairs in a suspension-bridge arrangement, the unsupported part of him curving downward. He had off a good deal more than just his shoes; in fact, his upper attire consisted solely of an oatmeal-colored union-suit with elbow-length sleeves, and immediately over that a pair of braces. Two white-toed socks tilted acutely upward from the chair-seat opposite him. He laid aside a pink racing-form and a rancid pipe as Lombard entered. "And what can I do for you, sirr?" he rumbled accommodatingly.

Lombard put his hat on the table and sat down without being asked. "A friend of mine wishes to get in touch with someone," he began confidentially. It would be poor policy, he felt, to overawe these people ahead of time with mention of death-sentences, consultations with the police, and all that; they might become intimidated and chary of telling him anything, even if they were able to. "It means a lot to him. It means everything. Now. This is why I'm here. Can you recall a man and woman getting out of a taxi in front of the theatre, while you were working there, one night in May? You held the door for them, of course."

"Well now, I held the door for everybody that drove up, that was my job."

"They were a little late, probably the last people you greeted that particular night. Now this woman had on a bright orange hat. A very peculiar hat, with a thin tickler sticking straight up from it. It swept right in front of your eyes as she got out, she passed so close to you. Your eyes followed it like this: slowly, from one side over to the other. You know, like when something passes too close to you, and you can't make out what it is."

"Leave it to him," his wife put in challengingly from the doorway, "if it was anything on a pretty woman he'd do that anyway, whether he could make out what it was or not!"

Neither of the men paid any attention. "He saw you do that," Lombard went on. "He happened to notice it at the time, and he told me about it." He pressed his hands to the oilcloth, leaned toward him. "Can you remember? Does it come back to you? Can you remember her at all?"

O'Bannon shook his head ponderously. Then he gnawed his upper lip. Then he shook his head some more. He gave him a reproachful look. "D'ye know what you're asking, man? All those faces night after night! Nearly always two by two, lady and gent."

Lombard continued leaning across the table toward him for long minutes, as though the intensity of his gaze would be enough to bring it back to him of itself. "Try,

O'Bannon. Think back. Try, will you, O'Bannon? It means everything in the world to this poor guy."

The wife began to draw slowly nearer, at that, but still held her peace.

O'Bannon shook his head once more, this time with finality. "No," he said. "Out of my whole season there, out of all them people I opened car-doors for, I can only recall today one single individjule. A fellow who showed up by himself one night, full of booze. And that was because he fell out of the cab face-first when I opened the door, and I had to catch him in me arms—"

Lombard stemmed the flow of unwanted reminiscence that he suspected was about to follow. He got to his feet. "Then you don't, and you're sure you don't?"

"I don't, and I'm sure I don't." O'Bannon reached for the reeking pipe and the racing-chart again.

The wife was at their elbows by now. She had been eying Lombard speculatively for some moments past. The tip of her tongue peered forth in calculation for an instant at the corner of her mouth as she spoke. "Would there have been anything in it for us, now, if he had been able to?"

"Well, yes, I don't suppose I would have minded doing a little something for you, if you'd been able to give me what I wanted."

"D'ye hear that, Mike?" She pounced on her husband as though she were going to attack him. She began to shake him strenuously by one shoulder, using both hands for the purpose, as though she were kneading dough or massaging a sprain. "Try, Mike, try!"

He tried to ward her off, backing an arm defensively before his head. "How can I, with you rocking me like an empty rowboat? Even if it was in me head somewhere, lying low, you'd shake it clean out of me mind!"

"Well—no go, I guess," Lombard sighed. He turned away and moved disappointedly down the long defile of hall-passage.

He heard her voice rise to an exasperated wail, there in the room behind him, as she renewed her assault on her husband's obdurate shoulder. "Look, he's going! Oh, Mike, what's the matter with you! All the man wants you to do is remember something, and you can't even do that!"

She must have vented her disappointment on the inanimate objects about him. There was a roar of anguished protest. "Me pipe! Me handicap-sheet!"

Their voices were loud in disputation as Lombard closed the outer door after him. Then, suspiciously, there was a sudden conspiratorial hush. Lombard's face took on a slightly knowing look, as he started down the stairs.

Sure enough, in a moment more there was a swift onrush of footsteps in his wake along the inner hall, the door was flung open, and O'Bannon's wife called hectically down the stairwell after him: "Wait, mister! Come back! He just remembered! It just now came to him!"

"Oh, it did, did it?" Lombard said drily. He stopped where he was and turned to look up at her, but without making any move to reascend. He took out his wallet, ran his thumb tentatively along its edge. "Ask him was it a black or a white sling she was holding her arm in?"

She relayed the question resoundingly back into the interior. She got the answer, sent it on down to Lombard —slight hesitancy of voice and all. 'White—for the evening, you know."

Lombard put his wallet away again unopened. "Wrong number," he said firmly, and resumed his descent.

12: *The Fourteenth, Thirteenth, Twelfth Days*
Before the Execution

THE GIRL

SHE'D already been perched on the stool several minutes when he first became aware of her. And that was all the more unusual, in that there were only a scattering of others at the bar as yet; her arrival should have been that much more conspicuous. It only showed how unobtrusively she must have approached and settled into place.

It was at the very beginning of his turn of duty, so her arrival must have occurred only moments after his own taking up of position behind the bar, almost as though she had timed it that way: to arrive when he did. She had not yet been there when he first stepped out of the locker-room in freshly-starched jacket and glanced about his domain-to-be, that much he was sure of. At any rate, turning away from waiting on a man down at the other end, he became aware of her sitting there quiescently, and immediately approached.

"Yes, miss?"

Her eyes held his in a peculiarly sustained look, he thought. And then immediately thought, in postscript, that he must be mistaken, he must be only imagining it. All customers looked at him when they gave an order, for he was the means of bringing it to them.

In this gaze of hers there was a difference, though; the impression returned a second time, after having been discarded once. It was a personalized look. A look in its own right, with the giving of the order the adjunct, and not just an adjunct to the giving of the order. It was a look at *him*, the *man* to whom she was addressing the order, meant for him in his own right. It was a look that said: "Take note of me. Mark me well."

She asked for a little whiskey with water. As he turned away to get it, her eyes remained on him to the last. He had a trivial and fleeting feeling of being at a loss, of being unable to account for her bizarre scrutiny, that evaporated again almost as soon as it had risen. That did not bother him much, that was just there and gone again, at first.

Thus, the beginnings of it.

He brought her drink, and turned away immediately to wait on someone else.

An interval elapsed. An interval during which he did not think of her again, had forgotten her. An interval during which there should have been some slight alteration in her position, if only a shift of her hand, a raising or edging of her glass, a look elsewhere about the room. There wasn't. She sat there not moving. As still as a pasteboard cut-out of a girl seated on a bar-stool. Her drink was not touched, remained where he had left it, as he had left it. Only one thing moved: her eyes. They went wherever he went. They followed him about.

A pause came in his activities, and he encountered them again, for the first time since his original discovery of their peculiar fixity. He found now that they had been on him all the while, without his guessing it. It disconcerted him. He could find no meaning for it. He stole a look into the glass, to see if there was anything awry with his countenance or jacket. There wasn't, he was as other times, no one else was looking at him in that prolonged steadfast way but she. He could find no explanation for it.

It was intentional, of that there could be no doubt, for

it moved about as he moved about. It was no glazed, dreamy, inward-mulling stare that just happened to be turned his way; there was intelligence behind it, directed at him.

Awareness of it having once entered his mind, it could not be dislodged again, it remained with him to stay, and trouble him. He began watching her covertly from time to time himself now, each time thinking himself unobserved. Always he found her already looking at him when he did, always he left her continuing to look at him after he had already desisted. His sense of being at a loss deepened, became discomfort, little by little.

He had never seen a human being sit so still. Nothing about her moved. The drink remained as neglected as though he had not brought it at all. She sat there like a young, feminine Buddha, eyes gravely, uninterruptedly on him.

Discomfort was beginning to deepen into annoyance. He approached her at last, stopped before her.

"Don't you care for your drink, miss?"

This was meant to be a hint, a spur to get her to move on. It failed; she blunted it.

Her answer was toneless, told nothing. "Leave it there."

The circumstances were in her favor, for she was a girl, and girls are under no compulsion to be repetitious spenders at a bar, as a man customarily is if he expects to continue to be welcome. Moreover, she was not flirting, she was not seeking to have her check lifted, she was not behaving reprehensibly in any way, he was powerless against her.

He drew away from her again, worsted, looking back at her all the way down the curve of the bar, and her eyes followed him as persistently as ever.

Discomfort was settling into something chronic now. He tried to shrug it off with a squirming of the shoulders, an adjustment of his collar about the nape of his neck. He knew she was still looking, and he wouldn't look over himself any more to confirm it. Which only made it worse.

The demands of other customers, the thicker they came, instead of harassing him, were a relief now. The necessary manipulations they brought on gave him something to do, took his mind off that harrowing stare. But the lulls would keep coming back, when there was no one to attend to, nothing that needed polishing, no glass that needed filling, and it was then that her concentration on him would make itself felt the most. It was then that he didn't know what to do with his hands, or with his bar-cloth.

He upset a small chaser of beer as he was knifing it atop the sieve. He punched a wrong key in the cash-register.

At last, driven almost beyond endurance, he tackled her again, trying to come to grips with what she was doing to him.

"Is there anything I can do for you, miss?" he said with husky, choked resentment.

She spoke always without putting any clue into her voice. "Have I said there is?"

He leaned heavily on the bar. "Well, is there something you want from me?"

"Have I said I do?"

"Well, pardon me, but do I remind you of someone you know?"

"No one."

He was beginning to flounder. "I thought maybe there was, the way you keep looking at me—" he said unsteadily. It was meant to be a rebuke.

This time she didn't answer at all. Yet neither did her

eyes leave him. He finally was the one had to leave them again, withdraw as discomfited as ever.

She didn't smile, she didn't speak, she showed neither contrition nor yet outright hostility. She just sat and looked after him, with the inscrutable gravity of an owl.

It was a terrible weapon she had found and she was using. It does not ordinarily occur to people how utterly unbearable it can be to be looked at steadily over a protracted period of time, say an hour or two or three, simply because it is a thing that never happens to them, their fortitude is not put to the test.

It was happening to him now, and it was slowly unnerving him, fraying him. He was defenseless against it, both because he was confined within the semi-circle of the bar, couldn't walk away from it, and also because of its very nature. Each time he tried to buffet it back, he found that it was just a look, there was nothing there to seize hold of. The control of it rested with her. A beam, a ray, there was no way of warding it off, shunting it aside.

Symptoms that he had never noted in himself before, and would not have recognized by their clinical name of agoraphobia, began to assail him with increasing urgency; a longing to take cover, to seek refuge back within the locker-room, even a desire to squat down below the level of the bar-top where she could no longer see him readily. He mopped his brow furtively once or twice and fought them off. His eyes began to seek the clock overhead with increasing frequency, the clock that they had once told him a man's life depended on.

He longed to see her go. He began to pray for it. And yet it was obvious by now, had been for a long time past, that she had no intention of going of her own accord, would only go with the closing of the place. For none of

the usual reasons that cause people to seek a bar were oper-
ating in her case, and therefore there was no reprieve to be
expected of any of them. She was not there to wait for
anyone, or she would have been met long ago. She was
not there to drink, for that same untouched glass still sat
just where he had set it hours ago. She was there for one
purpose and one alone: to look at him.

Failing to be rid of her in any other way, he began to
long for closing time to come, to find his escape through
that. As the customers began to thin out, as the number of
counter-attractions about him lessened, her power to bring
herself to his notice rose accordingly. Presently there were
large gaps around the semi-circle fronting him, and that
only emphasized the remorseless fixity of that Medusa-
like countenance all the more.

He dropped a glass, and that was a thing he hadn't done
in months. She was shooting him to pieces. He glowered
at her and cursed her in soundless lip-movement as he
stooped to gather up the fragments.

And then finally, when he thought it was never coming
any more, the minute-hand notched twelve, and it was
four o'clock and closing-time had arrived. Two men engaged in earnest conversation, the last of all the other customers, rose unbidden and sauntered toward the entrance,
without interrupting their flow of amicable, low-voiced
talk. Not she. Not a muscle moved. The stagnant drink
still sat before her, and she sat on with it. Looking, watching, eying, without even a blink.

"Good night, gentlemen," he called out loudly after
the other two, so that she would understand.

She didn't move.

He opened the control-box and threw a switch. The
outer perimeter of lights went out, leaving just an inner

glow coming from behind the bar where he was, a hidden
sunset creeping up the mirrors and the tiers of bottles
ranged against the wall. He became a black silhouette
against it, and she a disembodied faintly-luminous face
peering in from the surrounding dimness.

He went up to her, took the hours-old drink away, and
threw it out, with a violent downward fling of the hand
that sent drops leaping up.

"We're closing up now," he said in a grating voice.

She moved at last. Suddenly she was on her feet beside
the stool, holding it for a moment to give the change of
position time to work its way through her circulatory
system.

His fingers worked deftly down the buttons of his
jacket. He said cholerically, "What was it? What was
the game? What was on your mind?"

She moved quietly off through the darkened tavern
toward the street-entrance without answering, as though
she hadn't heard him. He had never dreamed that such a
simple causative as the mere sight of a girl quitting a bar,
could bring such utter, contrite, prostrate relief welling
up in him. His jacket open all down the front, he supported himself there on one hand planted firmly down
upon the bar, and leaned limply, exhaustedly out in the
direction in which she had gone.

There was a night-light standing at the outer entrance,
and she came back into view again when she had reached
there. She stopped just short of the doorway, and turned,
and looked back at him across the intervening distance,
long and solemnly and with purposeful implication. As if
to show that the whole thing had been no illusion; more
than that, to show that this was not its end, that this was
just an interruption.

He turned from keying the door locked, and she was standing there quietly on the sidewalk, only a few yards off. She was turned expectantly facing toward the doorway, as if waiting for him to emerge.

He was forced to go toward her, because it was in that direction his path lay on leaving here of a night. They passed within a foot of one another, for the sidewalk was fairly narrow and she was posted out in the middle of it, not skulking back against the wall. Though her face turned slowly in time with his passing, he saw that she would have let him go by without speaking, and goaded by this silent obstinacy, he spoke himself, although only a second before he had intended ignoring her.

"What is it ye want of me?" he rumbled truculently.

"Have I said I want anything of you?"

He made to go on, then swung around on his heel to face her accusingly. "You sat in there just now, never once took your eyes off me! Never once the live-long night, d'ye hear me?" He pounded one hand within the other for outraged emphasis. "And now I find you outside here waiting around—"

"Is it forbidden to stand here in the street?"

He shook a thick finger at her ponderously. "I'm warning you, young woman! I'm telling you for your own good—!"

She didn't answer. She didn't open her mouth, and silence is always so victorious in argument. He turned and shambled off, breathing heavily with his own bafflement.

He didn't look back. Within twenty paces, even without looking back, he had become aware that she was advancing in turn behind him. It was not difficult to do so, for she was apparently making no effort to conceal the fact. The ticking-off of her small brittle shoes was clear-cut if subdued on the quiet night-pavement.

An up-and-down intersection glided by beneath him like a slightly-depressed asphalt stream-bed. Then presently another. Then still another. And through it all, as the town slowly veered over from west to east, came that unhurried *tick-chick, tick-chick,* behind him in the middle distance.

He turned his head, the first time simply to warn her off. She came on with maddening casualness, as though it were three in the afternoon. Her walk was slow, almost stately, as the feminine gait so often is when the figure is held erect and the pace is leisurely.

He went on again, briefly, then turned once more. This time his entire body, and flung himself back toward her in a sudden flurry of ungovernable exasperation.

She stopped advancing, but she held her ground, made no slightest retrograde move.

He closed in and bellowed full into her face: "Turn back now, will ye? That's enough of this now, d'ye hear? Turn back, or I'll—"

"*I* am going this way too," was all she said.

Again the circumstances were in her favor. Had their roles been reversed— But what man has sufficiently stout armor against ridicule to risk calling a policeman to complain that a solitary young girl is following him along the streets? She was not reviling him, she was not soliciting him, she was simply walking in the same direction he was; he was as helpless against her as he had been in the bar earlier.

He maintained his stance before her for a moment or two, but his defiance was of that face-saving kind that only marks time while it is waiting to extricate itself with the least possible embarrassment from a false situation. He spun around finally with a snort through his nose, meant to convey belligerence, but that somehow sounded a bit like windy helplessness. He drew away from her, resumed his homeward journeying.

Ten paces, fifteen, twenty. Behind him, as at a given signal, it recommenced again, steady as slow rain in a puddle. *Tick-chick, tick-chick, tick-chick.* She was coming after him once more.

He rounded the appointed corner, started up the roofed-over sidewalk stairway he used every night to reach his train. He halted up above, at the rear of the plank-floored station gallery that led through to the tracks, scanning the chute-like incline he had just emerged from for signs of her.

The oncoming tap of her footfalls took on a metallic ring as her feet clicked against the steel rims guarding the steps. In a moment her head came into view above the midway break in the stair-line.

A turnstile rumbled around after him, and he turned there on the other side of it, at bay, took up a defensive position.

She cleared the steps and came on, as matter-of-factly, as equably, as though he wasn't to be seen there at all in the gap fronting her. She already held the coin pinched between her fingers. She came on until there was just the width of the turnstile-arm between them.

He backed his arm at her, swinging it up all the way past its opposite shoulder, ready to fling it loose. It would have sent her spinning about the enclosure. His lip lifted in a canine snarl. "Get outa here, now. Gawan down below where ye came from!" He reached down and quickly plugged the coin-slot with the ball of his thumb just ahead of her own move toward it.

She desisted, shifted over to the adjoining one. Instantly he was there before her again. She shifted back to the original one. He reversed himself once more, again blocked it. The superstructure began to vibrate with the approach of one of the infrequent night-trains.

This time he finally flung his arm out in the back-sweep he had been threatening at each confrontation. The blow would have been enough to fell her if it had caught her. She turned her head aside with the fastidious little quirk of someone detecting an unpleasant odor. It fanned her face.

Instantly there was a peremptory rapping on glass somewhere close at hand. The station-agent thrust head and shoulder out of the sideward door of his dingy little booth. "Cut that out, you. Whaddye trying to do, keep people from using this station? I'll run you in!"

He turned to defend himself, the tabu partially lifted since this intercession wasn't of his own seeking. "This girl's nuts or something, she ought to be sent to Bellevue. She's been follying me along the street, I can't get rid of her."

She said in that same dispassionate voice, "Are you the only one that can ride the Third Avenue El?"

He appealed to the agent once more, continuing to hang slant-wise out of the doorway as a sort of self-appointed arbiter. "Ask her where she's going. She don't know herself!"

Her answer was addressed to the agent, but with an emphasis that could not have been meant for him, that must have had some purpose of its own. "I'm going down to Twenty-seventh Street, Twenty-seventh Street between Second and Third Avenues. I have a right to use this station, haven't I?"

The face of the man blocking her way had suddenly grown white, as though the locality she had mentioned conveyed a shock of hidden meaning to him. It should have. It was his own.

She knew ahead of time where he was going. It was useless therefore to attempt to shake her off, outdistance her in any way.

The agent rendered his decision, with a majestic sweep of his hand. "Come on through, miss."

Her coin suddenly swelled up in the reflector and she had come through the next one over, without waiting for him to clear the way for her. A thing which he seemed incapable of doing at the moment, no longer through obstinacy so much as through a temporary paralysis of movement with which his discovery of her knowledge of his eventual destination seemed to have afflicted him.

The train had arrived, meanwhile, but it was on the opposite side, not theirs. It ebbed away again, and the station breastworks dimmed once more behind it.

She sauntered to the outer lip of the platform and stood there waiting, and presently he had come out in turn, but digressing so that he emerged two pillar-lengths to the rearward of her. Since both were looking the same way, in quest of a train, he had her in view but she did not have him.

Presently, without noticing what she was doing, she began to amble further rearward along the platform, relieving the monotony of the wait by aimless movement as most people are inclined to do at such a time. This had soon taken her beyond the agent's limited range of vision, and out to where the station roof ended and the platform itself narrowed to a single-file strip of runway. Here she came to a halt again, and would have eventually turned and retraced her steps back toward where she had come from. But while standing there, peering trainward and with her back still to him, an unaccountable tension, a sense of impending danger of some sort, began slowly to come over her.

It must have been something about the way his tread sounded to her on the planks. He too was straying now in turn, and toward her. He was moving sluggishly, just as she had. It wasn't that; it was that his tread, while distinct enough in the unnatural stillness that reigned over the station, had some sort of a furtive undertone to it. It was in the rhythm, rather than in any actual attempt to muffle it. It was somehow a leashed tread, a tread of calculated approach trying to disguise itself as a meaningless ramble. She could not know how she knew; she only knew, before she had even turned, that something had entered his mind in the few moments since her back had been turned. Something that had not been there before.

She turned, and rather sharply.

He was still little better than his original two stanchion-lengths away from her. It was not that that confirmed her impression. She caught him in the act of glancing down into the track-bed beside him, where the third rail lay, as he drifted along parallel to it. It was that.

She understood immediately. A jostle of the elbow, a deft, tripping side-swipe of the foot, as they made to pass one another. She took in at a glance the desperate position she had unwittingly strayed into. She was penned against the far end of the station. Without realizing it she had cut herself off from the agent's protective radius of vision altogether. His booth was set back inside to command the turnstiles, could not command the sweep of the platform.

The two of them were alone on the platform. She looked across the way, and the opposite side was altogether barren, had just been cleared by the northbound train.

There was no downtown train in sight yet, either, offering that dubious deterrent.

To retreat still further would be suicidal; the platform ended completely only a few yards behind her back, she would only wedge herself into a cul-de-sac, be more at his mercy than ever. To get back to the midsection where the agent offered safety, she would have to go toward him, *pass* him, which was the very act he was seeking to achieve.

If she screamed now, without waiting for the overt act, in hopes of bringing the agent out onto the platform in time, she ran a very real risk of bringing on all the faster the very thing she was trying to prevent. He was in a keyed-up state, she could tell by the look on his face, on which a scream, more likely than not, would produce the opposite effect from that intended. This temporary aberration was due to sheer fright on his part more than rage, and a scream might frighten him still further.

She had frightened him badly, she had done her work only too well.

She edged warily inward, back as far as possible from the tracks, until she had come up close against the row of advertisements lining the guard-rail. She pressed her hips flat against them, began to sidle along them, turned watchfully outward toward him. Her dress rustled as it swept their surfaces one by one, so close did she cling.

As she drew within his orbit he began to veer in toward her on a diagonal, obviously to cut off her further advance. There was a slowness about both their movements that was horrible; they were like lazy fish swimming in a tank, on that deserted platform three stories above the street, with its tawny widely-spaced lights strung along overhead.

He still came on, and so did she, and they were bound to meet in another two or three paces.

The turnstile drummed unexpectedly, around out of sight from them, and a colored girl of dubious pursuits came out on the platform just a few short yards away from the two of them, bent almost lopsided as she moved to scratch herself far down the side of her leg.

They slowly melted into relaxation, each in the pose in which she had surprised them. The girl, with her back to the billboards, stayed that way, slumped a little lower, buckled at the knees now. He leaned deflatedly against a chewing-gum slot-machine at hand beside him. She could almost see the recent fell purpose oozing out of him at every pore. Finally he turned away from his nearness to her with a floundering movement. Nothing had been said, the whole thing had been in pantomime from beginning to end.

That would never come again. She had the upper hand once more.

The train came flickering in like sheet-lightning, and they both boarded the same car, at opposite ends. They sat the full car-length away from one another, still recuperating from their recent crisis; he huddled forward over his lap, she with her spine held convex, staring upward at the ceiling-lights. In between there was no one but the colored girl, who continued to scratch at intervals and scan the station-numbers, as though waiting to pick one at random to alight at.

They both left the car at the Twenty-eighth Street station, again at opposite ends. He was aware of her coming down the stairs in his wake. She could tell that he was, although he didn't look back. The inclination of his head told her that. He seemed passively acquiescent now to letting her have her way, follow him the short rest of the way, if that was her intent.

They both went down Twenty-seventh Street toward Second, he on one side of the street, she on the other. He maintained a lead of about four doorways, and she let him keep it. She knew which entrance he would go into, and he knew that she knew. The stalk had now become a purely mechanical thing, with its only remaining unknown quantity the why. But that was the dominant factor.

He went in, was inked from sight, within one of the black door-slits down near the corner. He must have heard that remorseless, maniacally-calm *tick-chick, tick-chick* behind him on the other side of the street to the very last, but he refrained from looking back, gave no sign. They had parted company at last, for the first time since early evening.

She came on until she had used up the distance there had been between them, stood even with the house. Then she took up her position there, and stood in full sight on the sidewalk opposite, watching a certain two of the dozen-odd darkened windows.

Presently they had lighted, as in greeting at someone's awaited entry. Then within a moment they blacked out once more, as if the act had been quickly countermanded. They remained dark after that, though at times the grayish film of the curtains would seem to stir and shift, with the elusiveness of a reflection on the glass. She knew she was being watched through them, by one or more persons.

She maintained her vigil steadfastly.

An elevated train wriggled by like a glow-worm up at the far end of the street. A taxi passed, and the driver glanced at her curiously, but he already had a fare. A late wayfarer came by along the opposite side of the street, and looked over at her, trying to discern encouragement. She averted her face angularly, only righted it again after he was well on his way.

A policeman suddenly stood at her elbow, appearing from nowhere. He must have stood watching, undetected, for some little time before.

"Just a minute, miss. I've had a complaint from a woman in one of the flats over there that you followed her husband home from work, and have been standing staring at their windows for the past half-hour."

"I have."

"Well, y'd better move on."

"I want you to take hold of my arm, please, and walk me with you until we get around the corner, as though you were running me in." He did, rather half-heartedly. They stopped again when they were out of sight of the windows. "Here." She produced a piece of paper, showed it to him. He peered at it in the uncertain light of a nearby lamppost.

"Who's this?" he asked.

"Homicide Squad. You can call him and check on it, if you want to. I'm doing this with his full knowledge and permission."

"Oh, sort of undercover work, hunh?" he said with increased respect.

"And please ignore all future complaints from those particular people about me. You're apt to get a great many of them, during the next few days and nights."

She made a phone-call of her own, after he had left her.

"How is it working out?" the voice on the other end asked.

"He's already showing signs of strain. He broke a glass behind the bar. He nearly gave in to an impulse to throw me off the elevated platform just now."

"That looks like it. Be careful, don't go too close to him when there's no one else around. Remember, the main thing is, don't give him an inkling of what the whole thing's about, of what's behind it. *Don't put the question to him,* that's the whole trick. The moment he finds out what you're after, it goes into reverse, loses its effect. It's the not knowing that keeps him on edge, will finally wear him down to where we want him."

"What times does he start out for work, as a rule?"

"He leaves the flat around five, each afternoon," her informant said, as though with documentary evidence at his fingers to refer to.

"He'll find me on hand tomorrow, when he does."

The third night the manager suddenly approached the bar to one side of her, unasked, and called him over.

"What's the matter, why don't you wanna wait on this young lady? I been watching. Twenty minutes she's been sitting here like this. Couldn't you see her?"

His face was gray, and the seams were shiny. It got that way whenever he had to come this close to her now.

"I can't—" he said brokenly, keeping his voice muted so that others wouldn't hear it. "Mr. Anselmo, it's not human—she's torturing me—you don't understand—" He coughed on the verge of tears, and his cheeks swelled out, then flattened again.

The girl, less than a foot away, sat looking on at the two of them, with the tranquil, guiltless eyes of a child.

"Three nights she's been in here like this now. She keeps looking at me—"

"Sure she keeps looking at you, she's waiting to get waited on," the manager rebuked him. "What do you want her to do?" He peered closer at him, detected the strangeness in his face. "What's the matter, you sick? If you're sick and want to go home, I'll phone Pete to come down."

"No, no!" he pleaded hurriedly, almost with a frightened sob in his voice. "I don't want to go home—then she'll only follow me along the streets, stand outside my windows all night again! I'd rather stay here where there are people around me!"

"You quit talking crazy, and take her order," the manager said brusquely. He turned away, with a single verifying glance at her to confirm how well-behaved, how docile, how harmless she was.

The hand that set down the drink before her shook uncontrollably, and some of it spilled.

They neither of them said anything to one another, though their breaths all but mingled.

"Hello," the station agent said friendlily through the wicket, as she came to rest just outside it. "Say, it's funny, you and that guy that just passed through ahead of you always seem to get here at about the same time, and yet you're never together. Did y' notice?"

"Yes, I've noticed," she answered. "We both come out of the same place, each night."

She maintained contact with this shrine of his by resting the point of her elbow on the slab outside the wicket, as though there were some sort of protective virtue to be derived from the touch of it, while she chatted desultorily with him, whiling her train-wait away. "Nice night, isn't it? . . . How's your little boy getting along? . . . I don't think the Dodgers stand a chance." Occasionally she would turn her head and cast a glance at the platform outside, where a lone figure paced, or stood, or was lost to view at times, but she never ventured out on it herself.

Only when the train was in, and at a full stop, and the platform-gates stood open, did she break away and make a little dashing scamper that carried her aboard. On an insulated straight line, along which nothing could possibly happen to her, for the third rail was sheathed now by the undercarriages of the cars themselves.

An elevated train wriggled by like a glow-worm at the far end of the street. A taxi sloughed by and the driver glanced at her curiously, but he didn't want any more fares because he was taking his cab to bed for the night. Two late wayfarers passed, and one of them called over jocularly: "What's matter, Toots, did you get a rain-check?" Quiet descended again after they had lost themselves in the distance.

Suddenly without any warning the doorway, the doorway that belonged to the two windows, disgorged a woman, hair awry and rushing as though she were a projectile discharged by the long black bore of the hall. She had donned a coat over her night-dress, and her bare feet were thrust into improperly-secured shoes that made a clattering noise at each purposefully-quick step she took. She was brandishing the long pole of a denuded floor-brush, and she made unerringly for the lone figure standing across the way, with unmistakable intent to flail at her.

The girl turned and sped, down to the nearby corner and around it and along the next street, but with a neat economy of movement that robbed her going of all fear, made it just a precautionary withdrawal from someone in whom she had no interest.

The woman's railing screams, fleeter than their owner, winged after the girl, overtook her midway down the block. "For three days now you been hounding my momn!

Come back here and I'll give it to you! Let me get my hands on you and I'll fix you, I will!"

She stood there in view for a moment or two, just past the corner, gesturing threats of dire antagonism with pole and arm. The girl slowed, stopped, dissolved into the gloom.

Presently the woman went back around the corner, sought her own house again.

Presently the girl was back again too, standing where she had been before, and as she had been before, staring upward at two windows of the house across the way, like a cat watching a mouse-hole.

An elevated train wriggled by. . . . A taxi passed. . . . A late wayfarer came along, passed, receded. . . .

Those blank window-panes staring sightlessly down at her had a look of helpless frustration now, somehow.

"Soon," the voice on the telephone said. "One more day, to make sure he's completely pulverized. Maybe by tomorrow night—"

It was his day off, and he had been attempting to shake her off for well over an hour now.

He was going to halt again. She saw it coming before it had even occurred, she already knew the signs so well by now. He halted in full sunshine this time, stood back against a building-wall, with shoppers streaming to and fro before him. He had already halted two or three times before this, but each time it had ended inconclusively. As it always did. He had gone on again; she had too.

This time she detected a difference. This time the halt almost seemed to be involuntary. As though some mainspring of endurance had finally snapped, then and there, at just that point, as he was passing it, and he had suddenly found himself all unwound. As he backed to the wall the small flat parcel he had held bedded under his arm slowly overbalanced, slapped to the ground, and he allowed it to lie there unrecovered.

She halted a short distance from him, making no pretense, as usual, that her halt had anything to do but with him. She stood looking at him in her usual grave way.

The sun was streaming whitely into his face, and he was blinking his eyes against it. More and more rapidly, however.

Tears appeared unexpectedly, and suddenly he was weeping abjectly, in full view of all the passersby, his face an ugly, brick-red, puckered mask.

Two people stopped, incredulous. The two became four, the four, eight. He and the girl were both contained in the hollow core of the crowd that in no time at all had ringed them around, kept thickening, outer layer by outer layer.

He was past all ordinary sense of self-consciousness, humiliation; he appealed to the onlookers, almost as if asking help, protection against her.

"Ask her what she *wants* of me!" he bawled soddenly. "Ask her what she's *after!* She's been doing this to me for days now— Day and night, night and day! I can't stand it any more, I tell ya, I can't stand it any more—!"

"What is he, drunk?" a woman asked another, in a derisive undertone.

She stood there unshrinking, making no attempt to escape from the attention he was forcing her to share with him. She was so dignified, so grave, so fetching to the eye, and he was so grotesquely comical, it could have had only one result; the sympathies of the crowd could have gone only one way. Crowds are more often sadistic than not, anyway.

Grins appeared here and there. The grins became snickers. The snickers guffaws and outright jeers. In another moment the whole crowd was laughing pitilessly at him. Only one face in all that group remained impassive, sober, clinically neutral.

Hers.

He had only worsened his situation instead of bettering it, by making this spectacle. He had thirty tormentors now, instead of one.

"I can't stand it any more! I tell ya I'll *do* something to her—!" Suddenly he advanced on her, as if to strike her, beat her back.

Instantly men leaped forward, caught his arms, flung him this way and that with surly grunts. For a moment there was a confused floundering of bodies around her. His head suddenly forced its way through, lower than normal, straining to get at her.

It might easily have developed into a multiple onslaught —on *him.*

She appealed to them, self-possessedly but loudly enough to be heard, and the calm clarity of her voice stopped them all short. "Don't. Let him alone. Let him go about his business."

But there was no warmth nor compassion about it, just a terrible steely impartiality. As if to say: Leave him to me. He's mine.

Arms fell away from him, poised fists relaxed, coats were shrugged back into place, and the angry inner nucleus within the greater one disintegrated. Leaving him alone again within the hollow circle. Alone with her.

He made several false moves, in his torment and frustration, seeking an outlet through the massed figures around him. Then he found one, and forced his way through it, and went plunging out. He went *running* away from the scene full tilt, padding ponderously down the street; running away from the slender girl who stood there looking after him, her coat belted around her waist to the thickness of little more than a man's hand-span. The ultimate in degradation.

She didn't linger long behind him. She wasn't interested in the plaudits of the crowd, nor savoring any juvenile public triumph. She thrust those in her way aside with deft little passes of her arm, until she had gained clearance for herself. Then she set out after the heavily laboring figure ahead, at a blend of light running and graceful energetic walking that carried her rapidly forward in his wake.

Strange pursuit. Incredible pursuit. Slim young girl hurrying after a stocky barman, in and out, out and in, through the swarming midday streets of New York.

He became aware almost at once that she had taken up the chase once more. He looked back, the first time in dismal apprehension. She waited for him to look again. When he did, she flung up her arm straight overhead, in imperious summons to him to stop.

Now would be the time, now would be the moment Burgess would approve of, she felt sure. Now he was like wax as he ran through this bright midday sun. That crowd back there had taken away his last prop. He had tested it, found it no protection, and accordingly he no longer had a sense of immunity even in broad daylight on these bustling city streets.

The curve of his resistance might start upward again

from here on, if she didn't act now while she had the chance. The law of diminishing returns might set in from here on. Familiarity might very well breed contempt, for all she knew.

Now was the time; it was simply a matter of pinning him against the nearest wall, putting in a quick call to Burgess, and having him take charge in time to be in at the death. "Are you ready to admit now that you did see a certain woman at the bar that night in company with the man Henderson? Why did you deny having seen her? Who paid or coerced you to deny it?"

He had stopped for a moment, down there ahead at the next corner, looking all about him for a way of escape like a trapped, scurrying animal. Panic was on him at white heat. She could tell by the abortive, zig-zag, false starts he kept making, looking for sanctuary. To him she was no longer a girl, something he could have buffeted senseless with one arm if he chose. To him she was Nemesis.

She threw up her arm again, as the distance rapidly closed between them. It only stung him like the flick of a whip to an added spurt of frenzied disorientation. He was walled in there on the corner by a thin but continuous line of people waiting to cross over, standing elbow to elbow along the curb. There was an adverse light on above.

He gave one last look at her, rapidly nearing him now, and then plunged through them like a circus-performer tearing through a paper hoop.

She stopped short, as short as though both her flailing feet had caught simultaneously in a hidden crevice along the sidewalk. A brake keened out along the asphalt, scorching itself to death.

She flung up both hands, ground them into her eye-sockets, but not before she had seen his hat go up in the air, in a surprisingly high loop, clear over everyone else's head.

A woman screamed for prelude, and then a vast bay of horrified dismay went up from the crowd in general.

13: The Eleventh Day Before the Execution

LOMBARD

LOMBARD had been following him for the past hour-and-a-half, and there's nothing slower to be followed on the face of the earth than a blind mendicant. He moved like a tortoise that counts its life-span by centuries, instead of a man that counts his by years. It took him an average of forty minutes to traverse each block-length, from one corner to the next. Lombard timed it with his watch several times.

He didn't have a seeing eye dog. He had to rely on his fellow-pedestrians to get him safely over the crossings, each time he came to one. They never failed him. Cops held up traffic well into the green, if he hadn't quite made it by the time the change-over came. Hardly anyone that passed failed to drop something into his cup, so it paid him to walk slow.

It was painful to Lombard in the extreme; he was active, unhandicapped, and with an acutely-heightened sense of time-value these days. Several times it was all he could do to hang back in the wake of this endless, creeping progress, that was like a variation of the Chinese water-drop torture. But he curbed himself, kept him grimly in sight, sucking impatiently at cigarettes for a safety-valve, standing immobile for long stretches at a time in doorways and shopwindow indentations to let him accomplish some distance, then closing in rapidly again in a few hectic strides, and falling motionless once more, to once more let his quarry eke out a little further microscopic progress. Breaking it up that way into fits and starts took a little of the curse out of it.

It couldn't keep on forever, he kept reminding himself. It couldn't last through the whole night. That figure up ahead of him was a human being in a human being's body. He had to sleep sometime. He'd have to turn in out of the open and go behind walls and lie down to rest *sometime*. His kind didn't beg straight through the night-hours until daybreak, the law of diminishing returns alone would be enough to discourage that.

And finally it came. Lombard had thought it never would, but it did at last. He turned aside, went within walls, and quitted the open. It was in a sector that had unnoticeably become so derelict as they both advanced through it, that no bounty could be expected from it. It was in need of alms itself, instead of being able to bestow. It was blocked off at one end by overhead railway-tracks carried on a viaduct of rough-faced granite blocks.

His burrow was a mouldering tenement just short of this. Lombard had had to be careful, although he hadn't realized even yet that the end was this close at hand. He'd had to remain well-back, for the streets were desolate hereabouts, with few other footsteps to blur his own, and he knew they had supersensitive ears as a rule.

When he saw him enter, therefore, he was further back than he would have wished to be. He hurriedly closed in for the last time, trying to reach it in time to ascertain which floor it was, if possible. He stopped at the doorway and cautiously entered in turn, just deep enough within to be able to listen.

The cane-taps were still going up, with infinite slowness. They sounded a little like drops of water from a faulty spigot striking into an empty wooden bucket. He held his breath, listening. He counted four breaks in them, changes of tempo, one for each turn of the stairs. They were duller on the level-landings than on the incline of the stairs themselves. Then they dwindled off to the back, not the front, of the building.

He waited until he'd heard the faint closing of a door up there somewhere, then he started up in turn, treading stealthily but fast, with all the energy he'd had to hold suppressed until now unleashed at last. The acutely-tilted flights of worn stairs would have prostrated anyone else; he was hardly aware of them.

There were two of them at the back, but he could tell which it was, because one of them, even at this distance, was obviously a water-closet.

He waited a moment at the top step until his rapidity of breath was completely quelled again, then advanced carefully toward it. Again he reminded himself how acute of hearing they were said to be. But he accomplished his purpose to perfection; not a floorboard wavered, due more to his superb muscular co-ordination than to any particular lightness of weight. He was and always had been a swell machine; something that belonged under the hood of a racing car instead of in a flimsy sack of skin.

He put his ear over against the doorseam and listened.

There was no light coming from it, of course, because for him in there there was never any light, so it would have done him no good to put it on. But he could hear an occasional sound of moving about. It put him in mind of an animal that withdraws into a hole, and then keeps turning for some little time afterward, getting itself comfortable, before it finally settles down for good.

There were no sounds of voice. He must be in there alone.

This was long enough. Now for it. He knocked.

The moving-around died instantly, and there was nothing more. A cessation. A place trying to make itself seem empty. A frightened, bated stillness, that he knew would go on for as long as he was out there—if he permitted it to.

He knocked again.

"Come on," he said sternly.

His third knocking was harshly imperative. The fourth would be blows.

"Come on," he said brutally in the silence.

The flooring creaked timidly in there, and then a voice, almost with breath accompanying it, it was emitted so close to the doorseam, asked: "Who's out there?"

"A friend."

The voice became more frightened at that, instead of less. "I haven't any. I don't know you."

"Let me in. I won't hurt you."

"I can't do it. I'm alone in here and helpless. I can't let anyone in." He was worried about his day's gleanings, Lombard knew. You couldn't blame him for that. It was a wonder he hadn't lost them, in the way that he took this to be, long before now.

"You can let me in. Come on, open up a minute. I only want to talk to you."

The voice on the other side quavered, "Get away from

here. Go on away from my door or I'll holler down for help from the window." But it was pleading rather than threatening.

There was a short stalemate. Neither of them moved. Neither of them made a sound. They were acutely aware of each other's nearness. Fright on one side of the door, determination on the other.

Lombard took out his wallet finally, scanned it thoughtfully. The largest denomination in it was a fifty-dollar bill. There were some smaller ones he could have taken out in place of it; he chose the larger one instead. He dropped to his heels, worked it through the crack under the door until there was nothing left of it to hold onto any more.

He straightened up again, said: "Reach down and feel along the bottom of the door. Doesn't that prove I don't want to rob you? Now let me in."

There was a postcript of hesitancy, then a chain-head slid off its groove. A bolt sidled back, and last of all a key turned in the keyhole. It had been well-barricaded.

The door opened grudgingly, and the sightless black lenses that he'd first marked out on the streets hours ago stared at him. "Anyone else with you?"

"No, I'm alone. And I haven't come here to harm you, so don't be nervous."

"You're not an agent, are you?"

"No, I'm not a police-agent. There'd be a cop with me if I was, and there's nobody with me. I just want to talk to you, can't you get that through your head?" He pushed his way in.

The room was invisible in the darkness, non-existent, a pall of sightlessness, just as the other's whole world must be. For a moment a wedge of dull amber-tan lying along the floor from the hall-light outside helped a little, then that went too as the door closed.

"Put on a light, can't you?"

"No," the blind man said, "this makes us more even. If you just want to talk, what do you need a light for?" Lombard heard a decrepit bedspring sing out somewhere nearby, as he sank down on it. He was probably sitting on his day's take, nested under the mattress.

"Come on, cut out the foolishness, I can't talk like this—" He groped around him at knee-level, finally located the arm of a ricketty wooden rocker, shifted it over and sank into it.

"You said you wanted to talk," the other voice said tautly in the dark. "Now you're in, now go ahead and talk. You don't have to see to be able to talk."

Lombard's voice said, "Well at least I can smoke, can't I? You don't object to that, do you? You smoke yourself, don't you?"

"When I can get it," the other voice said warily.

"Here, take one of these." There was a click, and a small lighter-flame peered out in his hand. A little of the room came back.

The blind man was on the edge of the bed, his cane crosswise on his lap in case it should be required as a weapon.

Lombard's hand came away from his pocket holding, instead of cigarettes, a revolver. He held it in close, but pointed directly at the other. "Here, help yourself," he repeated pleasantly.

The blind man became rigid. The cane rolled off his knees and hit the floor. He made a spasmodic warding-motion of the hands, up toward his face. "I knew you were after my money!" he said hoarsely. "I shouldn't have let you in—"

Lombard put the gun away again, as calmly as he had taken it out. "You're not blind," he said quietly. "I didn't need that stunt to prove it to myself either. But I needed it to prove to you that I was already on to you. The mere fact that you opened the door for a fifty-dollar bill was proof enough. You must have struck a match for a minute and scanned it. How could you know it wasn't a one-dollar bill, if you weren't a fake? A one is the same size and shape, feels the same, as a fifty. A one wouldn't have made it worth your while to open the door, you probably came in with more than that on you yourself just now. But a fifty was worth taking a chance for; that was more than you'd collected."

He saw a misshapen remnant of candle, went over and touched the lighter to it while he was still speaking.

"You are an agent," the beggar faltered, wiping sweat from his forehead harassedly with the back of his hand. "I might have known—"

"Not the kind you mean, interested in whether you're out taking the public's money under false pretenses or not. If that's any consolation to you." He came back and sat down again.

"Then what are you? What do you want with me?"

"I want you to remember something you saw—Mr. *Blind Man*," he added ironically. "Now listen to this. You were hanging around outside the Casino Theatre, working the audience as it came out, one night last May—"

"But I've been around there lots of times."

"I'm talking about one night only, one particular night. That's the only one I care about, I don't give a damn about the rest. This night that I mean, a man and a woman came out together. Now here's the woman: she had on a

bright orange hat with a tall black feeler sticking up from
it. You put the bite on them as they were getting into a
taxi, a few yards down from the entrance. Listen carefully, now. Without thinking what she was doing, she
dropped a lighted cigarette into the cup you shoved at her,
instead of the donation she intended. It burned your finger.
The man quickly dug it out for you, and to make it up to
you, gave you a couple of dollars. I think he said something
like this: 'Sorry, old man, that was a mistake.' Now surely
you remember that. It isn't every night your finger gets
burned by a live cigarette landing in your cup, and it isn't
every night you get two dollars in a lick from just one
passerby."

"Suppose I say I don't remember?"

"Then I'm going to haul you out of here with me right
now and turn you in at the nearest police station as an im-
postor. You'll get a stretch in the work-house, you'll be
down on the police-blotter from then on, and you'll be
picked up each time they see you trying to work the
streets."

The man on the bed clawed at his own face distractedly,
momentarily displacing the dark glasses upward past his
eyes. "But isn't that like forcing me to say I remember,
whether I do or not?"

"It's only forcing you to admit what I'm sure you do
remember anyway."

"Then suppose I say I do remember, what happens
then?"

"First you tell me what you remember, then you repeat
it to a certain plainclothesman, a friend of mine. I'll either
bring him down here or take you up there with me to see
him—"

The mendicant jolted with renewed dismay. "But how

can I do that, without giving myself away? Especially to a plainclothesman! I'm supposed to be blind, how can I say I saw them? That's the same as what you were threatening to do to me if I *didn't* tell you!"

"No, you'll just be telling it to this one guy, not the whole force at large. I can strike a bargain with him, get him to promise you immunity from prosecution. Now how about it? Did you or didn't you?"

"Yes, I did," the professional blind man admitted in a low voice. "I saw the two of them together. I usually keep my eyes closed, even behind the glasses, when I'm near bright lights, like there were outside that theatre. But the cigarette-burn made me open them good and wide. I can see through the glasses, and I saw them both, all right."

Lombard took something out of his wallet. "Is this him?"

The blind man hitched his glasses up out of the way, scrutinized the snapshot critically. "I'd say it was," he said finally. "Considering how short a glimpse I had of him, and how long ago it was, it looks to me like the same guy."

"What about her? You'd know her again if you saw her?"

"I already have. I only saw him that one night, but I saw her at least once more after that—"

"What!" Lombard was suddenly on his feet, leaning over him. The rocker swayed emptily behind him. He grabbed him by the shoulder, squeezing as if trying to get the information out of his skinny frame in that way. "Let me hear about it! Come on, quick!"

"It was not very long after that same night, that's how I knew it was she. It was in front of one of the big swanky hotels, and you know how bright *they* are. I heard a pair

of footsteps coming down the steps, a man's and a woman's.
I heard the woman say, 'Wait a minute, maybe this'll bring
me luck,' and I knew she meant me. I heard her footsteps
turn aside and come over to me. A coin went in. A quarter.
I can tell the different coins by the sounds they make.
And then the funny part of it happened, that made me
know it was she. It's such a little thing, I don't know if
you'll be able to catch on like I did. She stood still for
just a tiny minute there in front of me, and they never do.
The coin was already in, so I knew she must be looking at
me. Or something about me. I was holding the cup in my
right hand, the one with the burn on it, and the burn was
one of those big water-blisters by that time. I think it
must have been that she saw, on the side of my finger.
Anyway, here's what happened. I heard her say under her
breath—not to me, but to herself— 'Why, how very
odd—!' And then her footsteps turned and went back to
where the man's were. That was all—"

"But—"

"Wait a minute, I'm not finished yet. I opened my eyes
just a slit, to look down at the cup. *And she'd added a
dollar-bill to the original quarter she'd put in the first time.*
I knew it was she, because it hadn't been in there until
then. Now why should she change her mind and add a
dollar-bill after she'd already put in a quarter? It must
have been the same woman; she must have recognized the
blister and remembered what had happened a few nights
be—"

"Must have, must have," gritted Lombard impatiently.
"I thought you said you saw her, could tell me what she
looked like!"

"I can't tell you what she looks like from the front, because I didn't dare open my eyes. The lights were too

bright around there, it would have been a give-away. After she turned away and I saw the dollar-bill, I peered up a little higher under my lashes and saw her from the back, as she was getting into the car."

"From the back! Well, tell me that at least, what was she like from the back!"

"I couldn't see all of her even from the back, I was afraid to look up that high. All I saw was just the seam of a silk stocking and one heel, as she raised it to step in. That was all that was in focus with my downcast eyelids."

"An orange hat one night. A stocking-seam and the heel of her shoe another night, a week later!" Lombard gave him a fling back onto the bed. "At this rate, after about twenty years we'll have a whole woman to stick in-between the two!"

He went over to the door, flung it open. He looked back at him balefully. "You can do a lot better than that, and I'm sure of it! What you need is the professional touch, to bring it out. You certainly did see her full eye-width the first night, outside the theatre. And the second time you must have heard the address given to the driver of the car, as she stepped in—"

"No I didn't."

"You stay here, get it? Don't move from here. I'm going down and call up this fellow I told you about. I want him to come over here and listen to this with me."

"But he's a bull, isn't he?"

"I told you that's all right. We're not interested in you, either one of us. You've got nothing to be nervous about. But don't try to run out before I get back, or then we will make it hot for you."

He closed the door after him.

The voice at the other end sounded surprised. "You got something already?"

"I've got something already, and I want you to hear it for what it's worth. I think you can probably get a lot more out of it than I can. I'm way up here at 123 St. and Park Avenue, the last house short of the railroad tracks. I'd like you to get over here as fast as you can, and see what you think of it. I've got the beat-cop posted at the door watching it for me until I can get back. I'm talking from around the corner, nearest phone I could find. I'll be waiting down there by the street-entrance for you."

Burgess dropped off a patrol-car with a running slow-down a few minutes later. The car went on without stopping and he came over to where Lombard and the cop were standing waiting in the doorway.

"In here," Lombard said, turning to go in without any further explanation.

"Well, I guess I can get back on the line," the cop said, turning away.

"Thanks a lot, officer," Lombard called out to him. They were already in at the stairs by that time. "All the way up at the top," he explained, taking the lead. "He's seen her twice, *that* night and another time, a week later. He's a blind man; don't laugh, phoney of course."

"Well, that was worth coming over for," Burgess admitted.

They made the first turning, one behind the other, hands coasting along the rail. "Wants immunity—about the blindness. Scared of cops."

"We can work something out, if it's worth it," Burgess grunted.

Second landing. "One more," Lombard checked off gratuitously.

They saved their breath for climbing on the next.

Third landing. "What happened to the lights from here on up?" Burgess heaved.

A hitch snagged the rhythm of Lombard's ascent. "That's funny. There was one still on when I came down. Either the bulb died, or it was tampered with, turned off."

"You sure it was still on?"

"Absolutely. I remember he had his room dark, but light from the hall came in through the open door."

"Better let me go first, I've got a pocket-light." Burgess detoured around him, took the lead.

He must have been still in the process of getting it out. At the middle turn, between floors, where the stairs changed direction, he suddenly went floundering down on all fours. "Look out," he warned Lombard. "Step back."

The moon of his torch sprang up, bleaching the little oblong between end-wall and bottom-step. Spanning it lay an inert figure, grotesquely contorted. Legs trailing downward off the last few steps, torso proper on the level landing-place, but head bent backward at an unnatural and acute angle by the impediment of the end-wall at the turn. Dangling from one ear, but miraculously unbroken, was a pair of dark glasses.

"That him?" he muttered.

"It's him," agreed Lombard tersely.

Burgess bent over the figure, probed awhile. Then he straightened up again. "Broken neck," he said. "Killed instantly." He shot his light up the stair-incline. Then he went up there, jittered it around on the floor. "Accident," he said. "Missed his footing up here on the top step, went all the way down head-first, and crashed head-on into that wall backing the turn. I can see the skid-marks up here, over the lip of the top step."

Lombard climbed slowly up to where he was, blew out his breath in a disgusted snort. "Fine time for an accident! I no sooner contact him—" He stopped short, looked at the detective searchingly in the batterylight-rays. "You don't think it could have been anything else, do you?"

"Did anyone pass you or that other guy, while you were waiting down there at the door?"

"No one, in or out."

"Did you hear anything like a fall?"

"No, we would have come in and looked if we had. But at least twice while we were waiting for you long trains went by on those overhead tracks, and you couldn't hear yourself think until they'd gone by. It might have been during one of those times."

Burgess nodded. "That's what probably kept others in the building from hearing it too. Don't you see, there's too much coincidence in it for it to be anything but an accident. He could have hit his head against that same wall down there ten times over and still lived; just been stunned without breaking his neck. He just *happened* to be killed instantly, but it couldn't have been counted on."

"Well, where does the bulb come in? I think that's too much coincidence, isn't it? I know what I'm saying, that light was still in working order when I tore down those stairs to phone you. If it hadn't been, I would have had to pick my way down, and I didn't; I went pretty fast."

Burgess shot his light along the wall until he'd found it; it was on a bracket, sticking out from the side. "I don't get what you mean," he said, staring up at it. "If he was supposed to be blind, or at least went around most of the time with his eyes closed, which amounts to the same thing, how does the bulb enter into it one way or the other? How would darkness be any disadvantage to him? In fact he'd be more sure-footed in the dark, probably, than with the light left on; because he wasn't used to using his eyes."

"Maybe that's just it," Lombard said. "Maybe he came out fast, trying to make his get-away before I got back, and in his hurry forgot to close his eyes, left them open. With them open, maybe he was no better off than you or me."

"Now you're getting yourself all tangled up. For his sight to be dazzled, the light would have had to be on. And your whole kick has been that it isn't. What would be the point, either way? How could anyone *count* on his missing a step, any more than they could count on his hitting in such a way that his neck snapped?"

"All right, it was a freak accident." Lombard flung his hand out disgustedly as he turned to go down. "All I say is, I don't like its timing. I no sooner catch up with him—"

"They will happen, you know, and they usually pick their own time for it, not yours."

Lombard went thumping frustratedly down the stairs, letting his whole weight down at each step. "Whatever you might have been able to drill out of him is gone for good now."

"Don't let it throw you down. You may be able to turn up somebody else."

"From him, it's gone for good. And it was practically there, waiting to be found out." He'd reached the landing where the body lay by now. He turned suddenly to look back. "What happened? What was that?"

Burgess pointed to the wall. "The bulb lit up again. Your vibration on the staircase jarred it on. Which explains what happened to it the first time: his fall broke the current. The wiring must be defective. That takes care of the light." He motioned him on. "You may as well clear out. I'll report it by myself. No sense of you getting all mixed up in it, if you want to keep working on the other thing."

Lombard's tread went dejectedly on down the rest of the way toward the street, all the lilt gone out of it. Burgess stayed behind up there, waiting beside the motionless form on the landing.

14: The Tenth Day Before the Execution

THE GIRL

It was on a slip of paper that Burgess had given her.

Cliff Milburn
house-musician, Casino Theatre, last season.
current job, Regent Theatre.

And then two telephone-numbers. One a police-precinct, up until a certain hour. The other his own home-number, in case she needed him after he'd gone off duty.

He'd said to her: "I can't tell you how to go about it. You'll have to figure that out for yourself. Your own instinct will probably tell you what to do, better than I can. Just don't be frightened, and keep your wits about you. You'll be all right."

This was her own way of going about it, here in front of the glass. This was the only way she could figure out, sight-unseen. The clean, tomboyish look was gone from her. The breezy sweep of the hair from an immaculate part over to the other side of her face, that was missing. In its place was a tortured surface of brassy rolls and undulations, drenched with some sort of fixative and then hardened into a metallic casque. Gone too was the youthful, free-swinging, graceful hang there had always been to her clothes. Instead she had managed to achieve a skin-tight effect that appalled her, even alone here in her own room. Excruciatingly short, so that when she sat down—well, she would be sure to catch his eye in a way that would do the most good. A big red poker-chip on each cheek, as obvious as a pair of stop-lights, but whose effect was intended to be the opposite: go ahead. A string of beads that clacked around her throat. A handkerchief with too much lace on it, saturated in a virulent concoction that made her own nose crinkle in distaste as she hastily stuffed it into her bag. She had made herself heavy-lidded with some blue stuff she had never used before.

Scott Henderson had been watching her throughout the proceeding, from a frame to one side of the glass, and she was ashamed. "You wouldn't know me, darling, would you?" she murmured contritely. "Don't look at me, darling, don't look at me."

And now one final ghastly item, to complete the catalogue of sleazy accessibility. She put up her leg and slipped a garter of violently-pink satin complete with a rosette up it, left it at a point just below visibility. At least when seated.

She turned away fast. His Girl shouldn't look like that thing she had just seen in the glass, not His Girl. She went around putting lights out, outwardly calm, inwardly keyed-up. Only someone that knew her well could have guessed it. *He* would have known it at a glance. He wasn't here to see it.

When she came to the last one of all, the one by the door, she said the little prayer she always said, each time she started out. Looking over at him there, in the frame, across the room.

"Maybe tonight, darling," she breathed softly, "maybe tonight."

She put out the light and closed the door, and he stayed behind there in the dark, under glass.

The marquee-lights were on when she got out of the cab, but the sidewalk under them was fairly empty yet. She wanted to get in good and early, so she'd have time to work on him before the house-lights went down. She only half-knew what was playing, and when it was over and she came out again she knew she wouldn't know very much more than she had when she went in. Something called "Keep on Dancing."

She stopped at the box-office. "I have a reservation for tonight. First row orchestra, on the aisle. Mimi Gordon."

She'd had to wait days for it. Because this wasn't a matter of seeing the show, this was a matter of being seen. She took out the money and paid for it. "Now you're sure of what you told me over the phone? That's the side of the house the trap-drummer is on, and not the other?"

"That's right, I checked on it for you before I put it aside." He gave her the leer she'd known he would. "You must think quite a lot of him. Lucky guy, I'd say."

"You don't understand; it's not him personally. I don't even know him from Adam. It's—how'll I explain? Everybody has some sort of a hobby. Well, mine happens to be the trap-drums. Every time I go to a show I try to sit as close to them as I can get, I love to watch them being played, it does something to me. I'm an addict of the trap-drums, they've fascinated me ever since I was a child. I know it sounds crazy but—" She spread her hands, "that's how it is."

"I didn't mean to be inquisitive," he apologized, crest-fallen.

She went inside. The ticket-taker at the door had just come on duty, the usher had just come up from the locker-room downstairs, she was so early. Whatever the status of the balcony, where the unwritten rule of being fashionable late did not hold sway, she was definitely the first patron on the orchestra-floor.

She sat there alone, a small gilt-headed figure lost in that vast sea of empty seats. Most of her gaudiness was care-fully concealed, from three directions, by the coat she kept huddled about her. It was only from the front that she wanted it to have its full lethal effect.

Seats began to slap down behind her more and more frequently; there was that rustle and slight hum that al-ways marks a theatre slowly filling up. She had eyes for one thing and one thing only: that little half-submerged door down there under the rim of the stage. It was over on the opposite side from her. Light was peering through the seams of it now, and she could hear voices behind it. They were gathering there, ready to come out to work.

Suddenly it opened and they began filing up into the pit, each one's head and shoulders bent acutely to permit his passage. She didn't know which one was he, she wouldn't know until she saw him seat himself, because she'd never seen him. One by one they dropped into the various chairs, disposing themselves in a thin crescent around the stage-apron, heads below the footlights.

She was seemingly absorbed in the program on her lap, head lowered, but she kept peering watchfully up from under her sooty lashes. This one, coming now? No, he'd stopped one chair too short. The one behind him? What a villainous face. She was almost relieved when he'd dropped off at the second chair down from her. Clarinet, or something. Well then this one, it must be he—no, he'd turned and gone the other way, bass viol.

They'd stopped emerging now. Suddenly she was uneasy. The last one out had even closed the door behind him. There weren't any more of them coming through. They were all seated, they were all tuning up, settling themselves for work. Even the conductor was on hand. And the chair at the trap-drum, the one directly before her, remained ominously vacant.

Maybe he'd been discharged. No, because then they'd get a substitute to take his place. Maybe he'd been taken ill, couldn't play tonight. Oh, just tonight this had to happen! Probably every night this week, until now, he'd been here. She mightn't be able to get this same particular seat again for weeks to come; the show was selling well and there was great demand. And she couldn't afford to wait that long. Time was so precious, was running so short, there was too little of it left.

She could overhear them discussing it among themselves, in disparaging undertones. She was close enough to catch nearly everything they said, to get in under the tuning-up discords that covered them from the rest of the house.

"D'jever see a guy like that? I think he's been on time once since the season started. Fining don't do any good."

The alto saxophone said, "He probably chased some

blonde up an alley and forgot to come out again."

The man behind him chimed in facetiously: "A good drummer is hard to get."

"Not that hard."

She was staring at the credits on her program, without their focussing into type. She was rigid with suppressed anxiety. Ironical, that every man in the orchestra should be on hand but the single one, the only one, that could do her any good.

She thought: "This is the same sort of luck poor Scott was in the night he—"

The lull before the overture had fallen. They were all set now, light-rods turned on over their scores. Suddenly, when she was no longer even watching it any more, it seemed so hopeless, the door giving into the pit had flickered open, closed again, so quickly it was like the winking of an intermittent light, and a figure scuttled deftly along the outside of the chairs to the vacant one before her, bent over both to increase its speed and to attract the conductor's attention as little as possible. Thus there was something rodent-like about him even at his first appearance within her ken, and he was to stay in character throughout.

The conductor gave him a sizzling look.

He wasn't abashed. She heard him pant in a breathless undertone to his neighbor, "Boy, have I got a honey for the second tomorrow! A sure thing."

"Sure, and the only sure thing about it is it won't come in," was the dry answer.

He hadn't seen her yet. He was too busy fiddling with his rack, adjusting his instrument. Her hand dropped to her side and her skirt crept up her thigh an unnoticeable fraction of an inch more.

He got through arranging his set-up. "How's the house tonight?" she heard him ask. He turned and looked out through the pit-railing for the first time since he'd come in.

She was ready for him. She was looking at him. She'd hit him. There must have been an elbow-nudge beyond her radius of downcast vision. She heard the other man's slurred answer. "Yeah, I know, I seen it."

She'd hit him hard. She could feel his eyes on her. She could have made a graph of the wavy line they traveled. She took her time. Not too fast now, not right away. She thought: "Funny how we know these things, all of us, even when we've never tried them before." She concentrated on a line on her program as though she could never get enough of its mystic import. It was mostly dots, running from one side of the page over to the other. It helped to keep her eyes steady.

"*Victorine* ....Dixie Lee"
She counted the dots. Twenty-seven of them, from character-name over to performer-name. There, that was about long enough. That had given it time to work. She let her lashes come up slowly and unveil her eyes.

They met his. They stayed with his. His had expected them to turn away, frost-over. Instead, they accepted his glance, sustained it for as long as he cared to give it. They seemed to say: "Are you interested in me? All right, go ahead, I don't mind."

He was a shade surprised for a moment at this ready acceptance. He kept on looking for all he was worth. He even tried a tentative smile, that was ready to be rubbed-out at a moment's notice too.

She accepted that in turn. She even sent him one back, of about the same degree as his. His deepened. Hers did too.

The preliminaries were over, they were getting into—
And then, damn it, the buzzer signalled from back-curtain.
The conductor tapped out attention, spread his arms holding them poised. Flounced them, and the overture was
under way, he and she had to break it off.

That was all right, she consoled herself. So far so good.
The show couldn't be straight music all the way through,
no show was. There would be rest-spells.

The curtain went up. She was aware of voices, lights,
figures. She didn't bother with what was going on onstage.
She wasn't here to see a show. She minded her own business strictly, and her business was making a musician.

He turned and spoke to her at the start of the intermis-
sion, when they were filing out for a rest and a smoke. He
was the furthest over, so he was the last to go; that gave
him the chance to do it undetected behind the others'
backs. The people next to her had gotten up and gone
out, so he could tell she was alone, even if her conduct had
left him any doubts on that point until now, which it certainly should not have.

"How do you like it so far?"

"It's real good," she purred.

"Doing anything afterwards?"

She pouted. "No, I only wish I was."

He turned to go out after his fellow-bandsmen. "You
are," he assured her smugly, "now."

She gave her skirt a corrective downward hitch with
considerable asperity as soon as he was gone. She felt as
though she could have used a scalding shower and plenty
of Lifebuoy.

Her face-lines slipped back to where they belonged.
Even the make-up couldn't hide the alteration. She sat
there, pensive, alone, at the end of the empty row of seats.

Maybe tonight, darling, maybe tonight.

When the house-lights went on again at the final curtain, she lingered behind, pretending to have dropped this,
pretending to be adjusting that, while the rest of the audience siphoned slowly up through the aisles.

The band finished playing them out. He gave the cym-
bal atop his drum a final stroke, steadied it with his fingers,
put down his drumsticks, snapped off the light over his
rack. He was through for the night, he was on his own
time now. He turned around to her slowly, as if already
feeling himself the dominant factor in the situation. "Wait
for me around at the stage-alley, lovely," he said. "Be
with you in five minutes."

There was ignominy attached even to the simple act of
waiting for him outside, for some reason she couldn't quite
ascertain. Perhaps it was something about his personality
that tinged everything that way. She felt crawly, walking
up and down out there. And a little afraid. And the way
all the other bandsmen, coming out ahead of him (he
couldn't even spare her that embarrassment, he had to be
the last one out), looked at her as they passed added to her
discomfort.

Then suddenly he'd swept her off with him by surprise.
That is to say, before she'd even seen him coming, he had
her arm possessively under his and was towing her along
with him, without even breaking stride. That was probably characteristic of him too, she thought.

"How's my new little friend?" he began breezily.

"Fine, how's mine?" she gave him back.

"We'll go where the rest of the gang goes," he said.
"I'd catch cold without 'em." She got the idea. She was
like a new boutonnière to him, he wanted to show her off.

This was at twelve.

By two o'clock she decided he'd been softened up enough by beer for her to begin to go to work on him. They were in the second of two identical places by then, the gang still in the offing. A peculiar sort of etiquette seemed to govern things of this sort. He and she had moved on when the rest of them moved, and yet once they were in the new place they continued their separateness, at a table by themselves. He would get up and join the others every once in awhile, and then come back to her again, but the others never came over and joined him, she noticed. Probably because she was his, and they were supposed to stay away from her.

She'd been watching carefully for her opening for some time. She knew she'd better get going at it; after all, the night wouldn't last forever, and she couldn't face the thought of having to go through another one like it.

One offered itself finally, just what she wanted, in one of the rancid compliments he'd been shovelling at her all evening—whenever he thought of it. Somewhat like an absent-minded stoker keeping a fire going.

"You say I'm the prettiest thing ever sat in that seat. But there must have been other times you turned around and saw someone you liked sitting there right behind you. Tell me about some of them."

"Not in it with you, wouldn't waste my breath."

"Well, just for fun, I'm not jealous. Tell me: if you had your choice, out of all the attractive women you ever saw sitting behind you, in that same seat where I was tonight, since you've been playing in theatres, which was the one you would have rather taken out?"

"You, of course."

"I knew you'd say that. But after me; which would your second choice be? I want to see just how far back you can remember. I bet you can't remember their faces from one night to the next."

"Can't I? Well just to show you. I turn around one night and there's a dame sitting there right on the other side of the rail from me—"

Under the table she was holding the soft inside curve of her arm with her own hand, squeezing it tightly as though it ached unendurably.

"This was at the other house, the Casino. I don't know, something about her got me—"

A succession of attenuated shadows slipped across their table one by one; the last one of all stood still for a minute. "We're going to pitch a jam-session downstairs in the basement. Coming?"

Her gripping hand relaxed its hold on her arm, fell away frustratedly down by the side of her chair. They'd all gotten up, were piling in through a basement-entrance at the back.

"No, stay up here with me," she urged, reaching out to hold him. "Finish what you—"

He'd already risen. "Come on, you don't want to miss this, snooks."

"Don't you do enough playing all evening at the theatre?"

"Yeah, but that's for pay. This is for myself. You're going to hear something now."

He was going to leave her anyway, she saw, this had a stronger pull than she had, so she rose reluctantly to her feet and trailed after him down narrow brick-walled stairs to the restaurant basement. They were all in a large room down there, with instruments in it already that they must have used at previous times. Even an upright piano. There was a single large but smoky bulb hanging on a loose wire from the center of the ceiling, and to supplement this they had candles stuck in bottles. There was a battered wooden table in the middle, and they put bottles of gin on it, nearly one to a man. One of them spread a piece of brown wrapping-paper out and dumped quantities of cigarettes onto it, for anyone to help themselves at will. Not the kind the world upstairs smoked; black-filled things; reefers, she heard them call them.

They closed and bolted the door, as soon as she and Milburn had come in, to keep themselves free from interruption. She was the only girl among them.

There were packing-cases and empty cartons and even a keg or two to sit on. A clarinet tootled mournfully, and mania had begun.

The next two hours were a sort of Dante-esque Inferno. She knew as soon as it was over she wouldn't believe it had actually been real at all. It wasn't the music, the music was good. It was the phantasmagoria of their shadows, looming black, wavering ceiling-high on the walls. It was the actuality of their faces, possessed, demonic, peering out here and there on sudden notes, then seeming to recede again. It was the gin and the marihuana cigarettes, filling the air with haze and flux. It was the wildness that got into them, that at times made her cower into a far corner or climb up on a packing-case with both feet. Certain ones of them would come at her at times, individually, crowding her back, driving her before them shrinking against the wall, singling her out because she was a girl, blowing their wind-instruments full into her face, deafening her, stirring her hair with them, bringing terror into her soul.

"Come on, get up on the barrel and dance!"

"I can't! I don't know how!"

"It don't have to be your feet. Do it with what else
you've got, that's what it's for. Never mind your dress,
we're all friends."

"Darling," she thought, sidling away from a rabid
saxophone-player until he gave up following her any
more with a final ceilingward blat of unutterable woe,
"Oh darling, you're costing me dear."

> "Futuristic rhythm, never on the beat,
> Any near drum, in my eardrum, throws me off my feet."

She managed to work her way around two sides of the
room until she got to the boiler-factory that was the trap-
drum. She caught his pistoning arms, held them down,
restrained them long enough to make herself heard. "Cliff,
take me out of here. I can't stand it! I can't stand any more
of it, I tell you! I'm going to keel over in another minute."

He was already doped with marihuana. She could tell
by his eyes. "Where'll we go, my place?"

She had to say yes, she could see that was the only thing
that would get him out of there.

He got up, guided her before him toward the door,
stumbling a little. He got it open for her, and she fled
through it like something released from a slingshot. Then
he came out after her. He seemed free to leave at will,
without an explanation or farewell. The rest didn't even
seem to notice his defection. The closing of the door cut
the frenzied turmoil in half, as with the clean sweep of
a knife, and there was sudden silence, so strange at first.

> "You're the unexpected, disconnected time,
> Let me think in, sleep and drink in—"

The restaurant upstairs was dark and empty, save for
a night-light left burning far at the back, and when she

had gained the sidewalk in front, the open air made her almost light-headed, it was so cool and rare and crystal-clear after that fever-chamber. She thought she'd never breathed anything so sweet and pure before. She leaned there against the side of the building, drinking it in, her cheek pressed to the wall like someone prostrated. He took a moment longer to come out after her, adjusting the door or something.

It must have been four by now, but it was still dark and the town was asleep all around them. For a moment there was a temptation to flee for dear life down the street, away from him, and have done with the whole thing. She could have outrun him, she knew; he was in no condition to go after her.

She stayed there, passive. She had seen a photograph in her room. She knew that was the first thing that would meet her eyes when she opened the door. Then he was beside her, and the chance was gone.

They went over in a cab. It was in one of a row of old houses done over into apartments, a single one to a floor. He took her up to the second floor and unlocked it and turned on the lights for her. It was a depressing sort of place; age-blackened flooring underneath a thin application of varnish, remote ceilings, high, coffin-like window-embrasures. It wasn't a place to come to at four in the morning. Not with anyone, much less him.

She shivered a little and stood still, close by the door, trying not to be too aware of the over-elaborate way he was securing it on the inside. She wanted to keep her thinking as clear and as relaxed as she possibly could, and that thought would only muddy it.

He'd finished locking her in. "We don't need these," he said.

"No, leave it on," she said matter-of-factly, "I'm cold."

There wasn't very much time.

"What're you going to do, just stand there?"

"No," she said with absent-minded docility, "no, I'm not going to just stand here." She moved one foot inattentively forward, almost like a skater trying out the ice.

She kept looking around. Desperately looking around. What would start it? The color. Orange. Something orange.

"Well what're you looking for?" he said querulously. "It's just a room. Didn't you ever see a room before?"

She'd found it at last. A cheap rayon shade on a lamp far over at the other end of the room. She went over to it, turned it on. It cast a small glow in the shape of a halo above itself against the wall. She put her hand on it, turned to him. "I love this color."

He didn't pay any attention.

She kept her hand on it. "You're not listening. I said this is my favorite color."

This time he looked blearily over. "All right, what about it?"

"I wish I had a hat this color."

"I'll buy you one. T'morrow or the next day."

"Look, like this, this is how I mean." She picked up the small base bodily, held it riding on her shoulder with the light still on inside the shade. Then she turned toward him so that the shade seemed to be topping her head. "Look at me. Look at me good. Didn't you ever see anyone wearing a hat this color? Doesn't this remind you of someone you once saw?"

He blinked twice, with owl-like solemnity.

"Keep looking," she pleaded. "Just keep looking like that. You can remember if you want to. Didn't you ever see anyone sitting right behind you in the theatre, in the same seat I was in tonight, wearing a hat this color?"

He said, quite momentously, quite incomprehensibly. "Oh—that was that five hundred smackeroos I got!" And then suddenly shading his eyes with one hand as if in perplexity, "Hey, I wasn't supposed to tell anyone about that." Then he looked up and asked with a sort of trustful blankness, "Have I already told you?"

"Yes, sure." That was the only answer to give. He might balk at telling her the first time, but not at repeating it, if the damage was already done. Those cigarettes probably did something to their powers of memory.

She had to grab it on the fly, she daren't let it go by, even though she didn't know if this was it yet, or what this was. She put the lamp down fast, moved toward him equally fast, yet somehow managing to give an impression of leisureliness. "But tell me about it over again. I like to listen to it. Go on, you can tell me, Cliff, because you know I'm your new friend, you said so yourself. What harm is there?"

He blinked again. "What are we talking about?" he said helplessly. "I forgot for a minute."

She had to get his drug-disconnected chain of thought in motion again. It was like a feeder-line that slips its cogs every once in awhile and dangles helplessly. "Orange hat. Look, up here. Five hundred—five hundred smackeroos, remember? She sat in the same seat I did."

"Oh yeah," he said docilely. "Right behind me. I just looked at her." He gave a maniacal laugh, stilled it again as suddenly. "I got five hundred smackeroos just for looking at her. Just for looking at her and not saying I did."

She saw that her arms were creeping slowly up his collar, twining around his neck. She didn't try to stop them, they seemed to be acting independently of her. Her face was close to his, turned upward looking into it. How close you can be to a thought, it occurred to her, without guessing what it is. "Tell me more about it, Cliff. Tell me more about it. I love to listen to you when you're talking!"

His eyes died away in the fumes. "I forgot again what I was saying."

It was off again. "You got five hundred dollars for not saying you looked at her. Remember, the lady in the orange hat? Did *she* give you the five hundred dollars, Cliff? Who gave you the five hundred dollars? Ah, come on, tell me."

"A *hand* gave 'em to me, in the dark. A hand, and a voice, and a handkerchief. Oh yeah, and there was one other thing: a gun."

Her fingers kept making a slow sweep to the back of his head, and then returning each time. "Yes, but whose hand?"

"I don't know. I didn't know then, and I never found out since. Sometimes I ain't even sure it really happened, I think it musta been the weed made it *seem* like it happened. Then again, sometimes I know it did."

"Tell it to me anyway."

"Here's what happened. I came home late one night, after the show, and when I come in the hall downstairs, where there's usually a light, it was dark. Like the bulb went out. Just as I feel my way over to the stairs, a hand reaches out and stops me. Kind of heavy and cold, laying on me hard.

"I backed against the wall and says, 'Who's there? Who are you?' It was a man, I could tell by the voice. After awhile, when my eyes got a little more used to it, I could make out something white, like a handkerchief, up where his face should be. It made his voice sound all burry. But I could hear him all right.

"He gave me my own name first, and what my job was; he seemed to know everything about me. Then he asked me if I remember seeing a certain lady at the theatre a night ago, in an orange hat.

"I told him I wouldn't have if he hadn't reminded me, but now that he'd reminded me of it, I did.

"Then he said, still in that same quiet voice, without even getting excited at all: 'How would you like to be shot dead?'

"I couldn't answer at all, my voice wouldn't work. He took my hand and put it on something cold he was holding. It was a gun. I jumped, but he made me hold my hand there a minute until he was sure I got what it was. He said, 'That's for you, if you tell anyone that.'

"He waited a minute and then he went on speaking. He said, 'Or would you rather have five hundred dollars?'

"I hear paper rustling and he puts something in my hand. 'Here's five hundred dollars,' he says. 'Have you got a match? Go ahead, I'll let you light a match, so you can see it for yourself.' I did, and it was five hundred dollars all right. Then when my eyes started to go up to where his face was, about, they just got as far as the handkerchief, and he blew the match out.

" 'Now you didn't see that lady,' he said. 'There wasn't any lady. No matter who asks you, say no, keep saying no —and you'll keep on living.' He waited a minute and then he asked me, 'Now if they ask you, what is it you say?'

"I said, 'I didn't see that lady. There wasn't any lady.' And I was shaking all over.

" 'Now go on upstairs,' he said. 'Good night.' The way

it sounded through that handkerchief, it was like something coming from a grave.

"I couldn't get inside my door fast enough. I beat it upstairs and locked myself in and kept away from the windows. I'd been blazing a reefer already before it happened, and you know what that does to you."

He gave another of those chilling jangles of laughter, that always stopped dead again as suddenly. "I lost the whole five hundred on a horse the next day," he added abjectly.

He shifted harassedly, dislodging her from the chair-arm she'd been perched on. "You've brought it back again, by making me talk about it. You've made me scared again and all shaky, like I was so many times afterwards. Gimme another weed, I want to blaze again. I'm going down and I need another lift."

"I don't carry marihuana on me."

"There must be some in your bag, from over there. You were just over there with me, you must have brought some away with you." He evidently thought she'd been using them as well as he.

It was lying there on the table, and before she could get over and stop him he'd opened it and strewn everything out.

"No," she cried out in sudden alarm, "that isn't anything, don't look at it!"

He'd already read it before she could pull it away from him. It was the forgotten slip of paper from Burgess. His surprise was guileless for a moment, he didn't take in its full meaning at first. "Why, that's me! My name and where I work and ev—"

"No! No!"

He warded her off. "And to call the precinct house number first, if not there call—"

She could see the mistrust starting to film his face, cloud it over. It was coming up fast, almost like a storm, behind his eyes. Behind it in turn was something more dangerous; stark, unreasoning fright, the fright of drug-hallucination, the fright that destroys those it fears. His eyes started to dilate. The black centers of them seemed to swallow up the color of the pupils. "They sent you on purpose, you didn't just happen to meet me. Somebody's after me, and I don't know who, if I could only remember who— Somebody's going to shoot me with a gun, somebody said they'd shoot me with a gun! If I could only think what I wasn't supposed to do— You made me do it!"

She'd had no experience with marihuana-addicts before; she'd heard the word, but to her it had no meaning. She had no way of knowing the inflaming effect it has on emotions such as suspicion, mistrust and fear, expanding them well beyond the explosion-point, providing they are latent already in the subject. She could tell by looking at him that she had somebody irrational to deal with, that much was apparent. The unpredictable current of his thoughts had veered dangerously, and there was no way for her to dam it, turn it aside. She couldn't reach into his mind, because she was sane, and he—temporarily—wasn't.

He stood misleadingly still for a moment, head inclined, looking up at her from under his brows. "I been telling you something I shouldn't. Oh, if I could only remember now what it was!" He palmed his forehead distractedly.

"No you haven't, you haven't been telling me anything," she tried to soothe him. She had realized she'd better get out of the place without delay, and also, instinctively, that to make her purpose apparent was to

invite interception. She began moving slowly backward,
a surreptitious step at a time. She had placed her hands
behind her back, so they would be in a position to find the
door, try to unlock it, before he could realize her purpose.
At the same time she tried to keep her gradual withdrawal
from attracting his attention by staring fixedly into his
face, holding his gaze with her own. She realized she was
becoming increasingly taut at the horrible slowness of the
maneuver. It was like backing away from a coiled snake,
fearful that if you move too fast it will lash out all the
quicker, fearful that if you move too slow—

"Yes I did, I told you something I shouldn't. And now
you're going to get out of here and tell someone. Somebody that's after me. And they'll come and get me like
they said they would—"

"No, honest you haven't, you only think you have."
He was getting worse instead of better. Her face must be
growing smaller in his eyes, she couldn't keep him from
realizing she was drawing away from him much longer.
She was up against the wall now, and her desperately cir-
cling hands, groping secretly behind her, found only
smooth unbroken plaster-surface instead of the door-
lock. She'd aimed wrong, she'd have to change directions.
Out of the corner of her eye she placed its dark shape a
few yards to her left. If he'd only stand there like that,
where she'd left him, a second or two longer—

It was harder to move sidewise without seeming to
than it had been rearwards. She would sidle one heel out
of true, then work the ball of the foot over after it, then
do the same with the second foot, bringing them together
again, all without letting any motion show in her upper
body.

"Don't you remember, I was sitting on the arm of your

chair, smoothing your hair, that's all I was doing. Ah, don't!" she whimpered in a desperate last-minute effort to forestall him.

It was only a few seconds since this minuet of terror had begun. It seemed like all night. If she'd only had another of those devilish cigarettes to throw at him, maybe—

She grazed some small lightweight table or stance in her crabwise creep, and some little object fell off. That slight sound, that tick, that thud, that inadvertent betrayal of motion going on, did it; shattered the glaze, seemed to act as the signal his crazed nerves had been waiting for; unleashed what she'd instinctively known all along was coming from one moment to the next. He broke stance, like a figure in a waxworks toppling from its pedestal, came at her arms out, in a sort of off-balance lurch.

She floundered to the door with a muted, thin little cry that was no cry at all, only had time to ascertain one thing with her wildly-flailing hands—that the key still projected, had been left in. Then she had to go on past it, he gave her no time to do anything with it.

She broke away from the wall, cut the corner of the room and made for the window, which was set into that next side. There was a blind down over it, effacing the exact outline of its sash-frame, hampering the single, sketchy attempt to fling up the sash and scream out for help that was all his onrush allowed her. There was a stringy, dust-laden drape hanging on each side of the embrasure. She flung one behind her at him, and it slowed him for a moment until he could get its hampering folds off his neck and shoulder.

There was a derelict sofa standing out diagonally across the next wall-angle. She got in behind that, and before she could get out at the opposite end, he had sealed her in.

They backed and filed along its length twice, she on her
side, he on his, in a cat-and-mouse play, a Victorian
beauty-and-the-beast pantomime, that she would have
laughed at until five minutes ago as being something that
just didn't occur, that belonged in "East Lynne," but that
she would never laugh at again for the rest of her life—
although that apparently would only be for another two
or three minutes.

"Don't!" she kept panting. "No! Don't! You know what
they'll do to you—if you do this to me up here—you know
what they'll do to you!"

She wasn't talking to a man, she was talking to the after-
effects of a narcotic.

He suddenly took a short-cut by planting one knee on
the seat of the sofa and grasping for her across the top of
it. There wasn't any room in the little triangle for her to
withdraw far enough. His fingers caught under the neck-
line of her dress, at one shoulder. Before they could
tighten, close on it, she had freed herself by flinging her
body around in two or three complete revolutions. It
pulled the whole thing down off her shoulder on that side,
but the contact broke.

She flashed out past the gap at the lower end of the
sofa while his body was still prone across the top of it,
and skimmed along the wall on the fourth and final side
of the room. She had now made a complete circuit of it,
was coming back to the door again, on the next side. To
cut out into the middle was to go *toward* him again, at
any particular point, for he had the inside position.

There was an unlighted opening on this last side, the
doorway to either a closet or bath, but after her experience with the sofa just now she flashed past it without
stopping, fearful of being trapped even more quickly in

whatever narrower space was offered on the other side of it. Besides, the outer door, the only way to final safety, lay just ahead.

She caught at a spindling wooden chair in passage, swung it around, flung it down behind her, in hopes of over-throwing him. He saw it in time, went out around it. It only gained her five extra seconds.

She was wearing down now. As she reached the final wall-angle, turned to go along the side where this inter-minable game of puss-in-corner had first started, he cut out ahead of her, turned, and blocked her. She couldn't reverse in time, went almost into him. He had her in a pocket now, between him and the wall. His arms scis-sored for her. She could go neither forward nor back, so she went down, the only direction there was left. She had dropped down through them before they could close, and darted out from below them, so close she grazed his side as she went.

She screamed a name. The one name of all that was most powerless to help her right now. "Scott! Scott darling!" The door was ahead, but she'd never get to it in time. And she was too spent to go on past it any further—

The little lamp was still there, the one she'd tried to light his memory with before. It was too light to be able to harm him much, but she picked it up and flung it back at him. It failed even to hit him, dropped futilely wide of the mark, and the bulb in it didn't even shatter against the dingy carpeting. He came on undeterred in the final surge that they both knew—

And then something happened. His toe must have caught in something. She didn't see these things at the time, but remembered about them later. The unbroken lamp bucked violently on the floor behind him, there was a flash of bright blue from the foot of the wall, and he went sprawling down full-length between the two, arms at full reach.

There was a channel of clearance left between him and the blessed door. She was afraid to trust herself into it, but she was more afraid not to. Those hands of his, flat for a moment, lay partly in the way. She jumped around him, just past his clawing fingers, got to it.

An instant can be so long. An instant can be so short. For an instant he lay helpless like that, flat on his face, an instant only. She could feel her hands wrangling the key. Like something in a dream; they didn't seem to belong to her at all. She turned it the wrong way first, it wouldn't work; had to reverse it, bring it all the way around to the other side. He was rippling his belly along the floor, trying to close the couple of inches gap between them from where he lay, without getting up; trying to grab her by the ankles and bring her down to him.

The key clicked, she pulled, and the door swung in. Something pecked futilely across the rounded back of her shoe, it was like the tapping of fingernails, as she plunged out through the new-made opening.

Then the rest was a blurred welter of mingled horror and relief; horror at anticipated pursuit that didn't come. She was careening down dimly-lighted stairs, more by impetus than any clear sight of them. She found a door, opened it, and it was cool, and it was night, and she was safe, but she kept staggering on, away from that place of evil, that would haunt her a little bit forever. She was zig-zagging along an empty sidewalk, like a drunk, and she *was* drunk—with overpowering terror.

She remembered turning a corner, and she wasn't sure where she was any more. Then she saw a light ahead and went toward it, running now, in order to get to it quick, before he had a chance to overtake her. She went in and found herself looking at glass cases holding salami and platters of potato-salad, so it must have been an all-night delicatessen.

There was no one in it but a man dozing behind the counter. He opened his eyes and found her standing there dazedly, her dress still diagonally down off one shoulder where he'd torn it. He jumped, came forward, peered, palms to counter.

"What's the matter, miss? You been in an accident? Something I can do for you?"

"Give me a nickel," she sobbed brokenly. "Please give me a nickel—to use your phone."

She went over and dropped it in, still sobbing by reflex-diaphragm action.

The kindly old man called inside to the back: "Momma, come out front, yess? Is here a child in zome kind of trouble."

She got Burgess at his home; it was nearly five in the morning by now. She didn't even remember to tell him who she was, but he must have known. "Burgess, will you please come here for me? I've just had a terrible time, and I don't think I can manage it the rest of the way by my-self—"

The delicatessen-keeper and his wife, the latter in curl-papers and bathrobe, were holding a diagnostic consultation over her in the background, meanwhile. "Black coffee, you think?"

"Sure, iss the only thing. Aspirin we ain't got."

The woman went over and sat down across the table from her, patted her hand sympathetically. "What they do to you, dolling? You got a mudder?"

She couldn't help smiling wanly at the thought, even while she continued to sniff. The only mother she had was a supposedly hard-boiled detective.

Burgess came in alone, collar up around his ears, to find her huddled over a thick mug of steaming black coffee. Shivers that had nothing to do with the temperature had set in, but were now waning again. He'd come by himself because this was not official; it was personal, off-the-record stuff as far as he was concerned.

She greeted him with a little whimper of relief.

He sized her up. "Ah, poor kid," he said throatily, shoving out the chair next to her and sitting down on it sidewise. "Bad as all that, huh?"

"This is nothing; you should have seen me five or ten minutes ago." Then she brushed that aside, leaned over toward him absorbedly. "Burgess, it was worth it! He saw her! Not only that. Somebody came around afterward and bribed him. Some man, acting on her behalf I suppose. You can get all that out of him, can't you?"

"Come on," he said briskly. "If I don't it won't be for lack of trying. I'm going up there right now. I'll put you in a taxi first and—"

"No, no, I want to go back with you. It's all right now, I'm over it."

The delicatessen-couple came out to the doorway after them, watched them go down the street together in the paling dawn. There was a dark disapproval of Burgess plainly to be read on both their faces.

"Yah, fine brudder she's got!" the man snorted contemptuously. "First leaffs her out alone at fife in the morning! Now he comes when it's too late to make trouble with the fellow what done it! A loafer he iss if he can't look after her any better than that!"

Burgess moved stealthily up the stairs, well ahead of her, motioning her backhand to go easy. By the time she'd caught up to him he'd already been listening intently at the door for several moments, head bent over motionless against it.

"Sounds as if he's lammed out," he whispered. "Can't hear him. Get back a little, don't stand too close, in case he starts up with something."

She retreated a few steps lower down on the staircase, until only her head and shoulders were above floor-level. She saw him take something to the door and worked it carefully, with little sound if any. Suddenly a gap showed, he thrust his hand back to his hip, held it there, and trod guardedly forward.

She came on up in his wake, holding her breath for the flare-up of violence, even the ambushed onslaught, that she expected from one moment to the next. She was even with the threshold herself when the sudden flare of electric light through the opening made her jump spasmodically, though it was soundless. He'd lit the place up.

She peered through, in time to see him disappear into that doorway in the adjoining wall that she had by-passed herself in her mad circuit of the room a while ago. She ventured in past the door-sill, emboldened, for his uninterrupted transit showed this first room to be vacant.

There was a second soundless flare of electricity, and the dark place he'd gone into became a gleaming white-surfaced bathroom. She was in a straight line with it and him; for a moment she could see into it. She could see an old-fashioned four-legged tub. She could see the rump of a figure folded like a clothespin over the rim of it. The soles of its shoes were turned back and up, she could see them too. The tub could not have been marble, in such a place, and yet it gave a curious optical illusion of being marbled even on the outside. That might have been due to the thin red vein or two discernible down its outside surface. Red-veined marble—

For a moment she thought he'd gotten sick and passed out. Then as she moved to go in after him, Burgess' sharp "Don't come in here, Carol; stay where you are!" stopped her like the crack of a whip. He came back a step or two, gave the door a corrective push-to, narrowing it enough to keep her from looking in any more, without closing it entirely.

He stayed in there a long time. She remained where she was, waiting. She noticed her own wrist was shaking a little, but it wasn't due to fear any more, it was with a sort of emotional tension. She knew what that was in there, now. She knew what must have brought it about. A paroxysm of drug-magnified fear, insupportable once she'd made good her escape and the unseen tentacles of retribution seemed to be closing in on him. All the more dreadful because they were unidentifiable.

A scrap of torn paper lying there on the table that caught her eye confirmed it. Three almost illegible words, trailing off into a meaningless wavy line that overran the paper and ended in a pencil-stub lying on the floor. "Ther after me—"

The door widened grudgingly and Burgess came out to her again at last. His face looked whiter than before he'd gone in there, she thought. She noticed that he crowded her before him, without overtly seeming to, so that she found herself moving backward toward the outer door without any volition of her own. "Did you see that?" she asked, about the note.

"Yeah, on the way in."

"Is he——?"

For answer he poked a finger up under one ear, then swept it all the way around his neck to the other.

She drew in her breath sharply.

"Come on, get out of here," he said with kindly-meant gruffness. "This is no place for you." He was closing the outside door after the two of them, the way he'd found it just now. "That tub," she heard him murmur under his breath, as he guided her down the stairs to the fore of him with both hands to her shrinking shoulders. "I'll never be able to think of the Red Sea again without——" He realized that she was listening to him, and shut up.

He put her in a taxi around the corner. "This'll get you home. I've got to get right back and break out with the notification."

"It's no good now, is it?" she said almost tearfully, leaning toward him through the cab-window.

"No, it's no good now, Carol."

"Couldn't *I* repeat what he told me——?"

"That would be just hearsay. You *heard* somebody say he'd seen her, been bribed to deny it. Second-hand evidence. It's no good that way; they won't accept it."

He'd taken a thickly-folded handkerchief out of his pocket, opened it in the palm of his hand. She saw him looking at something resting within it.

"What's that?" she said.

"You tell me what it is."

"A razor-blade."

"Not enough."

"A——a safety-razor blade?"

"That's it. And when a man takes a swing at his throat with one of the old-fashioned open kind—such as I found lying under him at the bottom of the tub—what's one of

these doing overlooked under the shelf-paper in the cabinet? A guy uses either one type or the other, not both."
He put it away again. "Suicide, they'll say. And I think
I'll let them—for the present. You go home, Carol. Which-
ever it is, you weren't here tonight, you're staying out of
it. I'll see to that."

In the taxi, riding homeward through streets tin-plated
in the quickening dawn, she let her head hang futilely
downward.

Not tonight, darling, not tonight after all. But maybe
tomorrow night, maybe the night after.

15: The Ninth Day Before the Execution

LOMBARD

IT was one of those incredible luxury-hotels, its single
slender tower rising to disdainful heights above the mass
of more commonplace buildings like a tilted aristocratic
nose. It was a plush-and-jewelled perch on which birds of
paradise flying east from the movie colony were wont to
alight. Bedraggled birds of equally rich plumage, flying
west before the storm broke, had also sought refuge here
in droves while they were still able to make it.

This, he knew, was going to require a finesse all its own.
It needed just the right touch, just the right approach. He
didn't make the tactical mistake of trying to gain admission on demand, sight unseen. It wasn't the kind of place
in which anyone was ever received by anyone just at re-
quest or at first try. You had to campaign, pull wires.

He sought out the flower-shop first, therefore, entering

it from the lobby itself through a curved door of blue glass. He said, "What would you say are Miss Mendoza's favorite flowers? I understand you deliver a great many to her."

"I couldn't say," the florist demurred.

Lombard peeled off a bill, repeated what he'd just said, as though he hadn't spoken loudly enough the first time.

Apparently he hadn't. "Callers are always sending up the usual sort of thing, orchids, gardenias. I happen to know, though, that in South America, where she comes from, those flowers aren't highly regarded, they grow wild. If you want a tip of real value—" He dropped his voice, as though this were of incalculable import, "The few times she has ordered flowers for herself, to brighten up her apartment, they have *always* been deep salmon-pink sweet peas."

"I want your whole stock," Lombard said immediately. "I don't want a single one left over. And let me have two cards."

On one he roughed out a brief message in English. Then taking out a small pocket-dictionary, he transcribed it into Spanish, word for word, on the second card. Then he threw the first away. "Put this in with them, and see that they go right up. About how long should that take?"

"They should be in her hands within five minutes. She's in the tower and the page will take an express up."

Lombard returned to the lobby and poised himself before the reception-alcove, head bent to his watch like someone taking a pulse-count.

"Yes, sir?" the clerk inquired.

"Not yet," Lombard motioned. He wanted to strike her at white heat.

"*Now!*" he said after a moment's wait, so suddenly the

clerk gave a startled jump backward. "Phone Miss Mendoza's suite and ask if the gentleman who sent the flowers may come up for a moment. Lombard's the name, but don't leave out about the flowers."

When the clerk came back again he seemed almost stunned with surprise. "She said yes," he reported limply. Apparently one of the unwritten laws of the hotel had just been broken. Somebody had been received at first try.

Lombard, meanwhile, was shooting upward like a rocket into the tower. He got out slightly shaky at the knees, and found a young woman standing waiting at an open door to receive him. Evidently a personal maid, judging by her black taffeta uniform.

"Mr. Lombard?" she inquired.

"That's me."

There was evidently a final customs inspection to be passed before he was cleared for admission. "It is not a press-interview, no?"

"No."

"It is not for an autograph, no?"

"No."

"It is not to obtain a testimonial, no?"

"No."

"It is not about some bill that has, er—" She hesitated delicately; "—escaped the señorita's mind, no?"

"No."

This last point seemed to be the crucial one; she didn't go any further. "Just a moment." The door closed, then in due course re-opened again. This time all the way. "You may come in, Mr. Lombard. The señorita will try to squeeze you in between her mail and her hairdresser. Will you sit down?"

He was by now in a room that was altogether remarkable. Not because of its size, nor the stratospheric view from its windows, nor the breath-taking expensiveness of its décor, though all those things were unusual; it was remarkable because of the welter of sounds, the clamor, that managed to fill it while yet it remained unoccupied. It was in fact the noisiest empty room he had ever yet found himself in. From one doorway came a hissing and spitting sound, that was either water cascading from a tap or something frying in fat. Probably the latter, since a spicy aroma accompanied it. Mingled in with this were snatches of song, in a vigorous but not very good baritone. From another doorway, this one of double width and which opened and closed intermittently, came an even more vibrant blend. This consisted, to the best of his ability to disentangle its various skeins, of a program of samba music coming in over short waves, admixed with shattering shots of static; of a feminine voice chattering in machine-gun Spanish, apparently without stopping to breathe between stanzas; of a telephone that seemed not to let more than two-and-a-half minutes at a time go by without fluting. And finally, in with the rest of the mélange, every once in awhile there was a nerve-plucking squeak, acute and unbearable as a nail scratching glass or a piece of chalk skidding on a slate. These last abominations, fortunately, only came at widely-spaced intervals.

He sat patiently waiting. He was in now, and half the battle was won. He didn't care how long the second half took.

The maid came darting out at one point, and he thought it was to summon him, and half-rose to his feet. Her errand, however, was apparently a much more important one than that, judging by her haste. She flitted into the

region of the sputtering and baritone-accompaniment to
shriek warningly: "Not too much oil, Enrico! She says
not too much oil!" Then raced back again whence she
had come, pursued by malevolent bass-tones that seemed
to shake the very walls.

"Do I cook for her tongue or do I cook for the shaky
clock on the bathroom-floor she step on?"

Both coming and going she was accompanied by an
intimate garment of feathery pink marabou, held extended
in her hands as though someone were about to ensconce
themselves in it, but which seemed to have nothing whatever to do with her mission. All the way over and back
it shed generously, filling the air with small particles of
feather which drifted lazily to the floor long after she was
gone.

Presently the hissing stopped short with one final spit,
there was a deep-drawn "Aaah!" of satisfaction, and a
rotund coffee-colored little man in a white jacket, towering chef's cap on his head and weaving his head with satisfaction, marched out, around, and in again at the next door
up, carrying something on a domed salver.

There was a momentary lull after that. Momentary
only. Then an upheaval that made the previous clamor
seem to have been golden silence detonated. It had everything previous in it and some new additions of its own:
soprano shrieks, baritone bellows, nail-head squeaks, and
the deep gong-like clash of a violently-thrown chafing-
dish cover striking the wall and rolling halfway around
the room after that giving out fractured chimes.

The small rotund man came out, fast and outraged; no
longer coffee-complected but streaked with what looked
like egg-yolks and red peppers. His arms were going

around like wind-mills. "This time I go back! On the next ship I go back! This time she can get down on her broken knees to me and I do not stay!"

Lombard bent slightly forward in his chair and tried stopping up his ears with the points of his pinkeys, to give them a rest. After all, the human ear-drum is a delicate membrane, it can stand just so much abuse and no more.

When he uncovered them again he found to his relief that the establishment had toned down once more to the state of only partial frenzy that was seemingly its norm. At least you could hear what you were thinking again. Presently the doorbell had rung by way of variation, instead of the telephone, and the maid admitted a dark-haired, daintily-mustached individual who sat down and joined him in waiting. But with much less fortitude than Lombard himself was displaying. He got up again almost at once and began walking briskly back and forth, but with paces that were just a trifle too short to fit comfortably into the laps he was giving himself. Then he discovered one of the aggregations of Lombard's sweet peas, stopped, extracted one, and put it to his nose. Lombard at this point promptly broke off all further thought of entering into diplomatic relations, even if any had been contemplated.

"Will she be ready for me soon?" the newcomer demanded of the maid on one of her flying visits. "I have a new idea. I would like to get the feel of it between my hands before it escapes me."

"So would I," thought Lombard, eying his neck truculently.

The sweet-pea smeller sat down again. Then he stood up again, with every appearance of vibrating impatiently down around the knees. "It's leaving me," he warned. "I am losing it. Once it goes, I will have to go back to the old way again!" The maid fled inside with these dire tidings.

Lombard murmured half-audibly, "You should have gone back to the old way long ago."

It worked, at any rate. The maid came out again, beckoned with suppressed urgency, and he was in. Lombard swung at the sweet-pea he had dropped, caught it neatly with the toe of his shoe, and kited it upward with grim zest, as though doing that made him feel a lot better.

The maid came out and bent over him confidentially, to salve his impatience. "She will positively squeeze you in between him and her costume-fitter. He's hard to handle, you know."

"Oh, I don't know," Lombard demurred, twitching his extended foot slightly and eying it longingly.

There was a good long lull after that. At least, comparatively. The maid only came out once or twice and the telephone only rang once or twice. Even the machine-gun Spanish only came in disconnected salvos now. The private chef who had been going back on the next ship appeared, more rotund than ever in beret, muffler, and fuzzy overcoat, but only to inquire with injured mien: "Ask if she is dining in tonight. I cannot do it myself, I am not speaking with her."

Lombard's predecessor emerged finally, small kit in hand, and departed. Not without detouring first and hijacking another one of the sweet peas. Lombard's foot crept toward the receptacle that held the rest of them, as though he were aching to let him have all of them at once, but he conscientiously curbed the impulse.

The maid reappeared outside the holy of holies, announced, "The señorita will see you now." He found, when he tried to stand up, that his legs had gone to sleep. He slapped at them fore and aft a couple of times, straightened his tie, shot his cuffs, and stepped through.

He had no more than glimpsed a figure stretched out Cleopatra-like on a chaise-longue, when a soft furry projectile of some sort shot through the air at him and landed on his shoulder with a squeaking sound. One of those same nail-on-glass squeaks that had reached him outside every now and then. He shied nervously at the impact. Something that felt like a long velvet snake coiled itself affectionately around his throat.

The figure on the chaise beamed at him, like a fond parent watching its offspring cut up. "Don't be alarmed, señor. Is unly little Bibi."

Giving it a pet-name was only partial reassurance as far as Lombard was concerned. He kept trying to turn his head to get a look at it, but it was too close in. He managed a grin of strained geniality, for the sake of furthering his own cause.

"I go by Bibi," his hostess confided. "Bibi is, how you say it, my welcoam-committee. If Bibi don't like, he duck under sofa; I get rid of them queek. If Bibi like, he jomp to their neck; then is all right they stay." She shrugged disarmingly. "You he must like. Bibi, come down off the man's neck," she coaxed insincerely.

"No, let him stay, I don't mind him in the least," he drawled tolerantly. It would have been a faux pas of the first water, he realized, to have taken her reproach at face-value. His nose had identified the encumbrance as a small monkey by now, in spite of the cologne it had been saturated with. The tail reversed, to rewind itself the other way around. He had evidently made a hit. He could feel strands of his hair being painstakingly separated and examined, as if in search of something.

The actress crowed delightedly. If anything could put her in a receptive mood, this simian seemed able to, so Lombard felt he couldn't afford to resent the way it was getting personal with him. "Sit down," she urged cordially. He walked rather stiffly to a chair and sank into it, careful not to disturb his head-balance. He got his first good look at her. She had on a shoulder-cape of pink marabou over black velvet pajamas, each trouser-leg of which was the width of a full skirt. A somewhat horrifying arrangement that looked like molten lava had been deposited on top of her head by the sweet-pea fiend who had been in here before him. The maid was standing behind her fanning at it with a palm-leaf as if to cool it off. "I have a minute while this sets," the wearer explained graciously. He saw her surreptitiously consult the card he had sent up with the flowers a while ago, to remind herself of his name.

"How nice it was to get my flowers in Spanish for a change, Señor Lombard. You say you have just come up from *mi tierra*. We met down there?"

She had, fortunately, glided past this point before it was necessary for him to commit himself outright. Her large dark eyes took on a soulful expression, went searchingly upward toward the ceiling; she made a cushion of her hands and pressed one cheek against them. "Ah, my Buenos Aires," she breathed, "my Buenos Aires. How I miss it! The lights of the Calle Florida shining in the even-ning—"

Not for nothing had he spent several hours poring over

travel-folders before coming up here. "The beach at La Plata, down by the shore," he supplied softly—"the races at Palermo Park—"

"Don't," she winced. "Don't, you make me cry." She wasn't just acting. Or at least she wasn't entirely acting, he could tell. She was simply dramatizing emotions that were already there, that were basically sincere, as is the way with the theatrical temperament. "Why did I leave it, why am I opp here so far away?"

Seven thousand dollars a week and ten per-cent of the show might have had something to do with it, it occurred to him, but he wisely kept that to himself.

Bibi, meanwhile, having failed to find anything that required exterminating on his scalp, lost interest, ran down his arm, and took a flying leap off onto the floor. It made conversation a lot easier, even though his thatch was left looking like a haystack that had been hit by a high wind. He refrained from smoothing it down lest this give offense to the pest's mercurial mistress. She was now in as soft a mood as he could ever hope to get her into, on such short acquaintance, so he took the plunge.

"I have come to you because you are known to be as intelligent as you are talented and beautiful," he said, laying it on with a shovel.

"It is true, nobody has ever said I am a doll," the celebrity admitted with refreshing unselfconsciousness, studying her fingernails.

He hitched his chair slightly forward. "You recall a number you did in last season's show, in which you threw nosegays, little flowers, to the ladies in your audiences?"

She poised a warning finger toward the ceiling. Her eyes sparkled. "Ah, *Chica Chica Boom!* Si, si! You like? Wasn't it good?" she agreed warmly.

"Perfect," he assented, with a concealed fluctuation of
his Adam's apple. "Now one night a friend of mine—"

That was as far as he got on that try. The maid, who
had just quit fanning a moment before, stepped in again.
"William would like his orders for the day, señorita."

"Excuse me a minute." She turned her head toward the
doorway. A stalwart individual in chauffeur's uniform
stepped forward, stood at attention. "I won't nidd you
until twelve. I go to the Coq Bleu for launch, so you be
downstairs at ten-to." Then she added without any change
of inflection, "And you better take that with you while
you here, you left it behind."

He stepped over to the vanity-table she had indicated,
removed a hammered-silver cigarette-case, spaded it into
his pocket and stepped outside again, all with perfect non-
chalance.

"It didn't come from the five-and-ten, you know," she
called after him, with, it seemed to Lombard, a slight
touch of asperity. Judging by the snap in her eyes, he
didn't give William much longer.

She turned back to him again, let her filaments slowly
darken.

"I was saying, a friend of mine attended a performance
one night with a certain woman. That is why I have come
to you."

"Ah?"

"I am trying to find her for him."

She misunderstood. Her eyes corruscated with renewed
zest. "Ah, a romance! I loave a romance!"

"I'm afraid not. It's a matter of life and death." As with
all the rest, he was afraid to give her too many details, lest
she shy away from it.

She seemed to like this even better. "Ah, a mees-tirry!

I loave a mees-tirry—" She shrugged. "—as long as it don't happen to me."

Something suddenly stopped her dead. Apparently some calamity, judging by the effect it had. She eyed a tiny diamond-studded particle on her wrist. Suddenly she had reared upright, begun snapping her fingers all over the place, like a string of firecrackers going off. The maid came running in on the fly. Lombard thought he was about to be unceremoniously dismissed, in favor of the next-comer.

"You know what time is it?" the dancer said accusingly. "I don't have told you to watch it closely? You are very careless. You nearly let it go past too far. The doctor said once itch hour, on the hour. Get the calomel—"

Before Lombard knew it, another of those seasonal typhoons that seemed to occur regularly in here, was swirling around him full-blast. Machine-gun Spanish, nail-head squeaks, and the maid going around and around the room after Bibi, until Lombard felt as though he were the center-pole of a carrousel.

He finally raised his own voice and added it to the din. "Why don't you stop short, and turn back the other way?" he shouted above the racket.

That did it. Bibi ran into the maid—and the calomel ran into Bibi.

When that was over with, and the patient was clinging forlornly to his mistress, both arms about her neck, giving her a momentary resemblance to a bearded lady, he resumed his own job.

"I realize how hopeless it is to expect you to remember any particular individual, out of that sea of faces before you each night. I realize you played six nights a week and two matinees, all season long, to packed houses—"

"I have never play to an empty house in my hull career,"
she contributed, with more of her characteristic modesty.
"Even a fire cannot compete with me. Once in Buenos
Aires the theatre start to burn. You think they left—?"

He waited until that was out of the way. "My friend
and this woman were sitting in the first row, on the aisle."
He consulted something on a scrap of paper taken from
his pocket. "That would be on your left, as you faced the
audience. Now, the only help I can give you at all is this.
She stood up in her seat, oh along about the second or third
chorus of the song."

A speculative glint flickered across her eyes. "She stood
opp? While Mendoza was onstage? This interests me very
much. I have never known it to happen before." Her
shapely fingers, he noticed, were beginning to claw tentatively at the velvet of her trouser-leg, as if whetting
themselves for reprisal. "She did not care for my singing,
perhaps? She had a train to catch, perhaps?"

"No, no, no, you don't understand," he reassured her
hastily. "Who could do that to *you?* No, here's what it
was. It was during the *Chica Chica Boom* number. You
forgot to throw one of the little souvenirs to her, and she
stood up to attract your attention. For just a moment or
two she stood there right in front of you, and we were
hoping—"

She shuttered her eyes rapidly two or three times, trying
to recapture the incident. She even poked one long finger
just behind her ear, careful not to disturb the hair-do.
"I see if I can remember it for you." She obviously was
doing her best. She did all the things likely to be con-
ducive to memory-quickening. She even lit a cigarette,

although she was not, judging by the stiff way she handled it, an habitual smoker. She simply held it, letting it burn down in her fingers.

"No, I cannot," she said finally. "I'm sorry. I try hard. For me last season is like twenty years ago." She shook her head morosely, clicked her tongue compassionately a couple of times.

He started to return the futile scrap of paper to his pocket, glanced at it as he did so. "Oh, and here's another thing—although I suppose it's no more help than the first. She had on the same hat that you did, my friend tells me. I mean a duplication of it, an exact copy."

She straightened suddenly, as though she were on the point of getting something from that. He obviously had her whole undivided attention at last, if he hadn't before. Her eyes narrowed speculatively. Then they glittered behind their thread-like constriction. He was almost afraid to move or breathe. Even Bibi looked at her curiously from a fur-huddle on the carpet at her feet.

Suddenly it came. She stabbed her cigarette out with a single vicious lunge. She emitted a strident, macaw-like cry, that wouldn't have been out of place in a jungle. "A-a-ai! *Now* I remember! Now!" A flash-flood of Spanish swept her off his conversational-track. Finally, after a lot of eddying around, she got back onto it in English again. "That *thing* that stood up there! That *criatura* that stand in front of the hull house, in *my* hat, to show she is wearing it! She even stop the spotlight, clip some of it off from me! Hanh! Do I recall? You bet I recall! You think I'm going to forget a thing like that in a horry? Hanh! You don't know Mendoza!" She snorted with such violence that Bibi gave the appearance of being swept across the floor for a distance of several feet like a dried leaf, although it was probably a scuttle for shelter under his own power.

The maid chose this most unpropitious moment to intrude. "The costumer has been waiting for some time now, señorita."

She semaphored violently, crossing and recrossing her arms over her head. "She should keep on wetting some more! I am listening to something I don't like to hear!"

She climbed down the chaise-longue toward Lombard, balancing on one bent knee over the lower end of it. She even seemed to regard her own overheated state of mind as a prideful accomplishment. She flung out her arms to show him, then tapped herself like a woodpecker on the chest. "Look how I get! Look how angry it still make me, even sotch a long time after! Look what it do!"

After which she rose to her feet, squeezed herself tightly around the waist with both arms in a belligerent embrace, as if holding herself in, and began to stalk back and forth, turning at the end of each short heat with a great fanning-out of her wide trouser-bottoms. Bibi crouched in a far corner, head bowed in desolation and his skinny arms flung up over it.

"And what you want her for, you and this friend of yours?" she demanded suddenly. "You haven't told me yet!"

He could tell by her challenging inflection that if it was anything that had to do with making the style-pirate happy, he wasn't going to get any help from Mendoza, even if she had been in a position to give it. He wisely marshalled the facts in such a way that her purpose would swing over to coincide with his, even though both had not quite the same end in view. "He is in serious trouble, believe me, señorita. I won't bore you with the details, but she is the only one who can get him out of it. He has to prove that he was with her that night, and not where they say he was. He only met her that night; we don't know her name, we don't know where she lives, we don't know anything about her. That's why we're looking high and low—"

He could see her mulling it over. After a moment she informed him: "I like to help you. I give anything to tell you who she is." Then her face dropped, she spread her hands helplessly. "But I never see her before. I never see her after. I just see her stand opp like that. That's all, I can't tell you no more about her than that." At least facially, she seemed to be even more disappointed than he was about it.

"Did you notice him at all, the man with her?"

"No, I never even give him a look. I couldn't say who was with her. He stay in the shadow down below."

"You see, there's as big a link as ever missing, only it's the other way around now. Most of the others remembered him, but not her. You remember her, but not him. It's still no good, wouldn't prove anything. Just that a woman stood up in a theatre one night. Any woman. She might have been alone. She might have been with someone else entirely. It doesn't mean a thing. I've got to get the two linked up together by *one* witness." He clapped his hands to his knees frustratedly, rose to leave. "Looks like it ends there, where it began. Well, thank you for your time."

"I keep trying for you, anyway," she promised, giving him her hand. "I don't know what I can do, but I keep at it."

He didn't either. He shook hands briefly, passed through the outer room in a mist of depression. He felt the let-down, the sudden reversal, all the more keenly because he had come closer to getting onto something tangible just now than he had at any other time so far; it had been almost within his grasp, only to be snatched away at the last moment. Now he was right back where he'd been before.

The operator had turned and was looking at him expectantly, so he knew he'd come all the way down without feeling it, and was supposed to get out of the car. Somebody propelled a door for him and he was outside in the street. He stood there for a moment without moving away from the entrance, simply because he couldn't decide which direction to take next. One offered as little as the other, so they checkmated each other. And his ability to make even such a minor decision as that was wallowing helplessly in a trough just then.

A taxi came along and he hailed it. It had someone in it, he had to wait for another. That kept him there a minute longer. And sometimes a minute can make an awful lot of difference. He hadn't left any tracer with Mendoza, she wouldn't have known where to contact him.

He was already seated in the second taxi and it was just about to take off, when the revolving-door of the hotel blurred like a propellor in motion and a bellboy came darting out to him. "Are you the gentleman that just left Miss Mendoza's suite? She called down a minute ago after you'd gone by. She'd like you to come back again, if you don't mind."

He went inside again and up fast. The same fur snowball launched itself at him, in fond recollection. He didn't even mind that this time. The pajamas were gone and she was in the middle of trying something or other on. She looked like a half-finished lampshade standing in the middle of the floor, but he had no eye for any of that.

She was only mildly disconcerted, if at all. "I hope you're a married man? Pouf, if you're not, you will be some day, so it's all the same." He couldn't quite grasp the fine point of propriety involved, but let it go at that. She picked up a length of material and draped it negligently across one shoulder, where it would do the least good, as a protection. Then she dismissed some shadowy third person kneeling at her feet with a mouthful of pins.

"A minute after you left I got something," she told him as soon as they were alone. "I was still kind of—" She twisted her hand this way and that, as though she were trying a doorknob; "you know—sore."

"William," occurred to him unspoken at this point.

"So I let it out, like I always do when I'm sore, by breaking a couple of little things." She motioned with perfect unconcern to numerous crystal fragments littering the floor, with a disembodied atomizer-bulb lying in their midst. "Then the fonniest thing happen. It bring back another time I am sore, about that woman we were talking about. Because I throw things now, I remember how I throw things that other time." She hitched her shoulders. "Is peculiar, no? It remember to me what I do with the hat. I think maybe it help you to know."

He waited, shifting one foot out toward her in leashed intensity.

She shook an explanatory finger at him. "So that night, when that woman do like that to me, I go back to my dressing-room and, immh—" She inhaled deeply. "I nidd to be tied opp. I take everything on the table and I go like this!" She made a clean horizontal sweep with one arm. "You onderstand how I feel, no? You don't blem me?"

"I don't blame you at all."

She trip-hammered the flat of her hand between the
circumflex accents formed by the brassiere she had on.
"You think anyone is going to do that to me in front of
a houseful of people? You think I, Mendoza, let them get
away with that?"

He didn't, now that he'd had a sample or two of her
combustive temperament.

"They have to huld me back by both arms, the stage
manager and my maid, to keep me from rushing out the
stage-door in my wrapper just like I am, to see if I can find
her in front of the theatre, for to pull her to pieces betwinn
my two hands!"

He'd half hoped, for a minute, that that was what it was
going to develop had happened, that she'd tangled with
the cipher at the theatre-entrance. But he knew it hadn't,
or Henderson would have mentioned it to him, and she
herself would have recalled it sooner than this.

"I would have showed her a thing or two, you bet!"
She still looked capable of doing it even at this late day.
Lombard even drew back a precautionary step or two,
the way she was crouched facing him, fingers working
convulsively in lobster-claw formation. Bibi was clasping
and unclasping his own tiny digits in apprehensive sup-
plication.

She straightened, threw her arms outward in breast-
stroke position. "The next day I'm still sore. With me it
lasts. So I go to the modiste, the designer, that make opp
the hat for me, and I blow off stimm there instead. I throw
it in her face in front of hull room full of customers. I say,
'So you make *me* an original for my production-number,
ha? The only one of its kind, ha? Nobody else is going to

have one like it, ha?' And I wipe it all over her face, and when I leave she is still spitting out pieces of the material, she can't talk."

She shovelled her hands at him inquiringly. "So that's good for you, is no? That helps you, no? This cheat of a designer, she must know who is the person she sell the copy to. You go to her and you find out who this woman is you look for."

"Swell! Great! At last!" he yelled, so enthusiastically that Bibi dove head-first under the chaise and pulled his tail in after him. "What's her name? Give me her name!"

"Wait, I dig it opp for you." She tapped the side of her head apologetically. "I work in so many different shows, I have so many different costumers, I can't keep track." She called the maid in, instructed her: "Look among my bills for a hat, from last year's show, see you can find one."

"But we don't keep them that long, do we, señorita?"

"You don't have to go all the way back to when it start from, stupid," said the star, as unselfconsciously as ever. "Look it opp among last month's, it probably still kipp coming in."

The maid came back after a moderately lengthy—and to Lombard, excruciating—wait. "Yes, I found it, it did come in this month again. It says, 'One hat, a hundred dollars,' and the letterhead reads 'Kettisha.'"

"Good! That's it!" She passed it to Lombard. "You got it?" He copied the address, returned it to her. Her hands went into hysterics, and a blizzard of tiny pieces of paper snowed all over the floor. Then she ground her foot down into the middle of them. "I like the nerve! Still sending me bills a year later! She's got no shem, that woman!"

She looked up to find him already crossing the adjoining

room on his way out. He was an opportunist; after all, her contribution had been made, she was of no further value to him. On to the next link.

She hastened to the boudoir doorway to deliver a parting benediction on his enterprise. One motivated by spite, however, and not altruism. She would have followed him all the way to the outside door, only the uncompleted hoopskirt she wore got stuck in the opening, wouldn't let her pass through. "I hope you catch opp with her!" she shrilled after him vengefully. "I hope she find herself in plenty of trouble!"

A woman will forgive you anything—but wearing the same hat as she does, at the same time.

He felt like a fish out of water when he walked into the place, but he didn't let it deter him. He would have stalked into far more unlikely places than this to attain his goal. It was one of those establishments on a side-street, housed in a former private residence converted to commercial purposes, whose expensiveness and exclusiveness always seem to be in inverse ratio to their lack of conspicuousness. The entire ground floor was given over to the display-room, or whatever the trade-name for it was. Having stated his business, he took shelter in a secluded corner of this, the most secluded corner he was able to find.

He'd walked in right in the middle of a showing. Or maybe they had one every day at this hour, for all he knew. It didn't help to put him at his ease. He was the only man there, or at least the only one of service age. There was what appeared to be a desiccated septuagenarian present among the sprinkling of clients seated here and there. The charming young thing with him, his granddaughter no doubt, must have brought him in with her to help her select a wardrobe. "The mind," thought Lombard, regarding him with a bilious eye, "can certainly work wonders." But with that one exception, it was all distaff. Even a girl-doorman and girl-pages.

The mannequins would come forward slowly, one by one, from the rear, and make a complete circuit of the forepart of the room, turning this way and that with little graceful swirls. For some reason, it may simply have been the corner he had chosen, he kept getting swirls and even full halts, from every single one of them. He felt like saying "I'm not here to buy anything," but didn't have the nerve. It made him acutely uncomfortable, the more so since he had to keep staring into their faces and there were lots of other places he would have preferred staring.

The young woman he'd spoken to came back and rescued him at last. "Madame Kettisha will see you in her private office, upstairs on the second floor," she whispered. A girl-page showed him the way, knocked for him, then departed below again.

There was a buxom, middle-aged, readheaded Irishwoman sitting facing him from behind a large desk when he went in. She not only had nothing of the chic couturier about her, she even leaned slightly to the horsey, dowdy side. She probably had once been Kitty Shaw in some backstreet tenement and she deserved plenty of credit, he told himself, sizing her up. She probably was a wizard at making money; only an unqualified success could have afforded to flaunt such personal slovenliness as she was exhibiting. His first impression was altogether favorable and his relief was almost abject.

She was shuffling through a sheaf of crayon-colored fashion-sketches at lightning speed, discarding some to her right, okaying others to her left. Or vice versa. "Well, mike, what can I do for you?" she grunted brusquely without looking up.

He was all out of tact by now. It was still the same day as the Mendoza interviews, and he hadn't had time to recuperate from them yet. It was getting late, anyway; nearly five in the afternoon.

"I came straight down here from one of your former customers. The South American actress Mendoza."

She did look up at that. "Better use a whiskbroom," she suggested dourly.

"You did a hat for her, for last year's show, remember? One hundred bucks, and I want to know who got the chaser on it."

She put the sketches out of harm's way first, before she cut loose. The accepts into a drawer, the discards into a wastebasket. She had a temper, evidently, that could be turned off and on at will, and with a time-limit set to it. At that, he liked it better than Mendoza's brand. It was more forthright. Her hand came down on the desk-top with a bang like a hand-grenade. "Don't you gimme any of that!" she roared. "I've had enough trouble out of that hat! I said then there was no copy made, and I still say now there was no copy made. When I produce an original, it stays original! If there was a copy made, it wasn't run up in this establishment or with my knowledge, and I'm not responsible! I may soak 'em, but I don't doublecross them!"

"There was a copy made," he insisted. "It showed up in a theatre, face to face with hers across the footlights!"

She leaned down heavily over the desk, both elbows in air. "What does she want me to do, sue her for slander?" she shouted. "I will if she keeps this up! She's a liar, and you can go back and tell her I said so!"

Instead he took his hat and pitched it onto a chair over in the corner, to show her he intended staying until he had what he'd come here to get. He even unbuttoned his coat, to give himself plenty of free arm-action. "She has nothing to do with it, so let's just forget her. I'm here for purposes of my own. There was a copy, because a friend of mine was with the very woman that had it on in the theatre. So don't tell me there wasn't. I want to know who she is, I want her name from your list of customers."

"It isn't on it. It couldn't be, because there was no such transaction entered into by us. What're you going to do, keep this up all day?"

He hitched his chin out into second, brought his own hand down in an answering blow to hers that made the whole desk-structure jar. "For the love of God, there's a man counting his life by hours! What the hell do I care about your business ethics at such a time. You're not going to sit there and head me off, not if I've got to lock this door and stay in here with you all night! Don't you understand me? There's a man going to be executed in nine days' time! The wearer of that hat is the only one can save him. You've got to give me her name. It's not the hat, it's the woman I want!"

Her voice suddenly dropped to a reasonable level. She'd evidently turned her temper off. He'd caught her interest. "Who is he?" she asked curiously.

"Scott Henderson, for killing his wife."

She wagged her head in recognition. "I remember reading about that at the time."

He struck the desk again, less shatteringly than before. "The man's innocent. It's simply got to be stopped. Mendoza bought a certain specially-designed hat here, that couldn't have been reproduced elsewhere. Somebody popped up in the theatre with an exact copy of that same hat. He was with this somebody, he was with her all that evening, but he never found out her name or anything about her. Now I've got to find that person, at all costs. She can prove that he wasn't home when it happened. Is that clear enough for you? If it isn't I can't make it any clearer!"

She gave him the impression of being a person with few, if any, moments of indecision. She was having one of them now, but it was of brief duration. She asked one more question, to safeguard herself. "You're sure this isn't some legal trick on that spick hellcat's part? The only reason I haven't filed suit against her, for non-payment and also for assault that day she came down here, was so that she wouldn't file cross-suit against me. The publicity would be harmful to my establishment's good name."

"I'm not a lawyer," he assured her. "I'm an engineer from South America. I can show you who I am, if you're in any doubt." He took things out of his pocket for identification-purposes, presented them to her.

"Then I can talk confidentially to you," she decided.

"Absolutely. My only interest in the matter is Henderson. I'm sweating myself skinny to get him out of it. Your wrangle with her doesn't mean anything to me, from either party's side. It's just that it happens to lie across my own path of investigation."

She nodded. She glanced at the door to make sure it was discreetly closed. "Very well then. Here's something that I wouldn't admit to Mendoza for the world, that I can't afford to, understand? There must have been a leak around here someplace. The copying did originate here. But not officially; on the sly, by some member of the organization.

Now I'm telling *you* this, but I don't want it to go any
further. I'd have to deny it, of course, if it was ever
brought out publicly. My designer, the girl that does the
sketches, is in the clear; I know it wasn't she who sold us
out. She's been with me ever since I first opened my own
place, she's bought into it. It wouldn't pay her, for a
measly fifty, seventy-five, or whatever it was, to peddle
around her own ideas like that. She'd be competing against
herself. The two of us, she and I, investigated on the q.t.
after Mendoza was down here raising an uproar that day,
and we found that particular sketch gone from her album,
missing, when we went to look. Somebody had deliberately swiped it, to use over again. We figured it for the
seamstress, the girl who did the actual needlework on that
number in the shop. She denied it naturally, and we had
no evidence to prove it. She must have run the thing up
at home on her own time. I suppose we caught her before
she'd had time to slip the borrowed sketch back into the
album again. Well, to be on the safe side, to make sure we
didn't get into hot water like that again, we shipped her."
She thumbed over her shoulder.

"So you see, Lombard—that your name, again?—as far
as the sales records here in the office go, there never was
any second buyer for that particular hat. That's dead on
the level. I couldn't help you there if I wanted to. All I can
suggest is, if you want that woman, your best bet is to
tackle that former sewing-apprentice of ours. As I say,
I can't guarantee that she actually does know anything
about it. All I know is we ourselves felt strongly enough
convinced that she did, at the time, to dismiss her. If you
want to take the chance, it's up to you."

Again it had jumped a lap ahead of him, just when he
thought he was safely up to it at last. "I have to, I haven't

any choice," he said dismally.

"Maybe I can give you a hand with it," she said helpfully. She snapped on her desk-speaker. "Miss Lewis, look up the name of that girl we discharged right after we had all that trouble with Mendoza. Address too."

He leaned his head sideward, elbow to desk, while they were waiting. She must have seen something in his attitude. "You think quite a lot of him, I guess," she said, almost gently. It was a seldom-used inflection with her; she had to clear her throat to get it to transmit in the right key.

He didn't answer. That was one of those things that didn't need answering.

She shot a drawer, pulled out a squat bottle of Irish whiskey. "The hell with that sissy champagne they serve downstairs. A nip of this is what's in order when you're up against something that needs tall bucking. It's an example I learned from my old man, rest his bones—"

The speaker signalled back. A girl's voice said: "That was Madge Peyton. The address on record for her when she worked here is four-nine-eight Fourteenth Street."

"Yeah, but which Fourteenth Street?"

"That's all it says here: Fourteenth Street."

"Never mind," he said, "there's only two to choose from, east and west." He took it down, went over and reclaimed his hat, buttoned up with renewed purpose, the brief rest-period over.

She was sitting there shading her eyes lengthwise. "Let me see if I can give you an angle on her. She won't come through willingly, you know." She dropped her hand, looked up. "Yeah, I've got her now. She was one of these quiet mousey little things. Shirtwaist-and-skirt type, know what I mean? They're the kind that are always apt to pull a stunt like that for money, quicker than the good-lookers

are, because money don't come as easy to them. You'll find
they're usually scared of guys, and don't give themselves
a chance to get to know them; then when they do get in
with one, it's always the wrong kind, because they haven't
had any previous sampling-experience."

She was a shrewd woman, he had to admit. That was
why she probably wasn't Kitty Shaw in some backstreet-
tenement at this very moment.

"We soaked Mendoza a hundred for it originally. She
probably didn't get more than fifty for repeating on it.
There's an angle for you, right there. Try her with another
fifty, that ought to get it out of her—if you can find her."

"If I can find her," he agreed, plodding dispiritedly
down the stairs.

A rooming-house keeper opened a door painted black
to resemble ebony, with a square of glass set into the upper
half and a tawny roller-shade backing that. "Un?" she
said.

"I'm looking for a Madge Peyton."

She just shook her head to conserve energy.

"A girl that—well, a sort of plain-looking mousey girl."

"Yeah, I know who you mean. No, she's not here any
more. Used to be, but she's gone quite some time now."
She kept scanning the street while she was talking to him.
As if, now that she'd taken the trouble of coming to the
door, she might as well get something out of it before she
went back inside again. That was probably why she continued to stand there as long as she did, and not because of
any interest in his problem.

"Any idea where she moved to?"

"Just left, that's all I can tell you. I don't keep strings
on 'em."

"But there must be some sort of a trace. People don't just go up in smoke. What took her things away?"

"One arm and both her feet." She jerked a thumb. "Down that way, if it's any good to you."

It wasn't very much. There were three more intersecting avenues "down that way." And then a marginal thoroughfare. And then a river. And then fifteen to twenty States. And then an ocean.

She'd had enough air and sightseeing now. "I can make something up, if you want me to," she offered. "But if it's facts you're after—" She bunched fingers to her lips, blew them apart, to denote emptiness.

She started to close the door, added: "What's the matter, mister? You look kind of white."

"I feel kind of white," he assented. "Mind if I sit on your doorstep here a minute?"

"Help yourself, as long as you don't get in the way of anyone coming in or going out."

Slam.

16: The Eighth Day Before the Execution

17: The Seventh Day Before the Execution

18: The Sixth Day Before the Execution

HE got off the train at the end of a three hour ride from the city, looked around him doubtfully as soon as it had taken itself out of the way. This was one of those small outlying hamlets close to a large center that, for some reason or other, often give an impression of far greater sleepiness and rusticity than places that are actually much further out. Possibly because the contrast is too sudden, the eye hasn't become conditioned to the change yet. It was still close enough in to have certain typical features of the metropolitan scene; a well-known five-and-ten cent store, an A and P, a familiar chain orange-juice concession. But they only seemed to emphasize its remoteness from the originals, instead of tempering it.

He consulted the back of an envelope, with a list of names jotted down it perpendicularly, each with an accompanying address. They were all approximations of one another, although in two different languages. All but the last two had been lined-out. They ran something like this:

> Madge Payton, millinery (and address)
> Marge Payton, millinery (and address)
> Margaret Peyton, hats (and address)
> Madame Magdax, chapeaux (and address)
> Madame Margot, chapeaux (and address)

He crossed the tracks to a filling-station, asked the grease monkey: "Know of anyone around here makes hats and calls herself Marguerite?"

"There's a boarder down at old Mrs. Hascom's got some sort of sign in the window. I don't know if it's hats or dresses, I never noticed it very closely. It's the end house, on this side of the road. Just keep going straight down."

It was an unlovely-looking frame building, with a pitiful hand-printed placard in a corner of one of the lower windows. "Marguerite, hats." A trade-name, for a whistle-stop like this. Even in an out-of-the-way place like this, he reflected curiously, they still had to be French. Peculiar convention.

He went up under the gloomy porch-shed and knocked. The girl who came out was she herself, if Kettisha's description was to be trusted. Plain and timid-looking. Lawn shirtwaist and dark-blue skirt. He caught sight of a little metal cap topping one of her fingers; a thimble.

She thought he wanted the person who owned the house, told him unasked: "Mrs. Hascom's gone down to the store. She ought to be back in—"

He said, "Miss Peyton, I had quite a time finding you."

Instantly she was frightened, tried to withdraw and close the door. He blocked it with his foot. "I don't think you have the right person."

"I do think I have." Her fright alone was proof enough of that, although he couldn't understand the reason for it. She kept shaking her head. "All right, then I'll tell *you*. You used to work for Kettisha, in their sewing-room."

She got white as a sheet, so she had. He reached down and caught her by the wrist, to keep her from running in even without being able to close the door, as he saw she was about to do.

"A woman approached you and induced you to copy a hat that had been made for Mendoza, the actress."

She kept swinging her head faster and faster; that was all she seemed capable of doing. She was straining terrifiedly away from him, at an acute backward slant. His grip on her wrist was all that was holding her there in the door-opening. Panic can be as stubborn as courage, its opposite.

"I just want that woman's name, that's all."

She was beyond reasoning with. He'd never seen anyone plunged head-long into such depths of terror. Her face was gray. Her cheeks were visibly pulsing, as though her heart were in truth in her mouth, as the expression went. It couldn't be the design-theft that was doing this to her. Cause and effect were too unrelated. A major apprehension for a minor infraction. He could sense, vaguely, that he'd stumbled on some other story, some other story entirely, lying across the path of this quest of his. That was the most he was able to make out of it.

"Just the name of the woman—" He could tell by her fear-blurred eyes that she didn't even hear the words. "You're in no danger of being prosecuted. You must know who it was."

She found her voice at last. A strangled distortion of one, anyhow. "I'll get it for you. It's inside. Let me go a minute—"

He held the door so that she couldn't close it. He opened the hand that had been choking her wrist, and instantly he was alone. She'd gone like something windswept, blown from sight.

He stood there waiting for just a moment, and then something that he was unable to account for, some tension that she'd left behind her in the air, made him spurt forward, rush down the gloomy central hallway, fling open the door to one side she had just closed behind her.

She hadn't locked it, fortunately. He swept it back just in time to see the shears flash in air, a little over her head. He never knew how he got over in time, but he did. He managed to deflect the blow with an outward fling of his arm, slashing his sleeve and drawing a fleshy cut for his pains. He pulled them away from her and threw them over in the corner with a tinkle. They probably would have gone in deep enough to get her heart, at that, if she'd hit the right place.

"What was that for?" he winced, stuffing a handker-chief down his sleeve.

She caved in like a stepped-on ice cream cone. She dissolved into a welter of tears and incoherence. "I haven't seen him since. I don't know what to do with it. I was afraid of him, afraid to refuse him. He told me just a few days and now it's been months—I've been afraid to come forward and tell anyone, he said he'd kill me—"

He clamped his hand across her mouth, held it there a minute. This was that other story, the one he didn't want. Not his. "Shut up, you frightened little fool. I only want the name, the *name* of the woman for whom you made a plagiarized hat at Kettisha's. Can't you get that through your head?"

The reversal was too sudden, the prospect of renewed security too tantalizing for her to be able to believe in it fully at once. "You're just saying that, you're just trying to trick me—"

A muted wailing, almost unnoticeable it was so thin, had started in somewhere nearby. Everything seemed to have power to frighten her. He saw her cheeks get white all over again at that, although it was scarcely loud enough to penetrate the ear-drum.

"What faith are you?" he asked.

"I was a Catholic." The tense she gave it held some kernel of tragedy, he could tell.

"Have you a rosary? Bring it out." He saw he'd have to convince her emotionally, since he couldn't through rea-soning.

She offered it to him resting in her hand. He placed his own two over and under it, without removing it. "Now. I swear that all I want of you is what I've told you. Nothing else. That I won't harm you in any other matter. That I'm not here on any other matter. Is that enough?"

She'd grown a little calmer, as though the contact of the object was a steadying influence in itself. "Pierrette Douglas, Six Riverside Drive," she said unhesitatingly.

The wailing was beginning to grow louder little by little. She gave him one last look of dubious apprehension. Then she stepped into a small curtained alcove to one side of the room. The wailing stopped short. She came back as far as the entrance, holding a long white garment or garments trailing from her enfolded arms. There was a small pink face topping it, looking trustfully up at her. She was still frightened, vastly so, when she looked at Lombard. But when she looked downward at that face under her own, there was unmistakable love in the look. Guilty, furtive, but stubborn; the love of the lonely, that grows steadily stronger, more unbreakable, day by day and week by week.

"Pierrette Douglas, Six Riverside Drive." He was shuffling out money. "How much did she give you?"

"Fifty dollars," she said absently, as if speaking of a long-forgotten thing.

He dropped it contemptuously into a reversed hat-shape she'd been working on. "And next time," he said from the doorway, "try to use a little more self-control. You're only laying yourself wide open this way."

She didn't hear him. She wasn't listening. She was smiling, looking downward at an answering little toothless smile that met her own.

It didn't bear the slightest resemblance to hers, that other little face directly under her own. But it was hers, hers from now on; hers to have and hers to keep and hers to banish loneliness with.

"Good luck to you," he couldn't resist calling back to her from the outer door of the house.

It had taken him three hours to ride out. It only took thirty minutes to ride back. Or so it felt. The wheels racketed around under him, talking out loud the way train-wheels do. "Now I've got her! Now I've got her! Now I've got her!"

A conductor stopped beside him, one time. "Tickets, please."

He looked up, grinning blankly. "It's okay," he said. "Now I've got her."

Now I've got her. Now I've got her. Now I've got her. . . .

19: The Fifth Day Before the Execution

THERE was no sound of arrival. There was a sound of departure, the faint hum of a car drawing away outside past the glass doors. He looked up and there was someone already standing there in the inner entrance, like a wraith against the glass doors. She'd partly opened them to step through, was standing there half-in, half-out, head turned to look behind her at the receding vehicle that had brought her.

He had a feeling that it was she, with nothing further than that to substantiate it for a moment. The fact that she was coming in alone, like the lady free-lance he'd gathered she was. She was stunningly beautiful, so beautiful that all delight was taken from her beauty by its excess amount, as anything overdone is apt to. Just as the profile of a cameo or the head of a statue fail to move the emotions, except as an artistic abstraction, so did she. One had the feeling that, the law of compensation being what it is, she had few inner merits, must be full of flaws, to be that peerless on the outside. She was a brunette, and tall; her figure was perfection. Almost it must have made life barren, to be without so many of the problems, the strivings, that plagued other women. She looked that way, as though life was barren, a burst soap-bubble leaving the unpleasant taste of soap upon her lips.

Her gown was like a ripple of fluid silver running down the slender gap between the wings of the door, as she stood there between them. Then, the car having gone, she turned her head forward again and finished entering.

She had no look for Lombard, a wan "Good evening" without spirit for the hallman.

"This gentleman has been—" The latter began.

Lombard had reached her before he could finish it.

"Pierrette Douglas." He stated it as a fact.

"I am."

"I've been waiting to speak to you. I must talk to you immediately. It's urgent—"

She had stopped before the waiting elevator, with no intention, he could see, of allowing him to accompany her any further than that. "It's a little late, don't you think?"

"Not for this. This can't wait. I'm John Lombard, and I'm here on behalf of Scott Henderson—"

"I don't know him, and I'm afraid I don't know you either—do I?" The "do I?" was simply a sop of urbanity thrown in.

"He's in the death-house of the State Penitentiary, awaiting execution." He looked across her shoulder at the waiting attendant. "Don't make me discuss it down here. Out of common ordinary decency—"

"I'm sorry, I live here; it's one-fifteen in the morning, and there are certain proprieties— Well, over here then." She started diagonally across the lobby toward a small inset furnished with a settee and smoking-stands. She turned to him there, remained standing; they conferred erect.

"You bought a hat from a certain employee of the Kettisha establishment, a girl named Madge Peyton. You paid her fifty dollars for it."

"I may have." She noticed that the hallman, his interest whetted, was doing his best to overhear from the outside of the alcove. "George," she reprimanded curtly. He withdrew reluctantly across the lobby.

"In this hat you accompanied a man to the theatre, one night."

Again she conceded warily, "I may have. I have been to theatres. I have been escorted by gentlemen to them. Will you come to the point, please?"

"I am. This was a man you'd only met that same evening. You went with him without knowing his name, nor he yours."

"Ah no." She was not indignant, only coldly positive. "Now you can be sure you are mistaken. My standards of conduct are as liberal as anyone else's, you will find. But they do not include accompanying anyone anywhere, at any time, without the formality of an introduction first. You have been misdirected, you want some other person." She thrust her foot out from underneath the silver hem, to move away.

"Please, don't let's split hairs about social conduct. This man is under sentence of death, he's to be executed this week! You've got to do something for him—!"

"Let's understand one another a little better. Would it help him if I falsely testify I was with him, on one certain night?"

"No, no, no," he breathed, exhausted, "only if you rightly testify you were with him, as you were."

"Then I can't do it, because I wasn't."

She continued to gaze at him steadily. "Let's go back to the hat," he said finally. "You did buy a hat, a special model that had been made for somebody else—"

"But we're still at cross-purposes, aren't we? My admitting that has no bearing on my admitting that I accompanied this man to a theatre. The two facts are entirely unrelated, have nothing to do with one another."

That, he had to admit to himself, could very well be. A dismal chasm seemed to be on the point of opening at his feet, where he had seemed to be on solid ground until now.

"Give me some more details of this theatre-excursion," she had gone on. "What evidence have you that the person accompanying him was myself?"

"Mainly the hat," he admitted. "The twin to it was being worn on the stage, that very night, by the actress Mendoza. It was an original made for her. You admit that you secured a duplication of it. The woman with Scott Henderson was wearing that duplication."

"It still does not follow that I was that woman; your logic is not as flawless as you seem to believe." But that was simply by way of an aside; her thoughts, he could see, were busy elsewhere.

Something had happened to her. Something was having a surprisingly favorable effect on her. Either something that he had said, or something that had occurred to her in her own mind. She had suddenly become strangely alert, interested, almost one might say feverishly absorbed. Her eyes were sparkling watchfully.

"Tell me. One or two more things. It was the Mendoza show, is that right? Can you give me the approximate date?"

"I can give you the exact date. They were in the theatre together on the night of May twentieth last, from nine until shortly after eleven."

"May," she said to herself, aloud. "You interest me strangely," she let him know. She motioned, even touched him briefly on the sleeve. "You were right. You'd better come upstairs with me a minute, after all."

During the ride up in the car she only said one thing. "I'm very glad you came to me with this."

They got out at the twelfth floor or so, he wasn't sure just which one it was. She keyed a door and put on lights, and he followed her in. The red fox scarf that had been dangling over her arm she dropped carelessly over a chair. Then she moved away from him over a polished floor that reflected her upside down like a funnel of fuming silver being spilled out across it.

"May the twentieth, is that right?" she said over her shoulder. "I'll be right back. Sit down."

Light came from an open doorway, and she remained in there awhile, while he sat and waited. When she returned she was holding a handful of papers, bills they looked like, sorting them from hand to hand. Before she had even reached him, she had apparently found one that suited her purpose more than any of the rest. She tossed all but one aside, retained that, came over to him with it.

"I think the first thing to establish, before we go any further," she said, "is that I was not the person with this man at the theatre that night. Suppose you look at this."

It was a bill for hospitalization, for a period of four weeks commencing on the thirtieth of April.

"I was in the hospital for an appendectomy, from the thirtieth of April to the twenty-seventh of May. If that isn't satisfactory, you can check with the doctors and nurses there—"

"That's satisfactory," he said, on a long breath of defeat.

Instead of moving to terminate the interview, she joined him in sitting down.

"But it was you who bought the hat?" he said finally.

"It was I who bought the hat."

"What became of it?"

She didn't answer immediately. She seemed to become lost in thought. An odd sort of silence descended on the two of them alike. Under cover of it he studied her and her surroundings. She, also under cover of it, studied some inward problem of her own.

The room told him things. Luxury keeping its head above water only by the sheerest nerve. No compromise permitted. Outside, a good, if not the smartest of possible addresses. In here, not quite enough carpeting to cover the polished lake of the floor. Not quite enough period pieces to go around. Gaps, where perhaps some had been sold off, one by one. But no shoddier stuff allowed to fill out the spaces. And even on the woman herself, as he looked at her, there were the same tell-tale signs. Her shoes were forty-dollar custom-mades, but they had been worn too long. Something about the heels and lustre, you could tell that. The dress had lines that nothing in the lower brackets could have hoped for, but again it had been used too much. He could read it plainest of all in her eyes. They had an unhealthy alertness, as of one reduced to living by her wits; never knowing from which direction the next chance might come, and desperately afraid of not being quick enough to seize it when it did. These were the little things about her that stated the case, if one could read. All of them could be denied, singly, but taken together they told the tale irrefutably.

He sat there almost listening to her thoughts. Yes, listening to them. He saw her look at her hand. He translated it: she is thinking of a diamond ring that once adorned it. Where is it now? Pawned. He saw her raise one instep slightly and glance at it. What thought had occurred to her just then? Silk stockings, probably. Some daydream of being deluged with silk stockings, scores of pairs, hundreds of pairs, more than she could ever hope to use. He translated it: she is thinking of money. Money for all these things and more.

She has decided, he said to himself, watching her expression closely.

She answered his question. The silence ended. Only a moment had gone by.

"The story of the hat is simply this," she resumed. "I'd glimpsed it, it took my fancy, and I wangled a copy of it out of a girl down there. I'm a creature of impulse that way, when I can afford to be. I wore it once, I think, not more than that, and"—her shoulders glittered in a corruscating silver shrug—"it wasn't meant for me. It just wasn't, that was all. Something wrong about it. I wasn't the type. It wasn't very tragic, I didn't let it bother me too much. Then, a friend of mine was up here one day, just before I went to the hospital. She came across it, happened to try it on. If you were a woman you'd understand how that sort of thing goes. While one is waiting for the other to finish her dressing, we try on one another's latest buys. She fell in love with it at sight, and I let her have it."

Ending it, she shrugged again as she had near the beginning. As though that was all there was to it, there was to be no more.

"Who is she?" he asked quietly. Even as he spoke the simple, casual words, he knew they were both fencing with one another, that the answer wouldn't be given readily, that this was bargaining.

She answered him equally simply, equally casually. "Do you think that would be fair of me?"

"There's a man's life involved. He's dying Friday," he said, in such a low, expressionless voice that it was almost wholly lip-motion.

"Is it because of her, is it through her in any way? Is she to blame, has she caused it? Answer me."

"No," he sighed.

"Then what right have you to involve her? There can be a form of death for women too, you know. Social death. Call it notoriety, loss of reputation, whatever you will. It isn't over with as quickly. I'm not sure it isn't worse."

His face was getting continually whiter with strain. "There must be something in you I can appeal to. Don't you *care* if this man dies? Do you realize that if you withhold this information—"

"After all, I *do* know the woman and I don't know the man. She is my friend, he isn't. You're asking me to jeopardize her, to save him."

"Where does the jeopardy come in?" She didn't answer. "Then you refuse to tell me?"

"I have neither refused, nor agreed to, *yet*."

He was suffocating with a sense of his own helplessness. "You're not going to do this to me. This is home-base. It ends here. You know, and you're going to tell me!" They

had both risen to their feet. "You think because I can't hit
you, like I would a man, I can't get it out of you. I'm going
to get it out of you. You're not going to stand here like
this and—"

She glanced meaningfully down at her own shoulder.
"See here," she said with cold indignation.

He relaxed his grip on it. She readjusted the silver penin-
sula that clothed it. She looked him straight in the eye,
in withering disparagement. A blundering, easily-dealt-
with male. "Shall I call down and have you removed?"

"If you want to see a good brawl up here, try it."

"You can't *compel* me to tell you. The choice rests
with me."

That was true up to a point, and he knew it.

"I'm a free agent in the matter. What're you going to
do about it?"

"This."

Her face changed for a minute at sight of the gun, but
it was just the flicker of shock that would have crossed
anyone's. It changed right back again to normal. She even
sat down slowly, but not in the crumpled way of the van-
quished; in a way that expressed patient assurance: as
though this would take some time and she intended sitting
it out.

He'd never seen anyone like her before. After that first
momentary contraction of the facial muscles, she was still
the one remaining in control of the situation, not he, gun
or no gun.

He stood over her with it, trying to bear down on her
mentally if nothing else. "Aren't you afraid to die?"

She looked up into his face. "Very much," she said with
perfect composure. "As much as anyone, at any time. But
I'm not in any danger right now. You can't afford to kill

me. People are killed to *keep* them from telling something
they know. They are never killed to *force* them to tell
something they know. For then, how can they tell it afterward? That gun still leaves the decision with me, not
with you. I could do many things. I could call the police.
But I won't. I'll sit and wait until you put it away again."

She had him.

He put it away, scrubbed a hand across his eyebrows.
"All right," he said thickly.

She uttered a note of laughter. "Which one of us got
most of the effects of that? My face is dry, yours is shining.
My color is unchanged, yours is pale."

About all he could find to say, once more, was: "All
right, you win."

She continued to hammer the point home. Or rather,
tap it delicately, hammering being a heavy-handed pro-
cedure at best; and she was deft, she was chic. "You see,
you can't threaten me." She paused, to permit him to hear
between the lines. "You can interest me."

He nodded. Not to her, in inward confirmation to himself. He said, "Can I sit here a minute?" and motioned to
a small table-desk. He took something out of his pocket
and snapped it open. He carefully tore out something along
a punctured line. Then he snapped the folder closed again
and returned it to his pocket. A blank oblong remained
before him. He uncapped a fountain-pen and began to
write across it.

He looked up once to ask: "Am I boring you?"

She gave him the wholly natural, unforced smile that
comes when two people understand one another perfectly.
"You're being very good company. Quiet, but enter-
taining."

This time he was the one smiled, to himself. "How do
you spell your name?"

"B-e-a-r-e-r."

He gave her a look, then bent to his task once more. "Not quite phonetic, is it?" he murmured deprecatingly.

He had written the numeral "100." She had come closer, was looking down on the bias. "I'm rather sleepy," she remarked, and yawned artificially and tapped her hand over her mouth once or twice.

"Why don't you open the windows. It may be a little close in here."

"I'm sure it isn't that." She crossed over to them, however, and did so. Then came back to him again.

He had added another cipher. "How do you feel now, better?" he questioned with ironic solicitude.

She glanced briefly downward. "Considerably refreshed. You might almost say revivified."

"It takes so little, doesn't it?" he agreed acidly.

"Surprisingly little. Next to nothing at all." She was enjoying her own pun.

He didn't go ahead writing. He allowed the pen to flatten against the desk without taking his hand from it. "This is preposterous, you know."

"I haven't gone to you for anything. You've come to me for something." She nodded. "Good night."

The pen upended again in his hand.

He was standing in the open doorway, facing inward in the act of taking leave of her, when the car arrived and the elevator-door opened in answer to his ring. He was holding a small tab of paper, a leaf torn from a memo-pad, folded once and held within the pronged fingers of one hand.

"I hope I haven't been rude," he was saying to her. A rueful smile etched into his profile for a minute. "At least I know I haven't bored you. And please overlook the exceptional hour of the night. After all, it was rather an exceptional matter." Then in answer to something that she said, "You don't have to worry about that. I wouldn't bother writing a check if I were going to stop payment on it afterward. That's a pretty small dodge, any way you look at—"

"Down, sir?" the attendant reminded him, to attract his attention.

He glanced over. "Here's the car." Then back to her again. "Well, good night." He tipped his hat to her decorously and came away, leaving the door ajar behind him. She closed it lingeringly in his wake, without looking out after him.

In the car he raised the tab of paper and glanced at it.

"Hey, wait a minute," he blurted out, with a stab of the hand toward the carman. "She only gave me one name here—"

The operator slowed the car, prepared to reverse it. "Did you want to go back again, sir?"

For a moment he seemed about to assent. Then he scanned his watch. "No, never mind. I guess it'll be all right. Go ahead down."

The car picked up speed again and resumed its descent.

In the lobby below he stopped long enough to consult the hallman, flashing the paper at him for a moment "Which way is this from here, up or down, any idea?"

On it were two names and a number. "Flora," the number, and "Amsterdam."

"It's finally over," he was telling Burgess breathlessly on the phone a minute or two later, from an all-night drugstore on Broadway. "I thought I had it, and there was one last link, but this time it's the last. No time to tell you now. Here's where it is. I'm on my way there now. How soon can you be there?"

Burgess, overreaching himself in the headlong sweep of the patrol car that had brought him over, recognized Lombard's car standing out by itself in front of one of the buildings, at first sight empty; jumped hazardously off in full flight and came back. It was only when he'd gained the sidewalk and approached from that direction that he made him out sitting there on the running board, screened from the roadway by the car-body at his back.

He thought he was ill at first, the way he was sitting there in a huddle on the car-step; bowed over his own lap, head lowered toward the sidewalk underfoot. His posture suggested someone in the penultimate stages of being sick to his stomach; everything but the final climax.

A man in suspenders and undershirt was standing a few steps off, regarding him sympathetically, arrested pipe in hand, a dog peering out from around his legs.

Lombard looked up wanly as Burgess' hastening footfalls drew up beside him. Then he turned his head away again, as though it were too much effort even to speak.

"Is this it? What's the matter? You been in there yet?"

"No, it's that one back there." He indicated a cavernous opening, occupying almost the full width of the building it was set into. Within, to one side, could be made out a glistening brass upright, set into the bare concrete flooring. Across the façade, in gilt letters backed with black sandpaper, was inscribed the legend: "Fire Department, City of New York."

"That's Number—," Lombard said, flourishing the tab of paper he still held in his hand.

The dog, a spotted Dalmatian, edged forward at this

point to muzzle at it inquiringly.

"And that's Flora, these men tell me."

Burgess opened the car-door and pulled it out behind him, forcing him to his feet to avoid being unseated.

"Let's get back," he commented tersely. "And fast."

He was flinging himself bodily against the door, with futile wrenches of breath, when Burgess came up with the passkey and joined him outside it.

"Not a sound from in there. Has she answered them below on the announcer yet?"

"They're still ringing."

"She must have lammed."

"She can't have. They would have seen her leave, unless she went out some roundabout way— Here, let me use this. You'll never get it that way."

The door opened and they floundered inside. Then they stopped short, taking the scene in. The long living room, which was a continuation of the entrance-gallery with simply a one-step drop in height, was empty, but it was mutely eloquent. They both got it right away.

The lights were all on. An unfinished cigarette was still alive and working, sending up lazy spirals of bluish-silver from the rim of an ash-stand with a hollow stem. The floor-length windows were open to the night, showing an expanse of black, with a large star piercing it in one corner, a smaller one in another, like a black-out cloth held in place by a couple of shiny thumbtacks.

Directly before the windows lay a silver shoe, turned on its side like a small, capsized boat. The long narrow runner of rug that bisected the polished flooring, from just past the drop-step to just short of the windows, showed corrugated ridges, frozen "ripples" that marred its evenness, at one end. As though a misstep had sent a disturbance coursing along it.

Burgess went to the window, detouring around the side of the room to get there. He leaned out over the low, inadequate, decorative guard-rail on the outside of it, stayed that way, bent motionless, for long minutes.

Then he straightened, turned back into the room again, sent a quiet nod across it to where Lombard had remained, as if incapable of further movement. "She's all the way down below there. I can see her from here, in the service alley between two deep walls. Like a rag off a clothesline. Nobody seems to have heard it, all the windows on this side are still dark."

He didn't do anything about it, strangely enough, didn't even report it at once.

There was only one thing moving in the room, outside himself. And it wasn't Lombard. It was the skein from the cigarette. It was that fact, perhaps, that attracted his eye to it. He went over to it, picked it up. There was still enough to hold, a fraction of an inch. He murmured something under his breath that sounded like: "Must have just happened as we got here."

The next thing, he had taken out a cigarette of his own, was holding the two upright side by side, their bases even, with the fingers of the same hand. He took a pencil, notched off the length of the remnant against the intact one.

Then he put the latter into his own mouth, lit it, and took a single, slightly ritualistic puff to get it going. After which he carefully set it down in the same curved trough the former one had occupied, left it there, and glanced at his watch.

"What're you doing that for?" Lombard asked in the

listless voice of someone for whom nothing holds any interest any more.

"Just a home-made way of figuring out how long ago it happened. I don't know if it's reliable or not, if any two of these things burn down at the same rate of speed. Must ask some of the guys about that."

He went over, glanced closely at it once, moved away again. The second time he came back he picked it up, looked at it in air like a thermometer, looked at his watch, then tapped it out and discarded it, its purpose served.

"She fell out exactly three minutes before we got in here. That's taking off a full minute while I was looking out the window, before I got over to it and measured it. And that's giving her just one puff, as I took. If she took more then that brings it down even closer."

"It may have been King-size," Lombard said, from a great distance away.

"It's a Lucky, there's enough of the trade mark left down at the mouth end to be visible. Think I would have wasted my time doing it if I hadn't seen that before I started?"

Lombard didn't answer, was back in the distance again.

"This makes it look as though it was our very ring on the downstairs announcer that killed her," Burgess went on. "Startled her and caused her to make that false move in front of the window that sent her over. The whole story's here in front of our eyes, without words. She'd gone over to them and was standing there looking out, possibly in an expansive mood, drinking in the night-air, making plans, when the ring came from downstairs. She did something wrong. Turned in too much of a hurry, or with her weight thrown badly. Or maybe it was her shoes did it. This one looks a little warped, unsteady from overlong wear. Anyway, the rug skidded over the waxed flooring. One or both of her feet shot out from under her, riding the rug. The shoe came off completely, went up in the air. She overbalanced backwards. It wouldn't have been anything, if she hadn't been that close to the open windows. What would have been otherwise just a comical little sit-down became a back-somersault into space and a death-fall."

Then he said, "But what I don't get, is about the address part of it. Was it a practical joke, or what? How'd she act; you were with her."

"Nah, she wasn't kidding," Lombard said. "She was serious about wanting that money, it was written all over her."

"I could understand her giving you a spiked address that would take you a long time to investigate, so she'd have time to cash the check and beat it. But a thing like this, only a few blocks from here—she might've known you'd be back in five or ten minutes. What was the angle?"

"Unless she figured she could get more from the lady in question herself, more than I was offering, by warning her, tipping her off, and just wanted to get me out of the place long enough to dicker with her."

Burgess shook his head, as though he found this unsatisfactory, but he contented himself with repeating what he'd said to begin with. "I don't get it."

Lombard hadn't waited to listen. He'd turned away and was moving listlessly off to the side, with the dragging shamble of a drunk. The other man watched him curiously. He seemed to have lost all interest in what was going on around him, to have gone completely flat. He arrived at the wall and stood there for a moment before it, sagging, like someone who has been disappointed too often, is finally licked, finally ready to quit.

Then before Burgess could guess his purpose, he had tightened one arm, drawn it back, and sent it crashing home into the inanimate surface before him, as though it were some kind of an enemy.

"Hey, you fool!" Burgess yelped in stupefaction. "What're you trying to do, bust your hand? What'd the walls do to you?"

Lombard, writhing in the crouched position of a man applying a corkscrew to a bottle, his face contorted more by helpless rage than pain even yet, answered in a choked voice while he nursed his flaming hand against his stomach: "*They* know! They're all that's left that knows now—and I can't get it out of them!"

20: The Third Day Before the Execution

THE last-minute drink he'd gulped just now right after getting off the train at the prison-stop wasn't any help. What could a drink do? What could any number of drinks do? It couldn't alter facts. It couldn't turn bad news into good. It couldn't change doom into salvation.

He kept wondering as he trudged up the steep road toward the gloomy pile of buildings ahead: How do you tell a man he's got to die? How do you tell him there's no more hope, the last ray has just faded out? He didn't know, and he was on his way right now to find out—by first-hand experience. He even wondered whether it wouldn't have been kinder not to come near him again at all, to let him go without seeing him this useless one last time.

This was going to be ghastly, and he knew it. He was

in the place now, and he already had the creeps. But he'd
had to come, he couldn't be that yellow about it. Couldn't
leave him dangling in suspense for three agonizing days
more; couldn't let him be led out on Friday night still looking back over his shoulder the whole way, metaphorically
speaking, for the last-minute cancellation that would never
come now.

He passed the back of his hand slowly across his mouth
as he trudged after the guard up to the second-floor tier.
"Am I going to get drunk tonight after I leave here!" he
swore bitterly to himself. "I'm going to get so full I'll be
an alcoholic case at one of the hospitals until it's over and
done with!"

And now the guard was standing by, and he went in to
face the music. Funeral music.

This was the execution right now. A bloodless, white
one preceding the other by three days. The execution of
all hope.

The guard's footsteps receded hollowly. After that the
silence was horrible. Neither of them could have stood it
for very long.

"So that's it," Henderson said quietly at last. He'd understood.

The rigor mortis was broken, at least. Lombard turned
away from the window, came over and clapped him on
the shoulder. "Look, fellow—" he started to say.

"It's all right," Henderson told him. "I understand. I can
tell by your face. We don't have to talk about it."

"I lost her again. She slipped away—this time for good."

"I said you don't need to talk about it," Henderson
urged patiently. "I can see what it's done to you. For the
love of pete, let's drop it." He seemed to be the one trying
to buck Lombard up, instead of vice versa.

Lombard slumped down on the edge of the bunk. Henderson, being the "host," let him have it, got up and stood leaning the curve of his back against the wall opposite.

The only sound in the cell for awhile after that was the rustle of cellophane, as Henderson kept continuously folding over the edge of an emptied cigarette-package back on itself, until he'd wound it up tight, then undoing it again pleat by pleat until he had it open once more. Over and over, endlessly, apparently just to give his fingers something to do.

No one could have stood it for long in that atmosphere. Lombard said finally, "Don't, will you? It's making me go nuts."

Henderson looked down at his own hands in surprise, as though unaware until then what they'd been up to. "That's my old habit," he said sheepishly. "I never was able to break myself of it, even in good times. You remember, don't you? Any time I ever rode a train, the time-table would end up like that. Any time I had to sit and wait in a doctor's or a dentist's office, the magazines would end up like that. Any time I ever sat in a theatre, the program—" He stopped short, looked dreamily across at the wall, just over Lombard's head. "That night at the show with *her*, I can remember doing it that night too— It's funny how a little thing like that should come back to me now, this late, when all the more important things it might have helped me to remember all along— What's the matter, what are you looking at me like that for? I've quit doing it." He threw the tormented wrapper aside, to show him.

"But you threw it away, of course? That night with

her. You left it behind you, on the seat or on the floor, as people usually do?"

"No, she kept both programs, I can remember that. It's funny, but I can. She asked me to let her have them. She made some remark to the effect of wanting to glory in her impulsiveness. I can't recall just what it was. But I know she kept them, I distinctly saw her put them in her bag."

Lombard had risen to his feet. "There's a little something there, if we only knew how to get at it."

"What do you mean?"

"It's the only thing we know for sure she has in her possession."

"We don't know for sure she still has it in her possession, do we?" Henderson corrected.

"If she kept it to begin with, then it's likely she still has it. People either do or don't keep such things as theatre-programs. Either they throw them away at once, or they keep them indefinitely, for years after. If there was only some way we could make this thing the bait. What I mean is, it's the only common denominator linking her to you—because it will have its upper right-hand corners neatly winged back from cover to cover, without missing a page. If we could only get her to come forward with it, without guessing—she will stand revealed to us automatically."

"By advertising, you mean?"

"Something along those lines. People collect all sorts of things; stamps, seashells, pieces of furniture full of wormholes. Often they'll pay any price for things that to them are treasures but to others are trash. They lose all sense of proportion, once the collector's lust gets hold of them."

"Well?"

"I'm a collector of theatre-programs, say. A freak, an eccentric, a millionaire throwing my money away right and left. It is more than a hobby, it is an obsession with me. I must have complete sets of programs for every play produced at every theatre in town, all the way back, season by season. I suddenly appear from nowhere, I open a little clearing-depot, I advertise. Word spreads around. I'm a nut, I'm giving away something for nothing. There's a free-for-all to get in on it while it lasts. The papers'll probably puff it up, with pictures; one of those screwball incidents that pop up every now and then."

"Your whole premise is full of flaws. No matter how phenomenal the prices you offer, why should that attract her? Suppose she's well-off?"

"Suppose she no longer is well-off?"

"I still don't see how she can fail to smell a rat."

"To us the program is 'hot.' To her it isn't. Why should it be? She may never even notice those tell-tale little folds up at the corner, or if she does, never dream that they'll tell us what we want to know. You didn't remember about it yourself, until just a few minutes ago. Why should she? She's not a mind-reader; how is she going to know that you and I are here together in this cell talking about it right now?"

"The whole thing is too flimsy."

"Of course it's flimsy," Lombard agreed. "It's a thousand-to-one shot. But we have to take it. Beggars can't be choosers. I'm going to try it, Hendy. I have a strange feeling that—that this'll work, where everything else has failed."

He turned away, went over to the bars to be let out.

"Well, so long—" Henderson suggested tentatively.

"I'll be seeing you," Lombard called back.

As he heard his tread recede outside behind the guard's, Henderson thought: "He doesn't believe that. And neither do I."

Boxed Advertisement, All Morning and Evening Papers:

TURN YOUR OLD THEATRE-PROGRAMS INTO MONEY

Wealthy collector, in town for short visit, will pay over-generous amounts for items needed to complete his sets. Life-long hobby. Bring them in, no matter how old, no matter how new! Specially wanted: music-hall and revue numbers, last few seasons, missing because of my absence abroad. Alhambra, Belvedere, Casino, Coliseum. No job-lots nor second-hand dealers. J. L. 15 Franklin Square. Premises open until ten Friday night, only. After that I leave town.

21: *The Day of the Execution*

AT nine-thirty, for almost the first time all day, the line had dwindled to vanishing-point, a straggler or two had been disposed of, and there was a breathing-spell, with nobody in the shop but Lombard and his young assistant.

Lombard slumped limply in his chair, thrust out his lower lip, and blew breath exhaustedly up across his face, so that it stirred the disarranged hair overhanging his forehead. He was in his vest, shirt-collar open. He dragged a handkerchief out from the pocket he was sitting on and popped it at his face here and there. It came away gray. They didn't bother dusting them off before they dumped them in front of him. They seemed to think the thicker the dust, the more highly they would be valued. He wiped his hands on the handkerchief, threw it away.

He turned his head, said to somebody hidden from view behind him by towering, slantwise stacks of programs: "You can go now, Jerry. Time's about up, I'm closing in another half-hour. The rush seems to be over."

A skinny youth of nineteen or so straightened up in a sort of trench left between two parapets of the accumulation, came out, put on his coat.

Lombard took out some money. "Here's the fifteen dollars for the three days, Jerry.

The boy looked disappointed. "Won't you be needing me any more tomorrow, mister?"

"No, I won't be here tomorrow," Lombard said broodingly. "Tell you what you can do, though. You can have these to sell for waste-paper; some rag-picker might give you a few jits for them."

The boy looked at him pop-eyed. "Gee, mister, you mean you been buying 'em up for three days straight just to get rid of them?"

"I'm funny that way," Lombard assented. "Keep it under your hat until then, though."

The boy went out giving him awed backward glances all the way to the sidewalk. He thought he was crazy, Lombard knew. He didn't blame him. He thought he was crazy himself. For ever thinking that this would work, that she'd fall for it, show up. The whole idea had been harebrained to start with.

A girl was passing along the sidewalk as the boy emerged. That was the only reason Lombard happened to notice her, because his eyes were on his departing assistant and she cut between them. Nobody. Nothing. Just a girl. A stray pedestrian. She gave a look in, as she passed the doorway. Then, with just a momentary hesitation, probably caused by curiosity, went on again, passed from view beyond the vacant show-window. For a moment, though, he had almost thought she was about to enter.

The lull ended and an antediluvian in beaver-collared coat, black-stringed eyeglasses, and an incredibly high collar came in, walking-stick to side. Behind him, to Lombard's dismay, appeared a cab-driver dragging in a small ancient trunk. The visitor halted before the bare wooden table Lombard was using for a desk, and struck a pose so hammy that for a minute Lombard couldn't believe it was intended seriously, wasn't just a burlesque.

Lombard rolled his eyes upward. He'd been getting this type all day long. But never with a whole trunkful of them at a time, until now.

"Ah, sir," began the relic of the gas-lit footlights, in a richly resonant voice that would have been something if only he'd kept his hands down, "you are indeed lucky that I read your advertisement. I am in a position to enrich your collection immeasurably. I can add to it as no one else in this city can. I have some rarities here that will warm your heart. From the old Jefferson Playhouse, as far back as—"

Lombard motioned a hasty refusal. "I'm not interested in the Jefferson Playhouse, I've got a full set."

"The Olympia, then. The—"

"Not interested, not interested. I don't care what else you've got, I'm all bought up. I only need one item more before I put out the lights and lock up. Casino, 1941–42. Have *you* one?"

"Casino, bah!" the old man sputtered in his face, with a little more than just expelled breath. "You say Casino to me? What have I to do with trashy modern revues? I was

once one of the greatest tragedians on the American
stage!"

"I can see that," Lombard said drily. "I'm afraid we
can't do business with one another."

The trunk and the cab-driver went out again. The
trunk's owner stopped in the doorway long enough to
express his contempt by way of the floor. "Casino—*thut!*"
Then he went out too.

Another short hiatus, then an old woman who had the
appearance of being a charwoman came in. She had be-
decked herself for the occasion with a large floppy hat
topped by a cabbagy rose, that looked as though it had
either been picked up from an ashcan or taken out of a
storage-closet where it had lain forgotten for decades. She
had applied a circular fever-spot of rouge to the leathery
skin of each cheek, with the uncertain hand of one trying
to indulge in a long-forgotten practice.

As he raised his eyes to her, half-compassionately, half-
unwillingly, he caught sight over her rounded shoulder of
the same girl as before, once again passing outside the
shop, this time in the opposite direction. Again she turned
and glanced in. This time, however, she did more than
that. She came to a full halt, if only for a second or two;
even went back a single step to bring herself more fully in
line with the open entrance. Then, having scanned the
interior, she went on. She was obviously interested in what
was going on. Still, he had to admit, there had been enough
publicity attending the enterprise to make a chance
passerby conscious of it, cause her to give a second look.
There had even been photographers sent around early in
the event. And she may have simply been coming back
from wherever she had been bound the first time she
passed; if you went someplace, you usually followed the

same route on the way back, there was nothing unusual in that.

The old drudge before him was faltering timidly, "Is it on the level, sir? You really pay money for old programs?"

He brought his attention back to her. "Certain ones, yes."

She fumbled in a knitted market-bag hanging over her arm. "I have only a few here, sir. From when I used to be in the chorus myself. I kept them all, they mean a lot to me. The Midnight Rambles, and the Frolics of 1911—" She was trembling with apprehension, as she put them down. She turned one of the yellowed leaves, as though to add to the veracity of her story. "See, this is me here, sir. Dolly Golden, that used to be my name. I played the Spirit of Youth in the final tableau—"

Time, he thought, is a greater murderer than any man or woman. Time is the murderer that never gets punished.

He looked at her raw, toilworn hands, not the programs at all. "A dollar apiece," he said gruffly, feeling for his billfold.

She was nearly overcome with joy. "Oh, bless you, mister! It will come in so handy!" She had swept up his hand before he could stop her and put her lips to it. The rouge started to elongate into pink tears. "I didn't dream they were worth that much!"

They weren't. They weren't worth a plugged nickel. "Here you are, mother," he said compassionately.

"Oh, now I'm going to eat—I'm going to eat a big dinner—!" She staggered out almost drunk with the unexpected windfall. A younger woman was standing there quietly waiting, as she gave place before him. She must have come in unnoticed behind her just now, he hadn't seen her enter. It was the same one who had passed the doorway twice already, once in each direction. He was almost sure of it, although the previous optical snapshots he had had of her had been too brief to focus properly.

She had looked younger out there, in the middle distance, than she did now, directly before him at close range. That was because she had retained a slimness of figure, after almost everything else was gone. She was ravaged, almost as ravaged as the charwoman who had just preceded her, if in a different way.

A prickling sensation lightly stirred the fuzz below the hairline on his neck. He tried not to stare at her too blatantly, looked down again after one all-comprehensive sweep of the eyes, so she wouldn't detect anything on his face.

His composite impression was this: she must have been pretty until just recently. It was rapidly leaving her now. There was an air of sub-surface refinement, perhaps even culture, still emanating from her, but there was a hard crust, a shell of coarseness and cheapening, forming on the outside that would soon smother it, extinguish it for good. Probably it was already too late to save her from the process. It was being accelerated, as far as he could tell at sight, either by alcohol in destructive day-long floods, or by acute and unaccustomed destitution; or perhaps by an attempt to dull the one with the other. There were traces of a third factor still discernible, and this perhaps had been the predecessor, the causative, of the other two, but it seemed to be no longer the determining one, had been superseded by the other two: unbearable distress of mind, mental misery, fear admixed with some sort of guilt, and prolonged endlessly over a period of months. It had left its mark but it was dying out now; the strictly physical dissipations were the current ones. She was jaunty, now,

she was rubbery and unbreakable with the resiliency of the
gutters and the bars, and of those who can go no lower,
and that would suffice to see her through to the end. Probably a gas-tube in some rooming house.

She looked as though she hadn't been eating regularly.
There was a shadowed hollow in each cheek, and the
whole bone-structure of the face showed through the thin
covering. She was entirely in black, but not the black of
widowhood nor yet the black of fashion; the rusty black
of slovenliness, adhered to because it doesn't show soil.
Even her stockings were black, with a white crescent of
hole showing above the back of each shoe.

She spoke. Her voice was ruined, raucous with cheap
whiskey gulped inordinately all day and night. Yet even
here there was a ghost of cultivation left. If she used slang
now, it was from choice, from contact with those she
associated with, and not because she didn't know any better. "You got any jack left to pay out on programs, or
am I too late?"

"Let's see what you've got," he said guardedly.

There was a snap of her shoddy, oversized handbag,
and a pair of them were planked down. Companion-pieces,
from the same night. A musical show at the Regina, season before last. I wonder who she was with that night, he
thought. She probably was secure yet and comely, she
didn't dream—

He pretended to consult a reference-list giving his
needs, the gaps that remained to be filled in his "sets."

"I seem to be short that one. Seven-fifty," he said.

He saw her eyes glitter. He'd hoped that would get her.

"Got any more?" he suggested craftily. "This is your
last chance, you know. I'm closing up this place tonight."

She hesitated. He saw her eyes go to her bag. "Well, do

you bother buying just one at a time?"

"Any number."

"As long as I'm in here—" She opened the bag once more, tilted the flap over against her so that he couldn't look down into it, pulled an additional program out. She snapped the bag shut again, first of all, before she did anything else. He noted that. Then she spaded the folder at him. He took it, reversed it his way.

Casino Theatre

It was the first one that had showed up in the full three days. He leafed through it with pretended casualness, past the preliminary filler columns to where the play-matter itself began. It was dated by the week, as all theatrical programs are. "Week beginning May 17th." His breath log-jammed. That was the week. The right week. It had been on the night of the twentieth. He kept his eyes down so they wouldn't give him away. Only—the upper right-hand corners of the pages were untouched. It wasn't that they'd been smoothed-out, that would have left a tell-tale diagonal seam; they'd never been folded-over in the first place.

It was hard to keep his voice casual. "Got the mate to it? Most of them come in twos, you know, and I could make you a better offer."

She gave him a searching look. He even caught the little uncompleted start her hand made toward the snap of her pocketbook. Then she forced it down again. "What d'you think I do, print them?"

"I prefer to buy duplicates, doubles, whenever possible. Didn't anyone go with you to this particular show? What became of the other pro—?"

There was something about it she didn't like. Her eyes
darted suspiciously around the store, as if in search of a
trap. She edged warily backward a step or two from the
table. "Come on, one is all I got. Do you wanna buy or
don't you?"

"I can't give you as much as I could have given you for
a pair—"

She was obviously in a hurry to get outside into the
open again. "All right, anything you say—" She even
arched over to reach for the money from where she
was standing, he couldn't get her to close in toward the
purchasing-table again.

He let her get as far as the door with it. Then he called
after her, but in a quietly-modulated voice, unwarranted
to cause alarm: "Just a moment. Could I ask you to come
back here a moment, there's something I forgot."

She stopped short for a single instant, cast a look of
sharp distrust back over her shoulder at him. It was more
than just the look of automatic response one gives to a
summons; it was a look of wariness. Then as he rose,
crooking his finger at her, she gave a stifled cry, broke
into a scampering run, rounded the store-entrance, and
fled from sight.

He flung the impediment of the table bodily over to
one side to get quick clearance, dashed out after her. Behind him several of the topheavy stacks of programs reared
by the boy wavered from the vibration of his violent
exit, crumbled, and spilled all over the floor in snowdrifts.

She was chopsticking it down toward the next corner
when he got out on the sidewalk, but her high heels were
against her. When she glanced back and saw him coming
full-tilt behind her, she gave another cry, louder this time,

and was stung into an added spurt of velocity that carried her around into the next street before he had quite halved the distance.

But he got her there, only a few yards past where his own car had been standing waiting all day, in hopes of just such an eventuality as this. He overlapped her, blocked her off, gripped her by the shoulders, and then swung her in with him against the building-front, pinning her there in a sort of enclave of his arms.

"All right now, stand still—it's no use," he breathed heavily.

She was less able to speak than he was; alcohol had killed her wind. He almost thought she was going to choke for a minute. "Lemme—'lone. What—uf I done?"

"Then what did you run for?"

"I didn't like," her head hung over his arms, trying to get air, "the way you looked."

"Lemme see that bag. Open that pocketbook! Come on, open up that pocketbook or I'll do it for you!"

"Take your hands off me! Leave me alone!"

He didn't waste any more time arguing. He yanked it so violently from under her arm that the frayed loop-strap she had it suspended by tore off bodily. He opened it, plunged his hand in, crowding her back with his body so that she couldn't escape from the position he had her backed into. It came up again with a program identical to the one she had just sold him in the store. He let the pocketbook drop to free his hands. He tried to flutter the leaves to open it, and they adhered. He had to pry them away from one another. All the inner ones, from cover to cover, were notched, were neatly folded over at their upper right-hand tips. He peered in the uncertain street-light, and the date-line was the same as the other.

Scott Henderson's program. Poor Scott Henderson's program, returning at the eleventh hour, like bread cast upon the waters—

22: *The Hour of the Execution*

10.55 P. M. The last of anything, ah the last of anything, is always so bitter. He was cold all over, though the weather was warm, and he was shivering, though he was sweating, and he kept saying to himself over and over, "I'm not afraid," more than he was listening to the chaplain. But he was and he knew he was, and who could blame him? Nature had put the instinct to live in his heart.

He was stretched out face downward on his bunk, and his head, with a square patch shaved on the top, was hanging down over the edge of it toward the floor. The chaplain was sitting by him, one hand pressed consolingly against his shoulder as if to keep the fear in, and every time the shoulder shook the hand would shake in sympathy with it, although the chaplain was going to live many more years yet. The shoulder shook at regular-spaced intervals. It's an awful thing to know the time of your own death.

The chaplain was intoning the 23rd Psalm in a low voice. "Green pastures, refresh my soul—" Instead of consoling him, it made him feel worse. He didn't want the next world, he wanted this one.

The fried chicken and the waffles and the peach short-cake that he'd had hours ago felt like they were all gummed-up somewhere behind his chest, wouldn't go down any further. But that didn't matter, it wouldn't give him indigestion, there wouldn't be time enough for it to.

He wondered if he'd have time to smoke another cigarette. They'd brought in two packs with his dinner, that
had been only a few hours ago, and one was already crumpled and empty, the second half-gone. It was a foolish
thing to worry about, he knew, because what was the difference if he smoked one all the way down or had to throw
it away after a single puff? But he'd always been thrifty
about things like that, and the habits of a lifetime die hard.

He asked the chaplain, interrupting his low-voiced
chant, and instead of answering directly the chaplain simply said, "Smoke another, my boy," and struck the match
and held it for him. Which meant there really wasn't time.

His head flopped down again and smoke came out of the
hidden gray gash of his lips. The chaplain's hand pressed
down on his shoulder once more, steadying the fear,
damming it. Footsteps could be heard coming quietly and
with horrible slowness along the stone-floored passage
outside, and a sudden hush fell over Death Row. Instead
of coming up, Scott Henderson's head went down even
further. The cigarette fell and rolled away. The chaplain's
hand pressed down harder, almost riveting him there to
the bunk.

The footsteps had stopped. He could sense they were
standing out there looking in at him, and though he tried
not to look, he couldn't hold out, his head came up against
his will and turned slowly. He said, "Is this it now?"

The cell-door started to ease back along its grooves,
and the warden said: "This is it now, Scott."

Scott Henderson's program. Poor Scott Henderson's
program, returning like bread cast upon the waters. He
stared at it. The handbag he had wrenched from her lay
unnoticed at his feet.

The girl, meanwhile, was writhing there beside him, trying to break the soldered grip of his hand on her shoulder.

He put it carefully away in his inside pocket first of all. Then he took two hands to her, trundled her roughly along the sidewalk and over to where his car stood waiting. "Get in there, you heartless apology for a human being! You're coming with me! You know what you've nearly done, don't you?"

She threshed around for a moment on the running-board, before he got the door open and pushed her in. She went sprawling knees-first, turned and scrambled upwards against the seat. "Let me go, I tell you!" Her voice went keening up and down the street. "You can't do this to me! Somebody come here! Aren't there any cops in this town to stop a guy like him—!"

"Cops? You're getting cops! All the cops you want! You'll be sick of the sight of them before I get through with you!" Before she could squirm out at the opposite side, he had come in after her, yanked her violently back so that she floundered against him, and crashed the door shut after him.

He took the back of his hand to her twice to silence her; once in threat, the second time in fulfilment. Then he bent to the dashboard. "I never did that to a woman before," he gritted. "But you're no woman. You're just a bum in feminine form. A no-good bum." They swerved out from the curb, straightened and shot off. "Now you're going to ride whether you want to or not, and you better see that you ride quiet. Every time you howl or try anything while I'm bucking this traffic I'll give you another one of those if I have to. It's up to you."

She quit wildcatting, deflated sullenly against the seat-leather, glowered there, while they cut around corners,

by-passed car after car going the same way they were.
Once, when a light held them up for a minute, she said
defeatedly, without renewing her previous attempts to
escape, "Where're you heading with me?"

"You don't know, do you?" he said cuttingly. "It's all
news to you, isn't it?"

"*Him*, hunh?" she said with quiet resignation.

"Yeah, *him*, hunh?! Some specimen of humanity you
are!" He crushed the accelerator flat once more, and both
their heads went back in unison. "You ought to be beaten
raw, for being willing to let an innocent man go to his
death, when you could have stopped it at any time from
first to last, just by coming forward and telling them what
you know!"

"I figured it was that," she said dully. She looked down
at her hands. After awhile she said, "When is it—tonight?"

"Yes, tonight!"

He saw her eyes widen slightly, in the reflected dash-
board-light, as though she hadn't realized until now it was
that imminent. "I didn't know it was—going to be that
soon," she gulped.

"Well, it isn't now!" he promised harshly. "Not as long
as I've got you with me at last!"

Another light stopped them. He cursed it, sat there wiping his face with a large handkerchief. Then both their
heads flung back together again.

She sat there staring steadily before her. Not at anything before or beyond the car. Yet not at anything below
the windshield either, although it was there her eyes were
fixed. He could see her in the mirror on her side. She was
staring inwardly at something. The past, perhaps. Sum-
ming up her life. There was no bar-whiskey at hand now
to provide her with an escape. She had to sit and face it,
while the car raced on.

"You must be something made of sawdust, without any insides at all!" he told her once.

She answered, unexpectedly and at length. "Look what it did to me. You haven't thought of that, have you? Haven't I suffered enough for it already? Why should I care what happens to him, or to anyone else! What is he to me, anyway? They're killing him tonight. But *I've* been killed for it already! I'm dead, I tell you, dead! You've got someone dead sitting in the car next to you."

Her voice was the low growl of tragedy striking in the vitals; no shrill woman's whine or plaint; a sexless groan of suffering. "Sometimes in dreams I see someone who had a beautiful home, a husband who loved her, money, beautiful things, the esteem of her friends, security; above all, security, safety. That was supposed to go on until she died. That was supposed to *last*. I can't believe it was me. I know it wasn't me. And yet the whiskey-dreams, sometimes, tell me that it was. You know how dreams are—"

He sat eying the darkness that came streaming toward them, to part in the middle over the silver prow of the headlights and come together again behind them, like a mystic undulating tide. His eyes were gray pebbles, that didn't move, didn't hear, didn't give a rap about her trouble.

"Do you know what it means to be thrown out into the street? Yes, literally thrown out, at two in the morning, with just the clothes you have on your back, and to have the doors locked behind you and your own servants warned not to admit you again on pain of dismissal! I sat on a park-bench all night the first night. I had to borrow five dollars from my own former maid the next day, so that I could get a room, find shelter at least."

"Why didn't you come forward then, at least? If you'd already lost everything, what more did you have to lose?"

"His power over me didn't end there. He warned me that if I opened my mouth, did anything to bring notoriety or disgrace on his good name, he'd sign me over into an institution for alcoholics. He could easily do it too, he has the influence, the money. I'd never get out again. Strait-jackets and cold-water treatments."

"All that's no excuse. You must have known we were looking for you; you couldn't have avoided knowing it. You must have known this man was going to die. You were yellow, that's what you were. But if you never did a decent thing in your life before, and if you never do a decent thing in your life again, you're going to do one now. You're going to speak your piece and save Scott Henderson!"

She was silent for a long moment. Then her head went over slowly. "Yes," she said at last, "I am. I want to—now. I must have been blind all these months, not to see it as it really is. Somehow I didn't think of him all along until now, I only thought of myself, what I had to lose by it." She looked up at him again. "And I *would* like to do one decent thing at least—just for a change."

"You're going to," he promised grimly. "What time did you meet him at the bar that night?"

"Six-ten, by the clock in front of us."

"Are you going to tell them that? Are you willing to swear to that?"

"Yes," she said in an exhausted voice, "I'm going to tell them that. I'm willing to swear to that."

All he answered was, "God forgive you for what you've done to that man!"

Then it came. It was as though something fozen within her had melted, crumbled. Or maybe it was that hard crust that he had noticed forming on the outside of her, smothering her slowly to death. Her hands flew up to her already-lowered face, stayed that way, covering it. She made very little sound. He'd never seen anyone shake so. As though she was being torn apart internally. He thought she was never going to stop shaking like that.

He didn't speak to her. He didn't look at her, except by indirection in the mirror.

After awhile he could tell it was over. Her hands had dropped again. He heard her say, more to herself than him, "It makes you feel so clean, when you're going to do a thing you've been afraid to do—"

They raced on in silence, just the two of them in the faint dashlight. Traffic was thinner now, and all coming one way; toward them, instead of along with them, as heretofore. They were out past the city limits, flying along the sleek, straight artery that led upcountry. The cars passing them left streaks of light on their side-windows, they were going so fast.

"Why are we going this far out?" she asked presently, with only dulled awareness. "Isn't the Criminal Courts Building the place where—?"

"I'm taking you straight up there to the penitentiary," he answered tautly. "It's the quickest in the end. Cut through all the red tape—"

"It's right tonight—you said?"

"Sometime within the next hour-and-a-half. We'll make it."

They'd hit full wooded-country now; trees with white-washed waistbands to give the road a boundary in the dark. No more terrain lights, only an occasional inbound car blurring into incandescence as it approached, then dousing its lights in that wayside salute so reminiscent of an ambulant tipping his hat.

"But suppose something happens to delay us? A tire goes out or something? Wouldn't it be better to telephone?"

"I know what I'm doing. You sound quite anxious all at once."

"Yes, oh yes, I am," she breathed. "I've been blind. Blind. I see which was the dream, now, and which the reality."

"Quite a reformation," he said grudgingly. "For five months you didn't lift a finger to help him. And now all at once, within fifteen minutes, you're all hot and bothered."

"Yes," she said submissively. "It doesn't seem to matter, all at once. About my husband, or the threat of being put into an institution, or any of the rest of it. You've made me see the whole thing in a different light." She drew the back of one hand weariedly across her brow, said with infinite disgust: "I want to do at least one brave thing, I'm so sick of being a coward all my life!"

They rode in silence after that. Until presently she asked, almost with anxiety, "Will just my sworn testimony be enough to save him?"

"It'll be enough to postpone—what they have scheduled for tonight. Once that's been accomplished, we can turn it over to the lawyers, they'll see it through the rest of the way."

Suddenly she noticed they had swung off left, at a fork, onto a desolate, poorly-surfaced cross-country "feeder." It had already occurred several moments before, by the time she became aware of it. The motion of the car had become less even. The occasional passing road-mate had diminished to none. There was no sign of life on it.

"But why this? I thought the north-and-south highway

we were on was the one that takes you up to the State Prison. Isn't he at—?"

"This is a short-cut," he answered briefly. "A sort of shuttle, that'll save time."

The humming of the wind seemed to rise a little, take on an apprehensive moaning quality, as they rushed through, displacing it.

He spoke again, chin almost to wheel, eyes motionless and emotionless over it. "I'll get you where we're going in plenty of time."

There were no longer just two of them in the car. At some indeterminate point in the previous silence, a third presence had entered it, was in it now, sitting between them. The icy, shrouded shape of fear, its unseen arms enfolding the woman in cold embrace, its frigid fingertips seeking out her windpipe.

There hadn't been any lights but their own for ten minutes past now. There hadn't been any word between them. The trees were a smoky, billowing mass on each side of them. The wind was a warning message, unheeded until too late. Their two faces were ghosts reflected side by side on the windshield before them.

He slowed, backed, turned aside once more, this time onto an unpaved dirt lane, little better than a defile through the trees. They jounced along over its unevenness of surface, dried leaves hissing in their wake, stirred by the exhaust-tube; the wheels climbing over half-submerged roots, the fenders grazing trunks impinging on the right of way. The headlights played over a grotto-like profundity of trees, bleaching the nearer ones into dazzling stalagmites, leaving the inner ones black and enshrouded. It was like some evil, bewitched glade in a fairy-tale for children; woods of supernatural import where bad things were about to happen.

She said in a smothered voice, "No, what're you doing—?" Fear locked its embrace about her tighter, breathed glacially down her neck. "I don't like the way you're acting. What're you doing this for?"

Suddenly they'd stopped, and it was over. The sound of the brakes only reached her senses after the fact had been accomplished. He killed the engine, and there was stillness all around. Inside the car and out. They were motionless, all of them; the car, and he and she, and her fear.

Not quite; there was one thing moving. The three fingers of his hand, that had remained upon the wheel-rim, kept fluttering restlessly, rising and falling in rotation, like somebody striking successive keys on the piano over and over.

She turned and began to pummel at him, in impotent fright. "What is it? Say something! Say something to me! Don't just sit there like that! What did we stop here for? What are you thinking, why are you looking like that?"

"Get out." He gave the order with a hitch of his chin.

"No. What are you going to do? No." She sat there staring at him in ever-widening fright.

He reached across her and unlatched the door on that side. "I said get out."

"No! You're going to do something. I can see it on your face—"

He flung her before him with one stiffly-locked arm. A moment later they were both standing there beside the car, toe-deep in sandpapery tan and yellow leaves. He cracked the car-door shut again after him. It was damp

and penetrating under the trees, pitch-black around them
in all directions but one: the ghostly tunnel ahead made
by the projecting headlight-beams.

"Come this way," he said quietly. He started walking
down it. He held her by the elbow, to make sure that she
accompanied him. The leaves sloshed and spit under them
in the unnatural quiet. The carfender fell behind them,
they were clear of it now, walking ahead. She went turned
unnaturally sidewise, staring into his unanswering face.
She could hear her own breath, echoing under the canopy
of the trees. His was quieter.

They walked like that in silent, unexplained pantomime
until they'd reached a point where the projected headlight-
shine thinned out, was about to disappear. On this bound-
ary-line between light and shadows he stopped, took his
hand off her. She went down convulsively a few inches,
he caught her, straightened her, took his hand off her a
second time.

He took out a cigarette and offered it to her. She tried
to refuse. "Here," he insisted roughly, thrusting it at her
mouth. "Better take one!" He lit it for her, holding his
hands cupped over the match-flame. There was something
ritualistic about the little attention that only struck re-
doubled fear into her, instead of reassuring her. She took
one puff, then the cigarette dropped from her unmanageable lips, she wasn't able to retain it. He made a precautionary pass at it with his foot, ground it out because of the
leaves.

"All right," he said. "Now go back to the car. Walk up
that pathway of light from here, and get back in the car,
and wait for me in it. And *don't look around*, just keep
walking straight ahead."

She didn't seem to understand, or else was too undone

by terror to be able to move of her own volition. He had to give her a slight push away from him to start her off. She tottered a few uncertain steps through the shuffling leaves.

"Go ahead, keep walking straight back along those lights like I told you," his voice came after her. "*And don't look back!*"

She was a woman and a frightened one. The admonition had an opposite effect to that intended; it brought her head around, uncontrollably.

He already had the gun out in his hand, although he hadn't quite brought it all the way up yet, it was still at half-position. It must have come out silently behind her back as she was moving away.

Her scream was like a bird, clawed and dying, that manages to spiral up through the trees for one last flutter before it drops down dead. She tried to close in toward him again, as though nearness was a guarantee of immunity and the danger lay in being detached from him.

"Stay there!" he warned flintily. "I tried to make it as easy for you as I could, I told you not to look back."

"Don't! What for?" she wailed. "I told you I'd tell them everything you want me to! I *told* you I would! I will, I will—!"

"No," he contradicted with horrifying calm, "you won't, and I'll make sure you don't. Tell it to him instead, when he catches up to you in the next world, about half-an-hour from now." His arm stretched out at firing-position with the gun.

She made a perfect silhouette against the fuzzy head-light-glare. Trapped, unable even to flee aside into the protective darkness beyond the beams in time, for they were so wide, she floundered around where she stood in a complete, befuddled circle, that brought her around facing him once more as she had been before.

That was all there was time for.

Then the shot echoed thunderously under the ceiling of trees overhead. Her scream was its counterpoint.

He must have missed, as fairly close to one another as they were. There was no smoke at his end, as there should have been, though her mind had no time to reason about that. She felt nothing; she still stayed up, too dazed to run or do anything but waver there, like a ribbon-streamer before an electric fan. He was the one stumbled sideways against a nearby tree-trunk, leaned there inertly for a minute, face pressed against the bark, as though in remorse for what he had just attempted. Then she saw that he was holding his shoulder with the other hand. The gun winked harmlessly from the bed of leaves where he had dropped it, like a lump of coal in the light-flare.

A man's figure glided swiftly past her from the rear, went down the path of light toward him. He was holding a gun of his own, she saw, centered on the crumbling figure against the tree. He dipped for a minute, and the wink was gone from the leaves underfoot. Then he stepped in close, there was a flash of reflected light down by their wrists, and something made the sound of a twig snapping. Lombard's sagging figure came away from the tree, leaned soddenly against him, then straightened itself.

In the leaden quiet the second man's voice reached her clearly.

"I arrest you for the murder of Marcella Henderson!"

He put something to his lips, and a whistle sounded with doleful, long-drawn-out finality. Then the silence came down on the three of them again.

Burgess leaned down solicitously and raised her from the kneeling position she had collapsed into on the bed of leaves, hands pressed tightly over her sobbing face.

"I know," he said soothingly. "I know it was pretty bad. It's over now. It's over. You did the job. You've saved him. Lean on me, that's it. Have a good cry. Go to it. You've got it coming to you."

Woman-like, she stopped then and there. "I don't want to now. I'm all right, now. It's just that—I didn't think anyone would get here in time to—"

"They wouldn't have just by tailing the two of you. Not the way he drove." A second car had braked somewhere further up the lane only moments before; its occupants hadn't even reached the spot yet. "I couldn't take any chances on that. I was riding right with you the whole way out, didn't you know that? I was right in the trunk-compartment. I heard the whole thing. I've been in it ever since you first walked inside the store."

He raised his voice, shouted back to where flashlights were winking fitfully under the trees as the second party descended. "Is that Gregory and the rest of you fellows? Go back—don't waste time getting out and coming over here. Get over to the highway fast and get on the nearest telephone. Get the District Attorney's office. We only have a few minutes. I'll follow you in the other car. Tell them I'm holding a guy named John Lombard, self-confessed killer of Mrs. Henderson, to get word to the warden—"

"You haven't got a bit of evidence against me," Lombard growled, wincing with pain.

"No? What more do I need than what you've just given me? I caught you in the very act of murdering in cold blood a girl whom you never even set eyes on until just an hour ago! What could you have possibly had against her, except that her evidence was the one thing that could

have still saved Henderson, absolved him of the crime?
And why were you determined not to let that happen? Because that would have meant reopening the whole case, and
your own immunity would have been endangered. That's
my evidence against you!"

A State Trooper came thudding up to them. "Need a
hand here?"

"Carry the girl over to the car. She's just been through
a pretty rocky experience and needs looking after. I'll take
care of the guy."

The husky trooper picked her up bodily, cradled her
in his arms. "Who is she?" he asked over his shoulder, as
he led the way back along the glowing headlight-carpet.

"A pretty valuable little person," Burgess answered
from the rear, jarring his prisoner along beside him, "so
walk gently with her, officer, walk slow. That's Henderson's girl, Carol Richman, you're holding in your arms.
The best man of us all."

23: One Day, After the Execution—

THEY were together in the living-room of Burgess' small
flat in Jackson Heights. That was the scene of their first
meeting, following the release. He'd arranged it that way
for them. He'd had her there waiting for Henderson, when
the latter came down on the train. As he expressed it to
her, "Who wants to meet outside a prison-gate? You two
have had enough of that stuff already. Wait for him over
at my place. It may be only instalment-plan furniture, but
at least it's non-penal."

They were sitting close together on the sofa, in soft

lamplight, in a state of profound—if still somewhat dazed
—peace. Henderson had his arm around her, and her head
was resting in the notch of his shoulder.

Something about the two of them gave Burgess a choking feeling in the throat, when he came in and saw them.
"How's it coming, you two?" he asked gruffly, in order
not to show it.

"Gee, everything's so *good-looking*, isn't it?" Henderson marvelled. "I'd almost forgotten how *good-looking*
everything is. Carpets on the floor. Soft light coming from
a lampshade. A sofa-cushion behind me. And look, the
best-looking thing of all—" He nudged the top of her
head with his chin. "It's all mine, I've got it all back again,
and it's good for another forty years yet!"

Burgess and the girl exchanged a side-glance of unspoken compassion.

"I just came from the District Attorney's office," Burgess said. "They finally got the full confession out of him
down there. Sealed, signed, and delivered."

"I still can't get over it," Henderson said, shaking his
head. "I still can hardly believe it. What was in back of it?
Was he in love with Marcella? She'd never met him more
than twice in her whole life, as far as I know."

"As far as you know," Burgess said drily.

"You mean it was one of those things on the side?"

"Didn't you notice she was out a lot?"

"Yes, but I didn't think anything of it. She and I weren't
living on cordial terms any more."

"Well, that was it, right there." He took a turn or two
about the room. "There's one thing I think ought to be
made clear to you, though, Henderson. For what it's worth
at this late date. It was strictly a one-sided affair. Your
wife was not in love with Lombard. If she had been, most

likely she would still be alive today. She was not in love with anyone but herself. She liked admiration and flattery; she was the type that likes to flirt and string people along, without meaning it seriously. That's a harmless game with nine men. And with the tenth it's dangerous. To her he was just someone to go out with, and a handy way of getting back at you in her own mind: to show herself that she didn't need you. Unfortunately, he was the tenth man. He was the wrong type for it altogether. He'd spent most of his life around oil-fields in God-forsaken parts of the world; and he hadn't had much experience with women. He didn't have any sense of humor about things like that. He took her seriously. And of course she liked that part of it all the better, that made the game more real.

"There's no question about it, she gave him a raw deal. She led him on until the very last, long after she must have seen where it was leading. She let him arrange his whole future around her, knowing darn well she wasn't going to be there to share it with him. She let him sign on for five years with this oil company in South America. Why, he even had the bungalow they were going to live in down there picked out and furnished up for them. The understanding was she was to divorce you as soon as they got there, and marry him. After all, when a guy's that age, and not a kid any more, he takes it hard when you kick his heart around like that.

"Instead of tapering off, breaking it to him by degrees, giving him a sporting chance to get over it, she went about it the worst possible way. She hated to give up her cake any sooner than she had to; his rings on the phone, their luncheon-meetings, their dinner-dates, his kisses in a taxi. Her ego needed all that. She'd got used to it, and she would have missed it. So she put off and put off. *She*

*waited until the very night they were due to sail together
to South America;* waited until he called for her at the
flat—as soon as you'd gone—to take her to the pier with
him.

"I'm not surprised it cost her her life. I would have been
surprised if it hadn't. He says he got there even before you
left, side-stepped you by waiting on the upper flight of
stairs past your floor, until after you'd come storming out.
It just so happened there was no hallman on duty that
night; the former one had just been drafted, and they
hadn't gotten a replacement yet. So no one saw him come
in. And as we all very well know, no one saw him leave
again either.

"Well anyway, she let him in, went back to her mirror
again, and when he asked her if she was all packed and
ready, laughed at him. That seems to have been her day for
laughing at people. She asked him if he'd really seriously
believed she was going to bury herself in South America,
place herself at his mercy, to marry or not as he saw fit,
once her bridges were burned behind her? Above all, free
you to go to someone else? She liked the situation the way
it was. She wasn't giving up a sure thing for a gamble.

"But more than anything else, it was the laughter that
did it. If she'd cried when she told him all this, or even if
she'd just kept a straight face, he says he thinks he would
have let it go at that. Just gone out and drunk himself
stone-blind, maybe, but she would still have been alive behind him. And I think so too."

"So he killed her," Henderson said quietly.

"So he killed her. Your discarded necktie was still lying
there on the floor behind her, where you'd dropped it. He
must have absently picked it up at one point or another
just before this, been holding it in his hands without no-

ticing it, when the snap came." He gave an expressive snap
of his own fingers.

"I don't blame him altogether," Carol breathed, looking
down at the floor.

"I don't either," Burgess admitted. "But that was no
excuse for doing what he did next. For deliberately turning on the man who had been his life-long friend, going
out of his way to see that he was framed for it."

"What did I do to him?" Henderson asked, without any
trace of rancor.

"What it amounts to is this. He didn't understand then,
and he still doesn't today yet, even this long after, what
it really was that made her act the way she did. Jilt him
so heartlessly. He failed to see that it was in perfect keeping with her own character to do so, that that was the way
she was built. He mistakenly thought it must be because of
a renewal of her love for you. Therefore he blamed you
for it. You were responsible for his losing her. That made
him hate you. He wanted to take it out on you. A dis-
torted form of jealousy, that was only made more insane
by the coveted one's death, is about the closest you can get
to it."

"Whew," said Henderson softly.

"He came out of there, unseen, and he deliberately set
out after you, to try and overtake you. That quarrel which
he'd overheard from the stairs was too good an opportunity to be passed up. Too good an opportunity of sad-
dling you with what he'd just done. His original idea, he
says, was to join you as if by accident, as if he'd just happened to run into you, and stick around with you long
enough to give you a chance to convict yourself out of
your own mouth. At least implicate yourself seriously.
He would have said, 'Hullo, I thought your wife was

going to be with you.' And then, quite naturally, you
would have answered, 'I had a fierce row with her before
I left.' It was necessary for that row to come out. He
wanted it to. He couldn't bring it out, otherwise, without
implicating himself as having been within eavesdropping
distance out on the stairs. It had to come through *your*
telling *him*, in the first person, do you understand?

"He would have seen to it that you got quite tanked—
if you still needed any additional encouragement—while
he was with you. Then he would have accompanied you
back to your own door. So that when you made the grim
discovery, he'd be there; be on hand to reluctantly repeat
to the police what he'd heard you say about having a terrific blow-up with her just before leaving. You would
have been acting as a shock-absorber for him. That's a
neat little touch there, that idea of accompanying the husband back to where he's just finished murdering the wife.
Automatically relegating himself to the position of innocent bystander at someone else's crime. It would have been
practically foolproof as a suspicion disinfectant.

"All this he tells quite freely—and I've got to admit
quite unremorsefully even yet—in his confession."

"Nice," said Carol somberly.

"He thought you'd be alone. He already knew two of
the places you'd said you'd be. You'd mentioned that
afternoon, when you ran into him, that you were taking
the missis to the Maison Blanche for dinner, and then afterward to the Casino. The bar he didn't know about, because
you didn't yourself until you turned and went in there
on the spur of the moment.

"He went straight to the Maison, and he cased it cautiously from the foyer, without showing himself. He saw
you in there. You must have just arrived. He saw you

were with someone. That changed things around. He not
only could not join you now with any hope of profiting
from any possible revelation on your part, but this unknown third person might even provide you with a degree
of immunity altogether, depending on just how soon you'd
met her after leaving your own door. In other words, that
early, almost at sight, he sensed her paramount importance
in the matter, both from his point of view and your own.
And acted accordingly.

"He withdrew, and hovered around outside on the
street, far enough away to command the entrance without
any danger of being caught sight of himself. He knew
your next stop was slated to be the Casino Theatre, but
he couldn't be sure, of course. Couldn't afford to take it
for granted.

"The two of you came out, taxied over, and he taxied
over in your wake. He followed you *into* the theatre.
Listen to this, it's an exciting thing. He bought a standing-
room ticket, as people often do who have only time to
catch one act. He stood up back there, at the rear of the
orchestra, sheltered by a post, and kept the back of your
heads in sight throughout the performance.

"He saw you leave when you did leave. He almost lost
you in the crowd when you left, but luck was with him.
The little incident of the blind man he missed altogether,
for he dared not tread that closely behind you. Your taxi
had such a hard time pulling clear of the jam that he was
able to keep you in sight from another.

"You led him back to Anselmo's finally, although he
still didn't know that that was the pivot of the whole thing.
Again he loitered outside, for in the closer quarters of the
bar he couldn't have hoped to avoid your spotting him.
He saw you leave her there, presently, and could guess by

that fact alone, if he hadn't already, that you'd carried out the threat he'd heard you yell back at the apartment: that you'd invite the first stranger you met along in your wife's place.

"He had to decide quickly now whether to keep on after you, and run the risk of losing her in the shuffle, or to switch his attention to her, find out just how much good she could do you, how much harm she could do him.

"He didn't hesitate long. Again his good luck held, and he did the right thing almost by instinct. It was too late to attach himself to you any more with any degree of plausibility. Instead of helping to incriminate you, he'd only be incriminating himself. His ship was being warped out of the pier at that very minute, and he should have been on it by this time.

"So he let you go and he chose her, never dreaming how unerringly right he was, and he bided his time outside, watching her covertly, knowing she could not stay in the bar all night, knowing she would have to have some final destination.

"Presently she emerged, and he drew back out of sight to give her leeway enough. He was shrewd enough not to accost her then and there; he would only be identifying himself to her. In case it turned out she could absolve you, he would only be incriminating himself indelibly for later on by the mere fact of having questioned her on the subject at all, shown any interest in it. So he wisely decided that this was the thing to do: learn her identity and destination first of all, so that he would know where to find her again when he wanted her. That much done, leave her undisturbed for a short while. Then discover, if possible, just how much protection she was able to give you. This by retracing your steps of the evening, seeking to ferret out if possible your original meeting-place, and above all how soon after your leaving the apartment the meeting had taken place. Then thirdly, if the weight she could throw in the matter was enough to count, take care of it by a little judicious erasing. Seek her out wherever it was he had traced her to the first time, and ascertain whether or not he could persuade her to remain silent. And if she proved not amenable, he admits there was already a darker method of erasure lurking in the back of his mind. Immunizing one crime by committing a second.

"So he set out after her. She went on foot, for some inscrutable reason, late as the hour was; but this only made it easier for him to keep her in sight. At first he thought it might be because she lived in the immediate vicinity, a stone's throw away from the bar, but as the distance she covered slowly lengthened, he saw that couldn't be it. Presently he wondered if it mightn't be that she had become aware there was someone following her, and was deliberately trying to mislead them, throw them off the track. But even this, he finally decided, couldn't be the case. She showed absolutely no awareness nor alarm about anything, she was sauntering along too aimlessly, almost dawdling, stopping to scan the contents of unlighted showcases whenever she happened upon them, stopping to stroke a stray cat, obviously improvising her route as she went along, but under no outward compulsion whatever. After all, had she been seeking to rid herself of him, it would have been simple enough for her to have hopped into a cab, or stepped up to a policeman and said a word or two. Several of them drifted into sight along the way and she didn't. There was nothing left for him to ascribe her erratic movements to, finally, than that she had no fixed destination, she was wandering at random. She was too well-dressed to be homeless, and he was completely at a loss what to make of it.

"She went up Lexington to Fifty-seventh, then she turned west there as far as Fifth. She went north two blocks, and sat for some time on one of the benches on the outside of the quadrangle around the statue of General Sherman, just as though it were three in the afternoon. She was finally driven off from there again by the questioning slowing-up of about every third car that passed her on its way in or out of the park. She ambled east again through Fifty-ninth, absorbedly memorizing the contents of the art-shop windows along there, with Lombard slowly going mad behind her.

"Then at last, when he almost began to think she intended going over the Queensborough Bridge on foot into Long Island, she suddenly turned aside into a very grubby little hotel at the far end of Fifty-ninth, and he detected her in the act of signing the register when he peered in after her. Showing that this was as much of an improvisation as all the rest of her meandering had been.

"As soon as she was safely out of sight, he went in there in turn and, as the quickest way of finding out what name she'd given and what room she'd been assigned to, took one for himself. The name immediately above his own, when he'd signed for it, was 'Frances Miller' and she'd gone into 214. He managed to secure the one adjoining, 216, by a deft process of elimination, finding fault with the two or three that were shown him at first until he'd secured the one he had his eye on. The place was in the last stages of deterioration, little better than a lodging house, so that was excusable enough.

He went up for a short while, chiefly to watch her door

from the hallway outside his own and convince himself that she was finally settled for the rest of the night and would be here when he came back. He couldn't have hoped for more proof than he obtained. He could see the light in her room peering out through the opaque transom over the door. He could, without any difficulty in that weatherbeaten place, hear every move she made, almost guess what she was doing. He could hear the clicking of the wire hangers in the barren closet as she hung her outer clothing up. She had come in without any baggage, of course. He could hear her humming softly to herself as she moved about. He could even detect now and then what it was she was humming. *Chica Chica Boom*, from the show you had taken her to earlier that night. He could hear the trickle of the water as she busied herself preparing to retire. Finally the light went out behind the transom, and he could even hear the creak of the springs in the decrepit bed as she disposed herself on it. He goes into all this at great and grim length in the final draft of his confession.

"He crossed his own unlighted room, leaned out the window, which overlooked a miserable blind shaft, and scrutinized what he could see of her room from that direction. The shade was down to within a foot of the sill, but her bed was in such a position that by straddling the sill of his own and leaning far out, he could see the glint of the cigarette she held suspended over the side of the bed in the darkness in there. There was a drain-pipe running down between their two windows, and the collar-like fastening which held it to the wall offered a foot-rest at one point. He made note of that. Made note it was possible to get in there in that way, if he should find it necessary, when he came back.

"Sure of her now, he came out of the place again. This was a little before two o'clock in the morning.

"He hurried straight back to Anselmo's in a cab. The place was going into the death-watch now, and there was plenty of opportunity to become confidential with the bartender and find out what, if anything, he knew. In due course he let drop some casual remark about her, you know the sort of thing. 'Who was that lonely-looking number I saw sitting up at the end there all by herself a little while ago?' or something on that order. Just as an opening wedge.

"They're a talkative race anyway, and that was all the barman needed to go the rest of the way under his own speed. That she'd been in there once before, around six, gone out with someone, he'd brought her back, and then he'd left her.

"An adroit further question or two brought out the point he was mainly interested in. That you had accosted her without any time-lag, immediately upon coming in, and that it had been only a very few minutes past six. In other words, his worst fears were exceeded. She was not only a potential protection to you, she was your absolute, unqualified salvation. It would have to be taken care of. And without delay." He broke off to ask, "Am I boring you by rehashing it at this length?"

"It was my life," Henderson observed drily.

"He didn't let any grass grow under his feet. He made the first deal then and there, under the very eyes of the few remaining customers still lingering in the place. The barman was the type that bribes easy, anyway, as the saying goes; he was ripe and ready to fall into his hand. A few guarded words, a palming of hands across the bar, and it was done. 'How much would you take to forget you saw that woman meet that fellow in here? You don't need to forget *he* was in here, just forget she was.' The barman allowed he'd take a modest enough sum. 'Even if it turned out to be a police matter?' The barman wasn't quite so sure after he'd heard that. Lombard made up his mind for him with a sum of fifty times larger than he'd expected to get out of it. He gave him a *thousand dollars in cold cash.* He had a considerable wad of it on him, ready at hand, the stake he'd been intending to use to set the two of them up in South America. That cinched it as far as the barman was concerned, of course. Not only that, Lombard cemented it with a few quiet-spoken but blood-chilling threats. And he was evidently a good threatener. Maybe because his threats weren't idle, they were the McCoy, and his listener could sense that.

"That barman stayed fixed from then on, long after he knew all the facts in the case, and nothing we nor anyone else could do could get a word out of him. And it wasn't entirely due to the thousand dollars by any means. He was good and frightened, and so were all the rest of them. You saw the effect it finally had on Cliff Milburn. There was something grim about this Lombard. He was a man with absolutely no sense of humor. He'd stayed too close to nature all his life.

"The barman taken care of, he went on from there, backtracking over the route you had taken not very many hours before. There's no need of giving you all the details at this late date. The restaurant and the theatre were closed, of course, by that time of night, but he managed to learn the whereabouts of the individuals he was after and seek them out. In one case he even made a quick trip all the way out to Forest Hills and back, to get one of them out of bed. By four o'clock that morning the job was complete; he'd contacted three more of the key figures whose collusion it was necessary for him to have: the taxi-driver Alp, the headwaiter from the Maison Blanche, and the box-office man from the Casino. He gave them varying amounts. The taxi-driver simply to deny having seen her. The headwaiter to give a split to the table-waiter, whose job depended on him after all, and make sure that he stayed in line. The box-office man he fixed so liberally he practically made him an ally. It was through him that Lombard learned one of the house-musicians had been heard shooting his mouth off, bragging what a hit he'd made with this particular woman—as he saw it—and added a suggestion that perhaps he'd better be taken care of too. Lombard wasn't able to get around to that until the second night after the murder, but luckily for him, we had overlooked the man entirely, so there was no harm done by the delay.

"Well, now it's an hour before daybreak and his job's done, he's caused her to disappear from view, as far as it's humanly possible. The only one who remained to be taken care of was she herself. He went back there where he'd left her, to attend to that part of it. And he admits, his mind was already made up. He wasn't going to buy her silence, he was going to make sure of it in a more lasting way— by death. Then the rest of his structure wouldn't be in any danger. Any of the others could welsh, but there wouldn't be any proof left.

"He let himself back into the room he'd taken next to hers, and sat there in the dark for a moment or two, thinking it out. He realized that he ran a far greater risk of being detected as the murderer in this case than in the case of your wife, but only as an unknown man who had signed the register downstairs under an assumed name, not as John Lombard. He intended overtaking his ship, he would never be seen around here again, so what chance was there of identifying him later? It would be suspected that 'he' had killed her, but it wouldn't be known who 'he' was. See what I mean?

"He went outside and listened at her door. The room was quiet, she was asleep by now. He tried it very carefully, but as he'd half-expected, the door was locked, he couldn't get in that way. There remained that drainpipe-stepping-stone outside their two windows, which had been in the back of his mind all along anyhow.

"The shade was still down to within a foot of the sill, as it had been before, when he looked out. He climbed quietly and agilely out the window, rested his foot on the necessary drainpipe support, and was able without very much difficulty to swing himself onto her sill and lower himself into the room under the shade. He didn't take anything with him, he intended using just his bare hands and the bedclothes.

"In the dark he edged his way to the bed, and he poised his arms, and he gripped the tortured mass of the bedclothes tight to prevent any outcry. They collapsed under him; they were empty. She wasn't there. She'd gone. As erratically as she'd come into this place, she'd gone again, in the hour before dawn, after lying in the bed awhile. Two cigarette-butts, a few grains of powder on the dressing-stand, and the rumpled bedclothes, were all that was left of her.

"When the worst part of the shock had worn off and he went downstairs again and asked about it more or less openly, they told him she'd come down not long before his return, handed in her key, and calmly walked out to the street once more. They didn't know which way she'd gone, nor where she'd gone, nor why she'd gone; only that she'd gone—as strangely as she'd come.

"His own game had boomeranged on him. The woman whom he had spent all night and hundreds of dollars in trying to turn into a ghost as far as you, Henderson, were concerned, *had* turned into a ghost—but as far as he himself was concerned now. Which wasn't what he'd wanted at all. It left things too dangerously indefinite. She might pop back into the picture at any moment.

"He went through hell in those few short hours that were all he could spare before he had to plane out, if he was still to overtake his ship. He knew how hopeless it was. He knew, as you and I know, what a place New York is to find someone in, on short order.

"He hunted for her high and low, with the remorselessness of a maniac, and he couldn't find her again. The day went, and the second night went, and his time was up, he couldn't stay behind any longer. So he had to let it go under the heading of unfinished business. An axe hanging over him from then on, threatening to fall at any moment.

"He planed out of New York the second day after the murder, made the short overwater hop from Miami to Havana that same day, and was just in time to board his own ship when it touched there on the third day out. His excuse to the shipboard officials was that he'd got drunk the night of sailing and missed it.

"That was why he was so ripe for that come-on message I sent in your name; that was all he needed to drop everything and come back. He'd been panicky all along, and that gave him the finishing-touch. They talk about murderers being drawn back to the scene of their crime. This pulled him back like a magnet. Your asking for help gave him just the excuse he needed. He could come back openly now and help you 'look' for her. Finish the death-hunt he hadn't had time to complete the first time. Make sure that if she was ever found, she'd be found dead."

"Then you already suspected him when you came to my cell that day and drafted that cable in my name. When did you first begin to suspect him?"

"I can't put my finger on it and give you the exact day or hour. It was a very gradual thing, that came on in the wake of my change of mind about your own guilt. There was no conclusive evidence against him from first to last, that's why I had to go at it in the roundabout way I did. He left no fingerprints at the apartment; must have wiped the few surfaces he touched off clean. I remember we found several doorknobs without any marks on them at all.

"To start off with, he was just a name you'd dropped, in the course of being questioned yourself. An old-time friend, whose invitation to join him in a farewell tour of the town you'd conscientiously passed up, much to your regret, on *her* account. I had a routine inquiry made for him, more to have him help us fill in a little of *your* background for our record than anything else. I learned he'd sailed, as you'd mentioned he intended to. But I also found out, quite unintentionally, from the steamship line, that he'd missed the sailing here and caught up with his ship at Havana three days later. And one other thing. That he'd originally booked passage for two, himself and a wife, but that when he'd overtaken the ship he was alone, and had finished out the rest of the trip unaccompanied. Incidentally, there was no record of his ever having been married or having had a wife up here, when I checked a little further.

"Now there was not necessarily anything glaringly suspicious in all that, you understand. People do miss ships, especially when they celebrate too copiously just before sailing-time. And people's brides-to-be do change their minds at the last minute, back out, or the contemplated marriage is postponed by mutual consent.

"So I didn't think any more about it. And yet on the other hand I did. That little detail of his missing the ship and then overtaking it alone, lodged in the back of my mind and stayed with me from then on. He had, a little bit unluckily for himself, managed to attract my attention. Which seldom turns out to be beneficial, with cops. Then later, when my belief in your own guilt began to evaporate, there was a vacuum left behind. And a vacuum is something that has to be filled, or it will fill by itself. These facts about him began to trickle out, and before I knew it, the empty space had begun to fill up again."

"You sure kept me in the dark," Henderson admitted.

"I had to. There wasn't anything definite enough, until just recently. In fact until that night he drove Miss Richman into the woods with him. Confiding in you would have been a bad risk. Most likely you wouldn't have shared my feelings about him, and for all I knew might have warned him off in some burst of misguided loyalty. Or even if you had strung along with me, had shared my belief, knowledge of what was up might have made you a poor actor. He might have detected something in your manner toward him, and our hands would have been tipped. You were under a terrific strain, you know. I felt the safest thing to do was to work *through* you, using you as a sort of unconscious medium, without letting you realize the purpose of what you were doing yourself. And it wasn't easy. Take that stunt with the theatre programs, for instance—"

"I thought you were crazy—or I would have if I was normal myself—the way you rehearsed me and rehearsed me and rehearsed me, every little act, every little word, that was to lead up to it. You know what I thought you were doing it for? As a pain-killer, to keep my mind off the approaching deadline. So I fell in with it, and did as you told me, but with my tongue in my cheek."

"Your tongue in your cheek, and my heart in my mouth," Burgess chuckled grimly.

"Did he have anything to do with those peculiar accidents that kept dogging you all along the way, as far as you were able to find out?"

"Everything. The strange part of that is, the one that seemed most like a murder, the Cliff Milburn affair, proved to be a bona fide suicide when we got through investigating it; and of course the barman was killed accidentally. But the two that seemed most like accidents turned out to be murders. Murders that he committed. I'm speaking of the deaths of the blind man and Pierrette Douglas. Both were murders without weapons, in the usual sense. The death of the blind man was a particularly horrible piece of business.

"He left him there in the room for a moment or two, ostensibly to chase down to the street and call me. He knew the man had an aversion to the police, typical of his kind of fraudulent panhandling. He knew the first thing he'd do would be to try to escape from there. He counted on his doing that. As soon as he was on the other side of the door he attached a strong black thread, the kind tailors use, across the top step, at about ankle-height. Knotted it around the bannister-leg on one side, a projecting nail-head on the other. Then he turned out the light, knowing now the blind man had the use of his eyes, made a receding drum-beat of his footsteps, you know that old stunt, and crouched there waiting on the lower flight, just out of sight below the landing.

"The blind man came out fast and incautiously, in a hurry to put himself out of reach before Lombard returned with his police-friend, and the thing worked just as he'd intended it to. The thread caught him short and sent him toppling down the whole flight, and into the foreshortened landing-wall head-first. The thread had snapped, of course, but that didn't save him. The fall didn't kill him, he simply got a nasty crack on the skull and lay there stunned. And so Lombard hurriedly came back up to the landing again, stepped over him, went on to the head of the stairs, removed the tell-tale ends of loose thread from both sides.

"Then he went back to the senseless man, explored with his hands, found he was still breathing. His head was forced back at an unnatural angle by the wall against which it rested, and there was a strain on his neck. It was like a suspension-bridge, you understand, between his shoulders flat on the floor and his head semi-upright against the wall. He located the position of the neck, and then he straightened up, raised one leg so that his heavy shoe was poised just over it, and—"

Carol turned her head sharply aside.

"I'm sorry," Burgess murmured.

She turned back again. "It's part of the story. We should know it."

"Then and only then he went out and called me. And when he came back he stayed down at the street-door, and was careful to engage the cop on the beat in conversation the whole time he was waiting for me, to establish that he'd remained down there in full sight, if it became necessary."

"Did you get what it was right away?" Henderson asked.

"I examined the body down at the Morgue later that night, after I'd sent him home, and I saw the little red nick across each shin the thread had made. I saw the traces of dust on the back of his neck too. I figured what it was then. It was just a matter of building it up from those two points. It would have been hard to get him on it, though. It might have been done. I preferred to wait and get him for the main thing. I couldn't have got him for the main thing on the strength of that blind man incident, that was a cinch. And I didn't want to grab him prematurely only to see him get away again. Once I had him, I wanted to hang onto him. So I kept my mouth closed and went on paying out rope."

"And the thing about that reefer-smoker you say he had nothing to do with?"

"In spite of the discrepancy of razors, that was only what it seemed. Cliff Milburn slashed his own throat in a fit of drug-induced depression and fear. The safety-blade must have been a discard berthed under the shelf-paper either by a former tenant or by some friend of his who came in and used his bathroom to shave in. A behaviorist would be interested. Even when it came to suicide, he instinctively avoided using his own implement for anything other than what it was intended for. That's a trait common to all of us; that's why we get so sore when our wives sharpen pencils with them."

Carol murmured softly, "I'll never be able to go near one again, after that night."

"But the death of Mrs. Douglas was his doing?" Henderson questioned interestedly.

"That was even more adroit than the other one. A long strip or runner of carpeting ran across the highly-polished floor-surface, in her place, from the foyer step-down, at one end, to directly under the French windows, at the other. What first put the idea into his head was that he skidded slightly himself, on the quite dangerous flooring, a little earlier in the proceedings, and she had laughed at him. Eye-measurement did the rest, while he was talking to her. The straight line-sweep of the rug, of course, was almost an invitation. He marked an invisible X on it to show where she must stand in order to have the greater part of her length go outside the window when she was overbalanced, and carefully retained its exact location in his mind from then on. Which is not the easy feat it sounds, when you are engaged in moving about yourself and talking with someone, and can only give it part of your attention.

"This isn't a hypothetical reconstruction on my part, I have all this from him at first hand, in black and white. From that point on, there was a sort of minuet of death danced by the two of them, during which he delicately maneuvered her into just the right position. When he had completed writing out the check he stood up with it and returned toward the window, as if to have the fresh air hasten its drying. Then he shifted until he was precisely to one side of the position he wanted her to take, but off the rug. Then he drew her on from where she had remained by seeming to offer her the check. Passively extending it toward her, but without moving his own feet, so that she had to come forward for it. It's the same principle they use in bull-fighting. The bull follows the cape away from the fighter's body. She followed the check up to one side of his body. When she had fallen into the exact spot he wanted her to, he relaxed his fingers and let the check pass to her.

"Her attention was taken up in scanning it for a moment or two, she stood motionless. He quickly moved away from her, strode the whole length of the room, as if taking an abrupt departure then and there. Then when he'd reached the far end of it, and was on the step clear of it, he turned to look back at her and called 'Goodbye!' That brought her head up from the check, that caused her to turn toward him—and at the same time present her full back to the window. She was now in the exact position it was necessary for her to be. For if she'd gone out frontwards or sidewards she might have been able to cling to the window-frame and arrest herself. Backwards it was an impossibility, the human arm-socket doesn't work that way.

"He dipped down, flung up the rug at full arm's length overhead, let it drop again; that was all he had to do. She went out like a puff of wind. She didn't even have time to scream, he says. He must have caught her on the outbreath. She was already gone by the time her flown-off shoe ticked back again to the floor."

Carol crinkled up the corners of her eyes. "Those things are worse than the ones with knife or gun, there's so much more treachery involved in them!"

"Yes, but much harder to prove to a jury. He didn't lay a hand on her, he killed her from twenty or twenty-two feet away. The clue was still in the rug itself, of course. I saw it the minute I got in there. The ripples were at his end. Where she had stood it was smooth, only just shifted further back along the floor. If it had been an honest skid or misstep, it would have been the other way around. The pleats would have been at her end, where her feet kicked the rug back on itself. His end would have been flat and undisturbed, the agitation couldn't possibly have transferred itself that far over.

"There was a cigarette left burning there, as if by her. That was to make it seem that the fall had occurred just previous to our arrival, whereas he had telephoned me some fifteen minutes before. Or if I wanted to disregard that, he had been continuously in my company for fully eight to ten minutes before, counting from the time I met him in front of the fire-station.

"It didn't fool me for a moment, but the mechanics of how he'd done it gave me three full days' work before I could figure it out satisfactorily. The ashstand had an orifice in its center through which ashes were meant to drop, all the way down through the long stem into the hollow base which was meant for that purpose. There was supposed to be a trap, but he jammed that so it would stay open. He simply took three ordinary-size cigarettes, removed a little tobacco from the mouth end of the two foremost ones, and telescoped them together to form one triple the usual length but retaining the trademark of a small-size cigarette at the far end, in case there should be enough left to investigate. Then he lit it, left it spearing the top of the stand in a long inclined-plane, one end down into the open stem and resting against it. A cigarette left burning like that in a slanted position, and over an opening, will seldom go out, even when it's not fanned by the breath as in smoking. The slow ember simply worked its way back from cigarette to cigarette without a break. As the first two were consumed, they dropped off down the stem without leaving a trace. The third, which was resting wholly on the tilted perimeter of the smoke-stand, remained in place to the end, forming just what he wanted it to, a perfect one-cigarette butt by the time we got there.

"This alibi, however, handicapped him in another way. It would have been better if he'd skipped it. It limited how far away he could go on the fool's errand she was supposed to have sent him; he had to be sure of getting back soon enough for it to be of any use to him. He had to pick some place in the immediate vicinity, and he had to pick some place that would at sight be identifiable as a complete hoax, so there would be no excuse for the two of us to linger around investigating or asking questions. Hence the firehouse gag. One look was enough, and we beat it back again to her place.

"In other words, by tying himself down with that cigarette-alibi, he weakened the plausibility of his story in another respect. Why would she do a thing like that, send him just a stone's throw away and to a glaringly fake address? She would have either given him the real address, refused to give him any address at all, or—if she intended fleecing him out of the check—given him a fake address and name that would have taken him all the rest of the night and the better part of the next day to run down, thus giving herself a comfortable head-start. Well, he preferred to cauterize the murder-angle a little even at the expense of shooting the credibility of her behavior to hell. After all, there was the precedent of the blind man by this time, and I guess he was afraid to have the pitcher go to the well once too often.

"Apart from that one bad flaw, he did a fairly competent job. Let the elevator-boy overhear him talking to an empty room, even gave the door a delayed-action swing behind him so that she seemed to be closing it after he'd already left it.

"I suppose I could have pinned him down with it." Then

he concluded: "But that still wouldn't have meant getting him for the killing of your wife, necessarily. So I played dumb again. It was just a matter of getting him to repeat himself—but on someone that we sicked onto him, and held the strings to, instead of on someone that he'd picked for himself, without our full knowledge."

"Was that your idea, to use Carol like that?" Henderson queried. "It's a good thing I didn't know about it ahead of time. If I had, you wouldn't have gotten me to—"

"That was her idea, not mine. I'd arranged to hire some outside girl to play the part of decoy. She muscled in on it. She came storming in to where we were posted, watching him in the magazine-shop, that last night, just before the deadline, and told me flatly she was going to be the one to go in there and tackle him, or else! She said she was going ahead whether she had my okay or whether she didn't. Hell, I couldn't stop her, and I couldn't afford to have two of them walking in there one behind the other, so I had to let her have her way. We called in a make-up expert from one of the theatres and had him give her a good going-over, and we sent her on in."

"Imagine," she said rebelliously to the room at large, "I should sit back on my hands, and take a chance on some two-dollar extra gumming the whole thing up with her hamminess! There was no more time left by then to go wrong any more, we'd used it all up."

"She never did show up, did she?" Henderson mused. "I mean the real one. Strangest thing. Whoever she is, wherever she is, she sure played out her little game of hide-and-seek to the end."

"She wasn't trying to, she wasn't even playing one," Burgess said. "That's what's stranger about it still."

Henderson and the girl both jolted slightly, leaned forward alertly. "How do you know? You mean you finally got wind of her? You've found out who she is?"

"Yes, I got wind of her," Burgess said simply. "Quite some time ago. I've known it for weeks, months now—who she was."

"Was?" breathed Henderson. "Is she dead?"

"Not in the way you mean. But she's as good as, for all practical purposes. Her body's still alive. She's in an asylum for the hopelessly insane."

He reached slowly into his pocket, began to sift through envelopes and papers, while the two of them stared, transfixed.

"I've been up there myself, not once but several times. I've talked to her. You can hardly tell it in her manner. Just a little vague, dreamy. But she can't remember yesterday, the past is blurred, all fogged-out. She would have been no good to us, no good at all; she couldn't have testified. That's why I had to keep it to myself, play the thing out the way we did. It was our only chance, to get him to convict himself out of his own mouth, by substituting someone for her."

"How long—?"

"She was committed within three weeks after that night with you. It had been intermittent up to then, then the curtain dropped for good."

"How did you—?"

"In a roundabout way, that doesn't really matter now any more. The hat showed up by itself, in one of these bundle-shops. You know, thrift shops where they sell things for a few cents. One of my men spotted it. We traced it back link by link, just as he did later, working in the opposite direction. Some old hag had picked it up out of an ashcan, peddled it to the thrift-shop. We canvassed all the houses in the vicinity, after she'd pointed out the general site of the ashcan to us. It took weeks. Finally we found a maid who had thrown it out. Her employer had been committed to an asylum not long before. I questioned her husband, the members of her family. Nobody knew of the exact incident with you but herself, but they told me enough to show it was she, all right. She'd been behaving erratically like that for some time past, staying out alone all night, going to hotels by herself. Once they found her sitting on a park bench at daybreak.

"I got this from them."

He handed Henderson a snapshot. A snapshot of a woman.

Henderson looked at it long and hard. He nodded finally, but more to himself than to them. "Yes," he said softly, "yes—I guess so."

Carol took it away from him suddenly. "Don't look at her any more. She's done enough to you for one lifetime. Stay as you are, keep her unremembered. Here, here's your snapshot back."

"It helped, of course," Burgess said, putting it away again, "when we were getting Carol ready that night, to go in and pinch-hit for her. The make-up man was able to give her a superficial resemblance to this person. Enough to fool him, anyway. He'd only seen her at a distance and in uncertain light that night."

"What was her name?" Henderson asked.

Carol made a quick pass with her hand. "No, don't tell him. I don't want her with us. We're starting out new— no ghosts."

"She's right," Burgess said. "It's over. Bury it."

Even so, they fell silent for a few moments, the three of them, thinking about her, as they would probably continue to think about her, every so often, for the rest of their lives. It was one of those things that stays with you.

At the door when they were leaving, Carol's arm linked to his, Henderson turned back to Burgess for a minute, his forehead querulously creased. "But there should be some lesson in the whole thing, some *reason*. You mean she and I went through all we did—for nothing? There must be some moral in it somewhere."

Burgess gave him an encouraging slap on the back to speed him on his way. "If you've got to have a moral, I give you this: don't ever take strangers to the theatre unless you've got a good memory for faces."

THE END

Special Advance Preview!

From the Author of
***The Bride Wore Black* and**
***Phantom Lady* Comes a Selection**
of His Most Suspenseful Tales,
Including the Story that Inspired
Alfred Hitchcock's Classic 1954
Film

Rear Window

by

Cornell Woolrich

coming from ibooks, inc.
in September 2001

Waltz

She was sitting there in white, cool and crisp and pure-looking, with ten young men around her, waiting for the next number to begin. She knew what it was going to be because only a short while ago she had requested the orchestra leader to play it. "The Blue Danube." She knew whom it was going to be with, too.

As the opening bars were struck, a preamble started all around her. She laughed and kept shaking her head and saying, "Reserved, reserved. The next one, maybe." But the joke was, there wasn't going to be any next one. She knew that and they didn't.

When she saw him coming for her all the way across the enormous room, she stood up expectantly. There seemed to be a star twinkling behind both of her eyes. The strains of Strauss' lovely lilting music found an echo in her heart. The disappointed men put on long faces and drifted back to the stag line that stretched unbroken across one entire side of the ballroom, ruler-straight, like a regiment on dress parade: black shoulders, white shirt-fronts, pink faces. Under the sparkling crystal chandeliers, figures in blue and yellow and pink were slowly beginning to turn all over the room, like tops, each with its black-garbed complement.

The girl in white and the man she'd been waiting for met, stood poised for a moment, started off with a slow spin, their forms reflected upside down on the glass floor. Her voice was eager, confidential:

"This is the first chance I've had to say a word to you alone all evening, they've been watching me so. Especially mother. . . . You've got your car outside, of course? . . . Right after this dance? Yes, that's as good a time as any. They'll be going upstairs then. They'll let the party go ahead under its own momentum. She's starting to yawn already. . . .

"Yes, I'm all set. I sneaked up and finished my packing while the last dance was going on. Imagine me doing my own packing! I wasn't taking any chances on the maid giving me away to the family. I even carried my bags down the back stairs myself. They're hidden in a little closet off the servants' entrance. Just as soon as this piece is over, you slip out the front way, bring your car around to the back, and I'll meet you there. We'll be miles away before we're even missed. . . .

"I still can't believe it, it's all been so sudden. . . . The family'll probably throw fits, when they find out I've only known you ten days. . . . They think you have to know a person years before you can trust them. And even then, you're supposed to play safe and not trust them anyway, half the time. Anyone you know less than six months, to them, is an utter stranger. I guess it's our money that made them that way. . . .

"Well, suppose they do think it's that? Let them. We know better, don't we, Wes? . . . Oh, shall I? I never thought of that. I never stop to think of money. Well, about how much shall I bring along? There's a lot of it lying scattered around in my bureau drawer upstairs. I just throw it in and then forget about it. . . . I've never bothered counting. Maybe a thousand or two. Will that be enough? I mean, I haven't the faintest idea what things cost, gasoline and hotels and things like that. I've never had to pay for anything myself. . . . Oh, don't apologize, Wes—I understand perfectly. Of course, just until you can cash a check tomorrow or the next day. What difference does money make anyway when two people are as much in love as we are? . . . If you don't think two thousand will be enough, I could go to Father maybe and ask him— . . . No, I guess you're right, I'd better not. He *might* think it was a strange time, right in the middle of the party like this, and start asking all kinds of questions. . . .

"My jewels? Why, of course, I'm bringing them. They're in one of the valises right now. . . . Yes, I suppose they are worth a lot. . . . No, I haven't the faintest idea; seventy-five, a hundred thousand, somewhere around there, don't you think? . . . A lot? Why, I thought every girl had about that amount of jewelry. I mean, except *servant* girls and people like that. Don't they? Everyone I know has at least that much. . . .

"Oh, here we're wasting this whole lovely music talking about money and jewels and uninteresting things like that! It's the last time I'll ever dance in my own home, with people around me that I've known all my life, who have sheltered and protected me. By morning we'll be hundreds of miles away, without leaving a trace. No one'll know where I am, what's become of me. They'll never see me again. Isn't that romantic, dropping from sight in the middle of a big party right under your own roof?

"Regret it? Feel sorry? No, how can I, when I think what I do of you? No, these other men don't mean a thing to me. I grew up with most of them. I know every one of those twenty-five men on that stag line, and there's not one of them I— . . . Well, yes, there are twenty-six, but that third one from the end doesn't count. He's only a detective. . . .

"Oops, you went out of step there. My fault I guess, I'm so excited tonight. . . .

"No, I don't mean that kind of a *hired* detective, that you just have around to see that no valuables are stolen during a big party like this. This one's some special kind of a detective, who's hunting somebody. Imagine looking for somebody *here!* Isn't that rich? . . .

"There we go again; it must be these high heels of mine. . . . I didn't really bother listening. I just happened to overhear Father bawling him out as I was passing the door; that was all. . . . Father nearly had a fit. He wanted to have him thrown out bodily, from what I could gather. But you know how nervous Mother is. As soon as she heard about it, she insisted that Father let him stay—just in case. . . .

"No, not a thief. He gave it a funny word. Wait'll I see if I can remember. Oh yes—con-congenital murderer! That was it. What's a congenital murderer anyway, Wes? . . . Darling, have we been dancing too hard? Your forehead's all wet. . . . Now isn't that preposterous? I don't believe a word of it. I think he's just trying to sound important and frighten us. Well anyway, Mother talked Father into letting him hang around, as long as he minded his business and didn't spoil the looks of the party. She made him give his word that he wouldn't start any rough stuff inside the house here—that he'd wait until the person—if there is such a person—left, and he'd get him outside. . . .

"Oh no, he's not alone. I think he's brought a whole battery of others with him. They're probably spread out lurking outside around the house somewhere. Something asinine like that. Father put his foot down. He said one inside the house was all he'd stand for—the rest would have to stay out. I guess they're all out there right now, thick as bees. . . .

"There we go again. My, but I'm clumsy tonight! . . .

"No, of course not, Wes; why should they interfere with us? They wouldn't dare! They'll just stop this man, when and if they see him coming out. . . . He might be here at that. When you throw a large party like this and invite dozens and dozens of people, almost anyone can slip in unannounced. Like you did yourself, that night I first met you at Sylvia's party, ten nights ago. Only of course you did it just for the fun of it. I asked her who you were afterwards, and she said she didn't know herself. . . . You know, if I weren't so excited about what *we*'re going to do, I'd have myself a perfectly swell time trying to figure out just who it could be. . . . Isn't it thrilling? Somebody here at this party is a congenital murderer! Somebody right out on this floor dancing like we are this very minute! I wouldn't want to be in his partner's shoes. . . . Let's see now, Tommy Turner, over there with that girl in yellow, has always had a perfectly vile temper. Why he half killed a man once just for—but Tommy and I have been playmates since we were seven. He wouldn't have the time to go around murdering people. He's always too busy playing polo. . . . Or maybe it's that Argentine sheik that's been rushing Kay Landon so all season. I always did think he had kind of a murderous face. . . .

"Don't stare at him like that, Wes—the detective, I mean. He'll know I told you something, and he asked us not to. I know you're highly interested, but you haven't taken your eyes off him *once* the past five minutes. No, he's not looking at us. Why should he be? . . . Well, if he is, it's because you've been looking at *him* so hard. You're like all the men. You seem to think a detective is wonderful. Personally I find them very stupid and uninteresting. This one talks out of the side of his mouth. I wish you could hear— . . .

"Wes, you're breathing so hard. I must be difficult to lead. . . .

"So they know what he looks like? I'm not sure. They do and they don't. I mean, what they're counting on is a certain scar across the back of his hand. That seems to be one of the few definite facts they know about him. They're positive he has it. I suppose they'll make every man that leaves here tonight hold up his hand before his face or something before they let him through. Which just goes to show you how very stupid they are. As though there couldn't be two people with a scar— . . . What am I laughing at? Why, there are! I just remembered you your-self have one. *You* know, that scald you got trying to unscrew the overheated cap of your radiator. Don't you remember my asking you about it at Sylvia's that night, when you still had tape around it? Incidentally, how is it getting— . . . Wes, don't pull your hand away like that! You nearly tore my arm out of my socket! . . . Silly, are you afraid they'll mistake *you* for this murderer? As though *you* could be a congenital murderer! Why, I'd know one in a minute. At least I think I would. Of course I never saw one, but they're sort of pale and hollow-eyed and suspicious looking, aren't they? . . . Wes, what a peculiar smile you just gave me! . . . Darling, is it too warm for you in here? You've gotten so white. . . .

"Oh, let's forget this stupid detective and his murderer! How'd we ever start talking about him anyway? . . . There, Father and Mother are saying good night. They'll be starting upstairs in a minute. Now just as soon as this waltz is over, I'll make a beeline out of here before that bunch of stags jump on my neck again. I'll get the money I told you about, throw some-thing over this dress, and meet you by the rear entrance. . . . Father's private library? Why the library? Well all right, any-thing you say. You wait for me in there then. Keep the door closed so no one'll see you. . . . What? Why yes, I think Father *does* keep some kind of a gun in the table drawer in there. I remember seeing it once or twice, but how on earth did *you* know about it? . . . I still can't understand why you want me to follow you in there. The library is in the exact center of the whole house. There's only one door to it and no windows. And we'll be cut off, walled up, in there; it'll be terribly hard for us to get out again without being seen. . . . Well, you know best, Wes. It'd be terribly unlucky for me to start arguing with my future husband the very first night. . . .

"The waltz is ending. Lead me over toward the stairs, so I can make a quick getaway. . . . That stupid detective keeps watching so; he must have intended asking me for the next dance. Well, he'll have another guess! I bet he dances like a Mack truck. . . . One minute more. . . .

"There, it's over! Wasn't that a lovely waltz? I'll never forget it as long as I live. Maybe that won't be as long as I think it will—I'll leave you for just this minute, and then I'll never leave you again. Till death do us part."

* * *

The two shots came so close together they sounded like one; they shattered the after-the-waltz stillness. A girl or two bleated fearfully. Then with a patter like rain on the polished dancing floor the crowd began herding toward a single point, converging on the partly open library door, where a man was standing. There was a wisp of smoke just over his head. Then it blew away.

Beyond him a man's face was visible, chin on the long, narrow table. Then that too disappeared, like the smoke, and a dull sound came from the carpeted floor.

The detective was saying, to those behind him in the doorway; "Search me, I headed over for this private liberry to bum another of the old man's cigars—they're the finest I ever smoked. I open the door and he's standing there perfectly still on the other side on that table, with the drawer open and his hand in it. He don't say anything, just looks at me like I'm a ghost. So I reach out my paw to help myself from the big humidor standing there between us. With that, he jerks up this gun, misses my ear by an eighth of an inch, turns it to his own dome, and gives it the works!"

Voices cried excitedly, "He must be that murderer you wanted!" The story had evidently already gotten around in some way.

"How could he be?" the detective shrugged. "We got him over an hour ago—nabbed him outside the house as he was on his way in with some swell-looking dame that was next on his list. He's been safely in custody ever since ten o'clock, and the guys I had watching the place all went with him. Why did I come back and hang around like that afterwards? Well I'll tell you frankly, the punch and the sanwidges and the cigars were the best I ever tried, and does anybody feel like complaining?"

ALSO AVAILABLE

THE BRIDE WORE BLACK

by Cornell Woolrich

Cover illustration and design by Steranko

ISBN: 0-7434-1316-4

A HITCHCOCKIAN SUSPENSE STORY THAT BECAME A CINEMATIC CLASSIC!

His glass fell, crashed to the floor. He started to writhe, clutch at himself. "My chest—it's being torn apart. Get help, a doctor—"

He was on the floor now at her feet, moaning out along the carpet in a foaming exasperation: ". . . only wanted to make you happy . . ."

From far away, a voice whispered mockingly, "You have . . . you have . . ." Then trailed off into silence.

No one knew who she was, where she came from, or why she had entered their lives. All they really knew about her was that she possessed a terrifying beauty—and that each time she appeared, a man died horribly. . . .

THE RESURRECTION MAN

A Sarah Kelling and Max Bittersohn Mystery

by Charlotte MacLeod

ISBN: 0-7434-2377-1

THE FIRST IN A DEFINITIVE SERIES OF CLASSIC
MYSTERIES BY AMERICAN MYSTERY AND NERO
WOLFE AWARD-WINNING AUTHOR CHARLOTTE
MACLEOD

Boston-based art detectives Sarah Kelling and husband Max Bittersohn were hoping for some time off
after their last case, especially since Max is still recov-
ering from a broken leg he suffered during the investigation. That hope dies quickly, though, when they run
into Countess Lydia Ouspenska.

The Countess, an expert forger of Byzantine icons,
tells them that an old acquaintance, Bartolo Arbalest—
known in their circles as "The Resurrection Man"
because of his skills in restoring damaged works of
art—has set up a Renaissance-style "guild" in their fair
city, with a number of artisans working independently
under one roof. Nothing mysterious about that, of
course—except for the fact that some of Boston's
wealthiest citizens have been murdered shortly after
valuable *objets d'arts* restored by Arbalest's organization were returned to them.

When Sarah's old friend George Protherie becomes the
latest victim, her investigation—which, coming as no
surprise, ties in with Max's search into Arbalest's
background—reveals that Protherie was not the staid
Boston Brahmin he appeared. In fact, he was guarding
an array of secrets that stretch back to his old days as
an importer of oriental antiquities. . . .

THE LADY VANISHES
by Ethel Lina White

ISBN: 0-7434-1300-8

THE WORLD-FAMOUS SUSPENSE STORY
FROM WHICH ALFRED HITCHCOCK CREATED HIS
MOVIE MASTERPIECE,
REDISCOVERED BY EDGAR AWARD-WINNING
MYSTERY EXPERT OTTO PENZLER!

"The day before the disaster, Iris Carr had her first premonition of danger... There was nothing to warn her of the attack. When she least expected it, the blow fell. Suddenly, she felt a violent pain at the back of her neck. Almost before she realized it, the white-capped mountains rocked, the blue sky turned black, and she dropped down into darkness...."

Iris Carr is a beautiful, young socialite on her way back home to England after vacationing in Europe. Feeling terribly alone and afraid, she finds comfort in the company of a strange woman she knows only as "Miss Froy."

But comfort soon turns to horror when Miss Froy mysteriously vanishes without a trace. Fearing madness, risking death, Iris desperately tries to solve the sudden disappearance of her traveling companion—a woman no one else on the journey remembers seeing at all!